I0746195

Their NERD

ALLYSON LINDT

USA TODAY BESTSELLING AUTHOR

ISBN: 9781949986747

Manufactured in the United States of America
Acelette Press

For my eternal dragon

CHAPTER ONE

"CAN WE PUSH OUT the beta on this subset of rewards?" Justin pointed to a line item on the production schedule displayed on Antonio's monitor.

The men sat across from each other in Antonio's office, hammering out scheduling details that didn't want to be tamed. Antonio twisted the screen to face him, and frowned. "Not without drawing extra attention. And if I give any of my guys more work, I have to stop pretending these demands don't require overtime."

"Fuck." Justin didn't have a problem offering their salaried employees an incentive for working extra hours, but he and Antonio were already pushing their luck with their time demands. Trying to balance working on a project their board of directors explicitly turned down, with getting other work done, was taxing everyone as it was.

Justin stood and strolled to the other side of Antonio's desk. Justin leaned in to get a better view of the split screen, resting one arm on the back of the chair and his hand on the desk next to Antonio's. A flash of heat flowed between them, despite Justin not making contact, and he paused for a moment to let it pass. Years ago, when they started working together, Justin questioned the energy. Was it attraction? Lust?

It was common enough Justin wrote it off as nothing these days. Familiarity at the most. He focused on the development timeline. "There's nothing else to move."

"No. We're tapped." Antonio twisted in his seat. Muscle rippled along his back, stretching his shirt and hinting at a physique honed by a steady diet of gym-time. He faced Justin. "I need another person." Antonio's *r*'s rolled of his tongue. His accent wasn't heavy, but it was enough to reveal Italian was his first language.

That, combined with a strong jaw and brown eyes so dark they were almost black, got Antonio a lot of tail. Male. Female. He had his pick. If Justin were anything other than straight, and not worried about destroying a brilliant friendship and business relationship, he'd be tempted to see if the reality matched the promise of the packaging.

Justin shook the thought aside. It was better than dwelling on the work issue, but it would dead end just as quickly as this search for more development hours.

Antonio's phone rang, and *Rebecca* flashed on the screen. Justin reached past him to hit the *speaker* button. "What's up?"

"I had a feeling you were in there." Rebecca was Justin's assistant, and frequently knew better where Justin was supposed to be than he did. "Grant's looking for you."

Justin gritted his teeth as a dull throb started

behind his right eye. He didn't have to ask if she knew what Grant wanted. Justin had hoped to put off another *money* conversation until after the PrimeAssure contract was signed.

He grabbed the receiver. "Send him through." The line clicked. "Grant. Sorry to keep you waiting. What can I do for you?" He moved back to the opposite side of the desk and dropped into a seat, sharing a scowl with Antonio.

"How's the weather up there?" Grant's tone was pleasant. It was also disconcerting. This was a man who loathed small talk.

"Sunny. Warm. Perfect golf weather, if you like that sort of thing." Same as it was nine times out of ten in San Jose.

Antonio raised his brows.

Grant made a *tsk-tsk* sound. "Never cared for golf. Listen, about that conversation we had a few months back?"

"Which one?"

"You know which." The one where Grant was concerned about annual profit loss projections, and asked if Phase 3 would be out of beta in his lifetime. "Don't yank my chain on this. The solution to low numbers is not to put higher numbers on paper."

Damn Rebecca for being efficient. Justin would make sure next time to specify *don't send this until after the PrimeAssure visit* rather than *no rush to get this to Grant's office*.

"The projections are legitimate," Justin said. "Our alphas have all gone smoothly, and we've got a beta and contract in the pipes."

"In the pipes isn't signed."

"It will be. I wouldn't have slated the money if I wasn't confident."

Grant sighed. "The problem with you tech boys is you're always confident. It doesn't equal reality."

"In three weeks, I'll have signatures, I'll have a deposit, and those numbers you're looking at will be a modest estimate." Justin wasn't making things up for the sake of looking good. It might seem like smoke to someone not on the inside, but he had no doubt the deal was done. He smothered irritation that someone would question it. Grant had his reasons, and those were based in experience. This was a different beast, though.

Antonio had a small pocket of their developers working on the projects he and Justin wanted done. If they could get something out there, stay under the budget set for the entire company, meet their existing deadlines, and prove it was a worthwhile endeavor, he could justify expanding the company it into more. It was the *staying under budget and still meeting deadlines* that caused issues for Justin and Antonio.

Justin looked up. Antonio gave him a sympathetic smile and shrugged. At least that made for a reassuring view.

"Tell you what," Justin said to Grant. "Your next office visit is coming up. Make it three weeks from now, and I'll show you the contract personally, as well as let you sit with the developers and see how this flows."

"That sounds great. In the meantime, I'd like to give you some extra help, to ensure you meet your upcoming release date. I have the perfect retainer for your group."

Justin's stomach sank. "I don't think that's necessary."

"It's no trouble. It won't come out of your budget. Ms. Lowry is my best, and she'll be there to help you and reassure me. Nothing more." Grant kept a handful of contract developers on a small salary when they weren't working for him, and paid their standard hourly rate in addition to that when he needed their skills. It ensured they made him a priority when he called. For instance, when he lost faith in a company.

There were rumors he stayed vested in one or two companies over the years, after his retainers fixed their projects. No one remained solvent after Grant branded them as not viable, though. His investment was the equivalent of a gold rating, and his pulling that money was a death knell.

Justin scrubbed his face, then pinched the bridge of his nose. "When you put it that way, it sounds fantastic. I look forward to it."

"Great." Grant's voice was flat and seconds later, the line went dead.

Justin didn't put the receiver back in place. "Plans tonight?" He looked at Antonio.

"Same thing I do every night." It wasn't taking over the world, but he and Justin spent most of their free time hammering away at the programming work they didn't have enough staff for. It didn't matter that it was Friday; the answer was always the same.

"We'll take tomorrow night off." The impulse struck Justin, and while it wasn't a good idea to waste that time, they were going to need a little break before things got really busy. It had been too long since he and Antonio went out for fun. And watching Antonio pick someone up, especially when he hinted after at details, was as alluring to Justin as finding his own hookup.

Justin dialed another number. "Rebecca, as you're walking out tonight, will you call us in a delivery from Golden Dragon? Standard order and instructions. Thanks." He finally replaced the handset in its cradle, then leaned back in his seat. "I almost forgot. You're getting an extra developer."

*

WHEN ANTONIO WAS GROWING UP, it was a given that he'd take over the family business—his father's technology company—someday. That didn't stop people from asking him what he wanted to be when he got older. His answer changed weekly, but he was pretty certain what he did now was never on the list. Not that he knew how to describe what this was. Keeping the suits happy while trying not to lose grasp of the dream he and Justin built from the ground up? Not exactly a job title.

Another developer should be good news, but rumors about the type of extra staff provided told Antonio this wasn't news to celebrate. "I'd like to think you're joking."

"My sense of humor isn't that bad. She'll be here Monday morning. Grant assures me she's the best retainer he's got." Justin said the word *retainer* the same way someone might say *hitman*. In Grant's case, they were synonymous. Even with disdain dripping from Justin's voice and marring his expression, he was attractive.

Antonio would much rather admire the scenery for a few more minutes than have this conversation. Too bad that wasn't practical. "Do we pause the work on education?"

"*No*. Definitely not." Justin was toeing the line of carelessness with this project. It wasn't obvious at first, but after his fiancée dumped him six months ago, and as the work deadlines got tenser, he let more slide.

Sometimes Antonio worried Justin would throw away what they already had, to prove his education idea could work. Not that Antonio blamed him for pushing. Despite the title *Founder and CEO* that decorated Justin's business cards and email signature, Justin didn't have the kind of control he wanted over their finished product. Money talked, and they still needed someone else's to make the magic happen.

"Grant assured me she'll only be here to provide extra labor. She's not *a spy or anything of that sort*. My interpretation." Justin ground out the words with disgust. "Give her the tasks that require the least training, and leave the high-end work to the people who know the product. We still have full control."

"That sounds too simple."

Justin's smirk shown through pursed lips. Kissable, alluring… Antonio shook the thoughts aside to focus on when he was alone.

"It does, doesn't it?" Justin asked. "I don't think for a minute she won't report back to him, outside of whatever we tell him."

Normally Antonio tried to distract himself from things like the set of Justin's mouth when he was focused. Or the intense flash of Justin's blue eyes when passion—good or bad—simmered inside. Or the fact he was more handsome than was fair. Right now, Antonio preferred enjoying the eye candy to acknowledging Justin's creeping irritation, and his half of an awkward power struggle of a conversation.

"But you don't want to shut down the extraneous work while she's here." Antonio shifted the direction of his thoughts, and the big picture clicked into place. "That's what we're doing tonight—figuring out how to keep the other project off her radar."

"Yup. With a little maneuvering, she can shadow each of us as is expected, and never have to know we've split our resources." Some of the strain evaporated from Justin's voice. "I've got another meeting. We'll regroup this afternoon."

"Wait."

"Hm?" Justin paused.

"Never mind. I've got it." Antonio wouldn't give voice to the doubt whispering through his thoughts. The murmur that Justin might sabotage this on purpose. He might be nearing burnout, when it came to shelving his ideas in favor of the board, but this company was still his baby. Asking—even implying otherwise—would add a new layer of tension to the situation, and that was the last thing they needed.

Antonio dove back into his work. If he had a brand-new developer coming on, retainer or not, he had a lot to rearrange outside of what he and Justin would discuss tonight, and probably over the weekend. Like making sure the new person had enough work to keep busy for at least a couple of days, with minimal instruction, until Antonio figured out a longer-term schedule.

Fortunately, he had a mile-long list of minor bug fixes—the kind of thing that always got shoved to the last minute, because they were quick to fix, but somehow never got corrected before the initial release. They should be easy to hand off and get her familiar with the code, so Antonio could see what she was capable of.

A group chat message from his development team chimed over his speakers.

Picking up Mexican. Anyone want anything?

The question was followed by a series of lunch orders. He hadn't realized it was noon. With the schedule that loomed in front of him, eating at his desk seemed like the best option. He typed, *grab me whatever the special is today*, and turned back to his work.

Just as he was getting back into the right mindset, his cellphone chimed. So much for finding his focus. *Dad* flashed on the screen, and Antonio swiped *Answer* without hesitation.

"*Ciao*." It felt good to speak in his native Italian. It was nine in the evening back home, and this was usually when his parents called when they wanted to chat.

"How's it going?" His father's cheerful voice rang over the line.

Antonio wouldn't mind chatting, if he weren't strapped for time. "Great. Busy. Life as usual.

What's up?"

"Checking to make sure you still plan on being home for your mother's birthday."

Antonio had scheduled the time off months ago, and he was looking forward to seeing Milan again almost as much as he was seeing his family. "Of course." The trip was six weeks out. His development team would have either met their deadline by then or missed it by a mile. Either way, he wasn't skipping something as important as Mother's birthday. "We talked about this, though. Nothing's changed. You could have emailed." He stayed casual despite his suspicion. Dad wasn't much for idle chatter. "What's going on?"

"I've got a couple of business associates in the States this week, and I'd like you to show them around San Jose while they're out there. Also, I was hoping while you were home, we could discuss transition, and set aside some dates to make things happen."

Oh. That. Dad wanted to retire, and have Antonio take over his technology business. Move back home. Stop working for someone else, and pick up the reins of the family business. It was the one thing Antonio didn't need to be thinking about. He'd managed to put it out of his head for a few days. "Happy to take the gentlemen out to dinner. Give them my number, and we'll make arrangements. I'm not sure I'll have final dates for you by then."

"It's been more than a year since we started kicking this around. How much longer do you need, to set the wheels in motion? Have you started making transition plans with Justin yet?"

He hadn't. Justin was half the reason he didn't want to go. The other half was that Antonio wasn't interested in the family business. He and Justin built this one together, from the ground up. He'd worked for his father for a couple of years and never made it above the bottom rung. He didn't belong there; he did here. "The timing hasn't been great."

"We'll talk about it when you're back in Milan." The pleasantness vanished from his father's voice. "No excuses this time."

Antonio gritted his teeth, grateful no one could see his expression. "Sure. I'm looking forward to it. I have to get back to work. Talk to you later, Dad."

As he disconnected, consequences raced through his thoughts. Leaving meant surrendering too much, including the one thing he'd never dare admit to anyone—he barely allowed himself to think it. He loved Justin. Not that he had any illusions about the sentiment being returned. It was a pleasant fantasy when Antonio needed something more personal than porn to jerk off to, but for the most part, Antonio was content seeing Justin happy.

Which wasn't happening right now. The realization hit Antonio hard and tugged loose a series of other notions he didn't want to recognize. If this thing with the retainer didn't go well—if the company collapsed because of it—he wouldn't have a good excuse to stay. Then again, if they met their deadline and signed the PrimeAssure contract, he wouldn't want to leave.

He sank back in his chair with a sigh. Either way, he was going to let someone down.

CHAPTER TWO

EMILY POKED AT THE CHERRY in what was left of her Appletini. The bartender had teased her twice that he'd never before seen someone make a drink last two hours. Her phone buzzed and she grabbed it from her purse.

Not going to make it after all. Sorry.

Emily frowned at the text from her best friend. This entire night out was Cynthia's idea. Emily replied. *I'll be home soon. Help you figure out what's going on.*

The downside to Cynthia being her own boss was she frequently worked Saturday nights. She hadn't expected tonight's emergency to take long, but she must have misestimated. She needed to work out some kinks in her app before she met with her next round of investors on Monday.

Don't you dare leave, Cynthia wrote. *That defeats the purpose.*

Emily scowled at her phone. *I can be daring somewhere else.*

If you can't handle picking up a guy in a bar, how are you going to stash your doubt long enough to have fun halfway around the world?

Most of her life, Emily had poured her efforts into work of some sort. In school, it was studying full time—she'd always had trouble keeping her grades up. After graduation, it was work of the paying sort. There was always another bill to pay, or requirement to prove herself.

She wanted more, though. The desire to do and be and see more hit her several months ago, and refused to release its claws. She'd been saving her money, and when her next job was up, she'd have enough to take half a year off and go wherever she wanted in the world. Tonight was supposed to be a celebration of almost being at that point combined with a test run of leaving her inhibitions behind.

Fine. She sent back to Cynthia. *But I'm going to a different place.*

Coming here specifically was a mistake. The bar was San Jose's hot spot, frequented by everyone who wanted to be anyone. CEO's of Silicon Valley's startups.

Cynthia sent a follow-up text. *Where you are is the same as any other bar you'd go to. He doesn't have to be brilliant, he just has to be attractive and know when to not talk. Stop making excuses.*

What if I do meet someone, and in a few months I find myself across from him in a contract?

Then you deal with that when it happens. You run that risk anywhere you meet someone in this town.

Emily dropped her phone back in her purse. Sometimes Cynthia made more sense than Emily wanted to admit.

A raucous cheer went up from a table halfway

across the room, and her gaze drifted before she could stop it. The group had been there for maybe half an hour and got louder with each passing minute.

What kept drawing her eye, was the sexy guy sitting at the bar, a few feet from them. Dark hair, gorgeous blue eyes, and the way his button-down white shirt hugged the muscles of his torso was almost a sin. And she swore she saw a hint of ink scrawling above his collar. He wasn't with the group, but if she cast her irritation in their direction each time they made noise, she got to see him.

Someone at the table said something. From the way Mr. Sexy shook his head and took another drink, she was glad she couldn't hear it. He looked up, and when he saw Emily, his scowl melted into a smile.

Not fair. That made him more attractive. Maybe Cynthia was right; this bar was as good as any. Emily returned the look. When he pushed back his chair and strode in her direction, her pulse hammered in her ears.

Crap. Smiling worked? She didn't expect that. Now what?

He took the seat next to her and settled his arm against hers. "Can I buy you another of whatever you're drinking?"

He even had a sexy voice. This wasn't real. Was it? "No, thanks. I've had enough."

His brow furrowed for a moment, and he studied her. "That's good for me, then. If you're sober, I know you're genuinely interested. That means I can keep you up late." He winked.

Her thoughts ground to a halt, before spinning up at high speed and diving into the analytical. Was that meant to be innuendo? The wink said he was teasing. Or being seductive. Was he making conversation and nothing more? What was she supposed to say next?

The way he looked her over, attention lingering on her chest and then her lips, sent heat flooding across her skin. "You're new to this." His eyes flashed with amusement.

Her thoughts stalled, and she growled at herself. This was ridiculous. She knew how to be assertive. It had taken her a while to learn, but as a contract software developer who was frequently assigned to work for companies who didn't want her there, she'd learned how to walk that line between aggressive and friendly. "No, I'm not. I pick up confident, attractive guys all the time."

"I like it." His gaze was back on hers. Up close, his eyes weren't simply blue; they were cool and clear, like warm ice. "I'm curious. You're an attractive woman, who's made more eye contact with your phone tonight than with any person here. You're drinking alone in the middle of a bar full of sharks. Are you one of them, or looking to land one?"

She wasn't sure if she should be insulted by the shark comparison. His tone didn't imply he was being rude. It didn't matter. She was stepping outside of her comfort zone, and he didn't have to be a brilliant conversationalist to be a one-night stand. The thought left a bitter aftertaste that she tried to ignore. "Neither. I'm supposed to be celebrating with a friend, but she couldn't make it."

"She doesn't sound like a great friend."

Cynthia would do anything for her. "She's the

best, but sometimes work has to come first. What about you? You're obviously on the prowl. Are you showing off your fin or looking for guppies?" This was good. She'd keep him from stealing the conversation away.

He grinned. "Who? Me? What about me says *predatory*?"

"Besides the toothy, devour-me smile?" Damn it. Despite the voice insisting he didn't need to be anything besides attractive to be an option, she was as interested in what lay below the surface as the package it came in. Pretty paper shredded easily.

"Yes. Besides that."

"Everything."

"That's not super specific." He trailed a finger up her arm.

She lingered on the warmth of his touch, and the goosebumps he left behind. "In that case, I'm too polite to say."

"Except that you led with the observation, which means your tongue's not completely tied. Maybe I'm not a shark. What if I'm a complex book with enough pages no one will ever read them all?"

"Most people are." Or rather, most people preferred to think they were. The banter with him moved at a nice clip, and she liked that she had to think to keep up. Maybe he'd be one of the few who was that complex.

"I bet you're curious about my book's contents," he said.

"I'm still trying to decide if there are enough to make it worth my time."

"Ouch. But that's fair. Still, I think you've

already started to compile a history for me, as well as everyone else you've watched tonight, and you want to know if you're right."

How was she supposed to react to that? His words were confrontational, but his tone and posture were flirty. She let her mouth keep running without permission; it was doing all right thus far. "Because I know you're on the hunt tonight? I don't need a complete history to guess that. It's the same kind of observant as me reading the neon sign in the window and knowing they serve Bud Light here."

"If I'm that obvious, you tell me—am I showing off my fin, or am I looking for guppies? And what does that make you?"

"Still looking for more of those pages you mentioned." The back and forth was fun, but not if it didn't move beyond the fish analogies.

"You're right." He didn't reach for her, but the shift in his tone was enough to make her pause. "I tend to grab hold of an idea and run with it, but it's clear the whole shark thing isn't doing it for you. Let's start over."

"I'm pretty sure that's not the way this works. You don't get to find one woman and try every bad line you know on her until she caves."

"I'm not here to pick someone up. That's not a line; I promise. I saw you, and I couldn't help myself. Apparently in more ways than one."

That was flattering. It might be another line, despite his assurance, but it sounded genuine enough to draw her back into the conversation. "Why *are* you here, then?"

"I was supposed to meet a friend, too, but

something came up." He leaned back enough to draw his gaze over her again, this time lingering on her face.

"That's convenient. I tell you a story, then you parrot it back to me and spin it as unique, simultaneously convincing me we have something in common and that you're different from everyone else in here."

"Nope. I'm not unique." He nodded around the room. "Like every other suit here—and by *here* I mean the valley, not the bar—I own a tech startup. We wrote an app."

His reply was rooted in the harsh reality of living in a town where *everyone* had written an app. That he didn't mind admitting it made her smile. The release relaxed her.

"Until I saw you drinking alone, I was only in here for the white noise and to drown my sorrows," he said.

"Is that when you zeroed in on me as a gullible guppy?"

"Not even close. I always pictured guppies as the water equivalent of sheep, and you're most definitely neither. You strike me as more of a siren. Gorgeous and alluring from a distance, but dangerous if someone unsuspecting gets close."

Heat flooded her cheeks. "That's a bit over the top. Not quite at the level of the shark analogy, but close."

"I'm being sincere. I was before, as well, but like I said—sometimes I hold onto an idea longer than I should." He hovered a finger it millimeters from her lips before dropping his hand again. "I wanted to talk to you, and one-too-many drinks convinced me smooth and cocky was the way to go."

Talking to him was a new kind of captivating. He was sexy-as-fuck on the physical scale, and intriguing on top of that. She couldn't guess his intentions or next move, and she wanted to find out more. "Why are you drowning your sorrows?"

"Boring business stuff."

"That's not super specific." She intentionally mimicked his reply from earlier.

"I don't want to sound like everyone else in the room. But since you're prodding... My investors want me to do one thing with my business. I want to do something else. They won. First thing Monday morning, they're sending in a ruthless, heartless killer to determine how many ways we've fucked up. It's not the executioner, but the judge and jury. Someone to report back to the men up top, about whether our fuckup is small enough to gloss over or they should sacrifice my whole company." His bitter tone put most she'd heard to shame.

She pitied the poor person who got in his path Monday morning. "Sounds brutal."

"It is. I may be a shark, but I'm not the biggest one in my ocean." He frowned, then shook his head, and his smirk flitted back in. "I'm getting fucked, we've both been stood up by the people supposed to have our backs, and you're sure you don't want another drink?" He waved the bartender over.

"On second thought, I'd love one. Something with ice in it." Maybe that would cool the heat flowing over her. Then again, maybe she didn't want the warmth gone.

"Two Jack and Cokes on the rocks." He ordered, slid a bill across the bar, and turned back to her.

"Why the shark analogy?" she asked.

"I'm not sure. Maybe I'm in a *Jaws* kind of mood."

She pursed her lips. "Is this the point where you tell me we should compare scars? Am I Robert Shaw or Richard Dreyfuss?"

"It's not a bad suggestion, but…" He tugged down his collar, exposing more of the tattoos. They scrolled around the back of his neck and vanished beneath his shirt. This wasn't fair. Every new hint he showed of himself was another layer of tantalizing.

He exposed his right shoulder and—without looking—pointed to a shark in the middle of a collage of cartoon characters, map pieces, and foreign characters. "Really, I'm a fan of the movie. First tattoo I got was when I visited Martha's Vineyard. Some tourists collect shot glasses. I wanted my memories to be more permanent, so every tattoo is from a place I've been."

The glimpse she had said there were a lot of tattoos. "Wow." She reached up and traced the edges of color on his skin, some more distinct and others faded. He'd done the traveling she only dreamed of. Her fascination grew several notches. "I bet you have some amazing stories to go with each of these."

He covered her fingers and drew them down his collarbone and across his chest before letting go. "I do."

"I don't have anything to show you in return. I've only got the one scar, and it's going to take a couple more drinks, or a bit more witty banter, before I show you proof of my appendix surgery." Though at this point, she was hoping for a lot of the latter, and the opportunity to show him more than just the pale white line running along her side.

Something caught her eye, and she brushed his neck again. His skin was smooth against her fingertips, coaxing her nerve endings to life. She nudged aside the fabric of his shirt for a closer look at one of his tattoos. "A phoenix?"

"Shit. Now you've discovered my dorky side." Amusement sparkled in his eyes. His expression was mischievous, and a new level of alluring.

That didn't mean she understood why he thought the bird was dorky. "It's a symbol of death and rebirth. Of rising from the ashes. That's magnificent."

"And exactly what I'll tell the next person who asks why I got it. Your answer is a lot better than mine."

She laughed. "What's the real reason?"

"I love comics, and I've got a thing for redheads who have an uncanny ability to see past what's on the surface."

He could be talking about her or Jean Grey. Probably a little of both, and she wasn't sure she cared what the ratio was. The compliment danced over her skin and made her pulse race. "Sirens and psychics. You like your women exotic."

"I never thought of it that way. I prefer the term *unique*. But the right magic powers make for a good fantasy."

"I can't argue with that." In fact, visions filled

her mind as they spoke. Of how this man's lips would feel, pressed hard and hungry against hers. Of his fingers roaming her body, stripping away her clothing a piece at a time. Of what came next.

"What kind of fantasies have you got?"

She shook her head. "You're redeeming yourself from the bad start, but not enough to segue from comics to sex."

"I don't remember specifying the type of fantasy, but now that you mention it… I'm curious. I feel like I'm the only one sharing."

She was pretty sure she'd shared more than she intended to. It was working for her though, and she wasn't interested in turning back now. The only problem with that was she never meant to share details. "Nope. Even if you had broken my defenses down that far, I'd tell you, you'd be bothered, and the night would be over."

He frowned. "You don't get off on guys licking your shoes, do you? Because I've sworn off groveling outside of office hours. Especially if I'm not getting paid." His tone started as serious, but shifted back to playful by the end of the sentence.

Or she'd imagined it was anything but lighthearted. "It's not that. I promise."

"Now I'm curious. You've built it up enough that, once you tell me, it'll seem like nothing and we'll both laugh it off."

She doubted that, but the challenge to shock him was enough to loosen her tongue. The hope he would be put off after all made up her mind for her. "One of my favorites? Being with two guys at once."

"Why would that bother me?"

"It doesn't threaten your masculinity or make you feel inadequate?" She expected at least a hint of recoil.

He shrugged. "It's a fantasy. But if you'd like to make it real, I can see if my friend's done working for the night. Women love him. Italian accent. Tall, dark, and handsome. The two of us could make your night." He reached toward his jeans. "I'll call him."

She grabbed his wrist, and a jolt of want raced through her. "I appreciate the offer, but it's called *fantasy* for a reason."

"Then you don't want company?"

"In my fantasy? You're already there." She hadn't meant to admit that, but she was glad the confession was out there. Images of this man and his faceless friend teased and tempted her. Why had she stopped him from making that call? Right. She might be up for bold tonight, and would even say *yes* if he wanted to take this conversation somewhere more private, but she wasn't willing to shed *all* her inhibitions yet.

"I was thinking something more outside of your head but with less background noise than here. Like my place." He stood and offered his hand. When she grasped his fingers, he tugged her to her feet. He dipped his head and trailed his lips along the edge of her ear. "No expectations. Unless you're into lengthy arguments about whether Green Lantern was a better movie than Batman Forever."

"That's not a lengthy conversation. It was Batman." Who the hell was this guy? Cocky asshole, closeted geek, or something in between she couldn't quite place her finger on? It was enough to ratchet her curiosity up several notches. She wanted to find out more and had just enough Jack flowing through her veins to strip away her reservations.

He searched her face and asked, "*Yes* or *no*?"

"Yes."

CHAPTER THREE

THEY AGREED NEITHER ONE of them should be driving, so Justin scheduled an Uber to pick them up. He watched her, standing a few feet away, at the curb outside, looking everywhere but him. The pause in conversation was enough for her to withdraw, and he struggled to bring her back into the discussion.

He and Antonio had worked late Friday night, bringing everything together in preparation for Monday. Though tonight should have been their Saturday night respite, Antonio called at the last minute and said he needed to deal with some family business.

Justin was disappointed at being blown off. However, the sexy redhead with pale green eyes, who watched him from across the bar and looked away every time he tried to catch her gaze, was a pleasant distraction. Enough to make him forget for a few moments he'd been looking forward to watching Antonio work. The way his voice dropped and his accent grew heavier when he was flirting.

Rather than lingering on that, Justin needed to draw himself and his siren back into the conversation. "What was it that changed your mind about me? The promise of a sexy best friend? No, wait—it was the comic references, wasn't it?"

It was a bonus that she let him fly his geek flag. It had been a long time since he felt like he could let that side of him show with anyone besides Antonio, and being himself felt good.

Crinkles of laughter scrunched around her eyes. "Depends. Is your friend really as attractive as you say?"

He brought his hands to his chest. "You know how to squash a guy's ego. But I did ask. Truth is I'd switch teams for him." The casual statement snagged something in the back of his mind, but he couldn't grasp the thought. He shook it aside.

A car pulled up to the curb—blue Nissan Versa, like the app said it would be. The driver rolled down the passenger window. "You Justin?"

"That's me." Justin opened the back door for the woman and took the opportunity to study her legs—long and slender in something as simple as jeans—when she slid into the car. He sat next to her, grateful for a crowded back seat for the first time he could remember.

"Justin. Got it." She shifted enough to face him but made no effort to put space between them. Her thigh pressed against his, searing hot and tempting.

He shook his head. "Sorry—what?"

"Your name. I didn't catch it before. I'm Em."

The driver maneuvered them into traffic, and Justin was glad he wasn't chatty. Justin shook Em's offered hand, letting his touch linger. "Pleasure to meet you."

"Is it?" She was still smiling, the passing

streetlights and traffic adding a mischievous glint to her eyes. "Because when we left the conversation, you were going gay for your friend. Which is a hot visual—especially that you don't mind admitting it—but it leaves me out in the cold if I say he's the reason I'm going home with you. My final answer is it was actually the possibility of hearing you tell stories about your trips abroad. That, and I assume you have a massive home entertainment system, for playing those horrific movies you mentioned."

"I knew it. I need to lose that shark line in bars and start leading with *Hey, baby. Want to come back to my place and see my impressive equipment?*"

Her laugh was light and playful. "Sure. You should do that. Can I watch next time you try?"

"Is that where the appeal is?" It wasn't what he meant to ask next, and it took him a second for his brain to catch up to his mouth.

"The appeal in what?" she asked.

Might as well go with it, now that he brought it up. "The fantasy of two guys at once. Is the appeal in watching?" He kept his voice low, wanting this discussion to stay intimate and for their ears only.

"The *two guys* thing was meant to be a shock-value kind of statement. It didn't carry the impact I thought it would." Pink dotted her cheeks, and she bit her bottom lip.

She'd meant for her confession about being with two men to deter him. Why didn't it? "It was close enough to the front of your thoughts for you to grab it as a quick answer. You've considered it before."

"I think you're as fascinated with the idea as I

am."

"Then you *are* fascinated by it." Justin was as well, on an intellectual level. The idea of kissing Antonio, making out with him, more, was enough to raise his blood pressure. Justin had never been attracted to any other man, though, and he wasn't willing to risk what he had with Antonio for casual experimentation. He didn't even like entertaining the thought because it was so implausible.

Justin didn't know what was different about tonight—enough whiskey he'd lost track, the tantalizing woman next to him, or an extra kiss of humidity. The notion wouldn't leave him alone, especially with Em as part of the vision.

"You still haven't quite answered—what about the fantasy does it for you?" he asked. Maybe her answer would help him sort out his own curiosities, given he didn't have another outlet for them. "Is it the multiple points of contact?" He hovered his hand millimeters from her cheek, drawing a path along her face without making contact.

"There's some allure in that," she said, "but you were closer the first time." She tilted her head into his touch, and heat sparked against his fingertips, racing up his arm and igniting his pulse. Her sigh—so quiet he felt it on his palm, as much as heard it—added more fuel to the flames.

He struggled to flip back those few minutes and remember what he said. The fuzz of alcohol and all the blood rushing from his head made it a difficult task. "With what?"

"The watching. The being watched."

Snippets blinked through his thoughts. Sitting

at a distance, while she stripped down and ran her hands along her body in a private show. Making her moan, kissing along freckled skin and finding out where her sweet spots were, while someone else looked on. Being that *someone else*. Each new scenario danced along his skin and teased, asking which was most appealing. He lowered his head to her ear, inhaling a faint perfume. "In other words, there's a level of anticipation in knowing our driver is only a few feet away and might catch us if we misbehaved?"

"You're making it too simple." She rested her hand on his thigh. Did she know she traced tiny circles along the inside of his leg, making his cock twitch, or was it a subconscious tick?

"Help me understand."

"There's an intimacy to it. Two people are attracted to each other, and they do… *that*. There are sparks." She met his gaze and held it, licking her lips.

He had to stop himself from kissing away the shine, afraid it would stop her explanation.

"I can't believe I'm telling you this," she said. "Even my best friend doesn't know these things about me."

"With any luck, by the end of the night, I'll find out a bit more she's not privy to."

"Fair enough. Add a third to something that private, either participating or witnessing, and the intensity rises. It's kind of like vicariously feeling what they feel, but on a more personal, up-close level." Em frowned and looked away. "I'm not doing a very good job of explaining."

"We're here." The driver's sharp tone shattered

the immersive bubble around Justin and Em.

Sure enough, they were parked in front of a stucco, three-story house that looked like all the others sprawled along the winding street. Justin adjusted to the shock of being part of the real world again and forced a smile at the man looking back at them. "Thanks, man," Justin said and helped Em from the car.

His dick didn't get the signal the conversation was over, and rubbed against the seam of his jeans as he and Em strolled up the walk, their fingers intertwined. It loosed the floodgate on his desire again. When they reached the front door, he twirled her, to place her back against the frame, then cupped her cheek. He dipped his head enough to feel the warmth radiating from her lips. Her quiet gasp screamed in his ears. "I think you're doing a wonderful job of explaining," he whispered against her mouth, and kissed her.

The taste of sour apples and cola lingered on her tongue. She pressed into him, grinding her hip against his erection. He slid his hand to the back of her head, to twist his fingers in her hair. He tugged her head back and laid a row of kisses along her jaw and neck.

He managed to fish his keys from his pocket and not let go of her, and was surprised he got the door unlocked without dropping them. "Walk me through this daydream of yours." He kicked his shoes off, then pushed her back toward the couch. The reality of her body molded to his overlapped with images of Antonio sliding up behind her and joining in the fun.

"I don't know. Me, you, this friend of yours, and lots of naughtiness?" Hesitation filled her reply. "You know how it works. You've seen porn."

She had no idea how true that statement was. He glided his hands under her top, to dance his fingers up her spine. "I want to hear your interpretation. Are you watching or an active participant?"

"Depends on the day." More courage worked its way into her voice. She kept her gaze on her hands, as she moved up the front of his shirt, undoing buttons along the way. She trailed her mouth over his chest, tracing the lines of some of his tattoos. "Sometimes I'm watching the two of you make out." She dragged a thumb over his nipple. "Sitting back and playing with myself, while he covers you with attention."

Justin liked the way she pulled him into the description, and he had shed enough inhibition that the thought of Antonio's naked form against his added to his arousal.

It had been a long time since he let himself entertain that image, but tonight it was more vivid and intense than he ever remembered it being. "Playing with yourself? I like that. What next?" He dropped one hand below her waist and ground denim against her slit. She pushed into his hand with a moan, hips thrusting in time to his teasing.

"He kisses down your chest, undoes your pants, and works you free." She slid his zipper down as she talked. When she wrapped her cool fingers around his warm shaft, he hissed at the shock that raced through him.

"You're watching while he jerks me off?"

She bit her bottom lip. "Better. While he takes you in his mouth."

God. Justin could almost feel the heat against his cock, and they were Antonio's. "What if I want you to be an active participant?" he asked.

"You could kiss me while he was kneeling between your legs."

Justin liked that suggestion. He sought out her mouth again, bit at her lips, and devoured her groans, until they broke apart with a gasp. "What next?"

Eyes wide, he stared at him and shook her head. "I don't know."

"Don't know or won't say?"

"Both?"

He was immersed in the daydream, as it bled into this moment, and happy to pick up the slack. "I'll help. I want to see these full lips wrapped around his dick." He pulled his thumb along her bottom lip. She flicked out her tongue and drew the digit into her mouth, to trace along the pad, then draw circles, before releasing him.

"So we've moved on from him at your feet? If we shift position, does that put you behind me?" she asked.

He spun her and slid his hands to her breasts. "It does. And I'm taking advantage of it." He pinched her nipples through her bra and shirt, and she gasped.

Her back pressed into his chest, and her ass teased his cock until he thought he might come.

"You look gorgeous, giving him head. Trying to keep up the rhythm, as I roll these nubs between my fingers." He pulled harder, and she squirmed in time with his touch.

Her breathing grew shallower. Her pants rubbed against his exposed dick, creating enough friction it almost hurt, but still enticed. "I might lose track of what I'm doing if you keep that up," she said.

He dropped one hand to the button on her pants and undid them. "I've lost track of what I'm doing. Watching your ass wiggle in the air, I can't help but slide my fingers between your legs." He pushed under her panties and dipped into her folds. "*Fuck. You're soaked.*" In the fantasy and in real life—the combination kept him anchored.

"Because I've never done something this intense before."

Him either. "I can't let him have you all to himself. I need to be inside you."

She wiggled her ass one more time, then hooked her hands in the waist of her jeans and pushed her clothes to the floor. He barely had the presence of mind to grab a condom from his wallet and roll it on.

Hand on her back, he pushed her forward. She caught herself on her palms and knelt on the edge of the couch. Her gorgeous, round butt teased him, temptation hiding between her legs. Would this have been so potent without the verbal play? He was grateful he didn't have to find out.

He nudged her pussy, then thrust forward, pushing his cock deep inside her. Gripping her hip with one hand, he moved to the other to her clit.

When he found the swollen button and circled it, she cried out and drove back into him. He pumped against her while he rubbed her sex, using her gasps to pace himself. "Are you still sucking him off while I fuck you?" he asked.

"Yes. But not for long. He's close, and I'm too distracted by what you're doing. I have to pull back, but he's stroking himself."

Justin was too lost in the fantasy and in Emily, to keep talking. He pressed harder against her clit, and her pussy clenched around him when she came.

She didn't pull away, and he didn't ease up. The squeezing around his shaft mingled with her cries, drawing him toward climax. His legs threatened to give out, but he steeled himself. Digging his fingers into her pelvis, he pounded hard and fast, the slap of skin against skin filling the room.

He grunted as orgasm spread through him. His vision narrowed, his ears rang with their mingled sounds of pleasure, and the scents of sex and whisky teased his nose.

After he was spent and her screams faded to whimpers, he slowed down, then puttered to a stop.

"God damn." He bent at the waist, to lay kisses along her back, then pulled her upright.

She wobbled, and the lack of balance was enough to send them tumbling to the couch.

"I think you left a mark." She splayed her hand over her hip.

He pushed her back enough to kiss the pale flesh. "Better?"

"I don't think it will stop the bruising, but I'm not complaining."

"*Fuck*. That was incredible. And you felt amazing." As the endorphins from pleasure ebbed, logic seeped in. Did he really do that? Fantasize about his best friend sucking him off? About sharing this woman with Antonio? How was Justin supposed to face him again?

Em curled up against him and rested her hand on his stomach. Her gentle breath fell across his chest. "Thank you for the fantasy," she said.

Right. It was only a daydream. Antonio was attractive, but it wasn't as though Justin harbored a secret crush on him. This was fun and games and a one-night stand. Nothing more.

He didn't realize he'd dozed off, until sunlight struck his closed eyes, jarring him awake. He stretched and realized he was alone on the couch. That was a bit disappointing.

"Em? Are you still here?" he called through the house.

No answer.

Bummer.

There was a note on the coffee table. The flowing script said, *Thanks for the wonderful night and the memories. Good luck with your investors.*

The sentiment made him smile. He was glad he wasn't the only one who enjoyed it. Better still, her *good luck* meant she'd been listening to him last night. Even if he'd never see her again, it was nice to be heard beyond the sex.

His phone beeped. That must be what woke him up. He grabbed it from the floor, where it had tumbled at some point during their playtime. Antonio had left a voicemail saying they could start their day whenever Justin was ready.

Hearing Antonio's voice didn't make Justin squirm as much as he'd expect. He could push the fun of last night aside and brace himself for the long weeks ahead.

CHAPTER FOUR

ANTONIO MADE HIMSELF COMFORTABLE at Justin's kitchen table and opened his laptop. The motions were familiar and comforting—things he'd done dozens or possibly hundreds of times, since Justin bought the house a few years back.

"My apologies for last night." Antonio would have rather been working. Even though it shouldn't be necessary, it was better than showing his father's business partners around town and pretending he didn't recognize all the subtle attempts to remind him how much better things were back in Milan. Their efforts had the opposite effect.

Justin had offered to keep him company, but Antonio didn't want him knowing the real reason for the visit. He didn't intend to reveal his father urging him to come home, unless things got that bad here. Which they wouldn't.

Justin took a seat, tablet in hand for notes. "We needed a night off anyway, and I kept myself busy." There was the tiniest catch in his voice. It could have been a swallow, or a pause to breathe.

Antonio knew it was more. "What did you get up to?"

"You know—a bit of this, a little of that. A lot of gorgeous redheaded siren with a brain to match."

Antonio almost pushed for more, but something he couldn't define stopped him. "You and your redheads."

"*Anyway.*" Justin's voice was too sharp in the quiet room, echoing off polished stone and stainless steel. "What else do we need to cover before tomorrow?"

"We need to make sure we're not missing any tiny details." Last night didn't matter. Either Antonio's company or whatever Justin got up to that he hesitated to share. If they got this right—making the retainer and Grant happy, while still letting their side project continue—Antonio would remain in the States. He hated the idea of letting his father down, but proving this company was not only viable, but also cutting edge, would soften the blow of him staying here. With Justin.

* * * *

ANTONIO PAUSED OUT OF VIEW of the office lobby, taking a few seconds to steel himself for the day ahead. They had a plan. Whoever this woman was, she'd be shown what she needed in order to do her job, and he and Justin could carry on as necessary, to do theirs.

He didn't need to ask Reception who the retainer was. She was the only other person in the room. The redhead in a pinstriped suit, perched on the edge of her seat as if getting comfortable was the last thing she wanted. She was gorgeous, and exactly

Justin's type.

Lust surged through him, catching Antonio off-guard. Even with her mouth pinched in a flat line and her eyes dull and cast at nothing in particular, she was attractive. Cute in that deceptive way that probably fooled people into thinking there was nothing under the surface. Something told him she took advantage of that assumption. She must have some defense in place, to be in a position like hers.

"Ms. Lowry." Antonio stopped in front of her and extended his hand.

She stood and smoothed her skirt, before returning the greeting. "*Emily*, please. Mr. Conroy?" Her voice was lilting and pleasant, but didn't hold any traces of hesitation. That was sexy.

Which was completely inappropriate for Antonio to think. *Don't hit on the employees.* Usually be didn't need reminders like that. "His schedule is packed this morning, though he'll try to stop by later and introduce himself. I'm Antonio Bianchi. Co-founder and development manager. *Antonio* is fine. I'll be your primary contact while you're here." He gestured toward the elevator banks. "This way."

They crossed the room, her heels not echoing on the tile as loudly as they should. Was she walking with a light step on purpose?

"How much do you know about our business?" His question came out gruffer than he expected. He needed to find a balance between being polite and stowing his attraction. He took a deep breath and counted to three as they waited for the lift, forcing his racing thoughts to calm.

She pursed her lips and stood a little straighter.

She was only a few inches shorter than him and met his gaze, unwavering. "Grant gave me an overview of your specialties and what he'd like to see accomplished while I'm here, and I spent several hours on your website."

"In other words, not much of anything." Christ, he was being an asshole. They stepped into the waiting car, and he hit the button for the third floor, where his programmers sat.

Her scowl said she agreed with his assessment. "I'd like to hear the details from you. Someone in your position is more familiar with everything I need to know."

Justin would give her most of those details. He excelled at selling people on the dream that built this company. He had a vision and a compelling way of sharing it. Besides, they agreed Antonio's job was to give her enough to keep her busy and cut her out of everything else.

"I'm pressed for time this morning as well. I hope you understand. Things like company vision and real orientation will have to wait." At least until he could still his racing pulse enough to deal with her professionally. The doors slid open, and they stepped onto the office floor, rows of cubicles spanning in front of them.

"That's fine." Her voice was low but firm. She stepped in his path, forcing him to look her in the eye. "I'm not here to take work from you or take away this vast thing the two of you have built. My job is to make yours easier. To do whatever grunt work is related to the project."

He raised his brows at what sounded like a well-rehearsed speech. "That's good. How long did it take you to refine it?"

She looked away for a brief moment, before looking at him again. "This is my fourth attempt." Some of the formality vanished from her voice. "I close with offering to treat you and Mr. Conroy to dinner—on Grant's dime—so you see I'm like any other developer you'd hire."

"With the exception that we don't typically give our programmers that kind of expense account."

Her shoulders slumped, and her expression softened. "I don't want to argue with you, but I will. I'd prefer you give me a task, and I'll do it."

That was the opening he needed to put her to work, and out of his distraction range. "How familiar are you with Source Secure?"

"Intimately."

The single word triggered the last kind of thing he should be thinking. Whispers of how he'd approach her differently if she weren't working for him. If he'd met her at a bar, like Justin met his redhead Saturday night. The stunning woman with the light walk and the tempting hips that begged to be grasped, while he pushed her back and kissed away her shy smile and turned it into something mischievous.

That needs to stop now. "That's where we do source control. I flagged a series of files in there. Some are documentation. Others, the code that goes with it. Read through them, to familiarize yourself with the system."

The creases in her brow deepened.

"Do you have any questions or concerns?" he

asked. A voice in the back of his mind screamed that he was being unreasonably harsh, but he wasn't in the mood to listen.

"I don't have a problem learning, but I may absorb more if you sit me with someone, rather than give me a series of notes without a point of reference."

"Did my accent make me difficult to understand? You're here to do whatever we need, are you not?" Antonio asked.

"I am."

"That's what we need. Your desk is right there." He led her to a cubicle set up with its screen facing his door, that allowed zero privacy, and she followed his gaze. "Your Active Directory login and temporary password are on a sticky note, and there's a number to call if you need helpdesk support."

She looked back at him, face pinched. "And if I have questions about what I'm reading?"

"Make a list. I'll see if I can find a resource for you later. Anything else?"

"No. I'm on it." She walked the short distance to her new work home.

He wouldn't watch her ass in that skirt. He had his own work to do. He headed to his office and settled in front of his computer. Sitting in a spreadsheet in front of him was his actual backlog of work. It started with bug fixes—things that could introduce her to the code much more effectively. Tasks that needed to be done but kept getting put off. This was what he and Justin agreed on, though.

Jackass. The word echoed in Antonio's head, taunting him. Not only did he shove real help aside, he also ogled her in the process. She was knowingly a contractor for a man who took some sort of perverse joy in making his investments jump through hoops. Antonio was surprised she didn't call him on the menial labor. Was she really that amicable, or was she keeping track of every slight and misstep she could report back to Grant?

It didn't matter how many directions Antonio tried to drive his thoughts in, he kept coming back to the fact he hadn't given Emily a chance. He really was being an asshole. A horny, spiteful—

A knock drew his attention, and he looked up, to see Emily standing in the doorway. She didn't look any happier than when he shooed her away, nearly an hour ago.

He forced a blanket over his mind, to at least be civil. "Yes?"

"Is this what you have all your developers do when they start working for you?" The quaver in her words vanished by the end of her question.

"No."

"Do you think I'm not qualified for the job?" She crossed her arms.

There was no reason to make this worse, but he struggled to find an apology. "I assume you're quite qualified."

She shifted her weight from one foot to the other. "Then give me something to do that will teach me and will actually help you meet your deadline."

"How do you know this won't?"

"It doesn't matter how anal a company is when it comes to documentation—and few even bother to make it a priority—unless they're about to be audited, they don't care about shi— things like this. And if you *are* about to be audited, you don't expect someone to code from your documentation; it only has to be readable."

"What is it you expect of me, Ms. Lowry?"

Several seconds passed before she replied. "Give me a real task list, and if I need orientation before I dig into your code, hand me over to someone who can provide that."

He glanced at his screens, and his project timeline mocked him. He dragged the spreadsheet over to his primary monitor, then turned the second screen to face her. "Grab your laptop, and you can follow along."

She relaxed her shoulders, and a smile ghosted across her lips. "Be back in two seconds." When she returned, she set up her machine so she could see both it and his screen, and looked at him. "Whatever you do, don't go easy on me."

His helpful mind summoned a new interpretation for her statement, of pushing her onto the desk, shoving her skirt to her waist, and sliding between her legs. *What the fuck is wrong with me today?*

She didn't know what she was asking, and he needed to stop letting his mind wander. He'd give her the same orientation all new developers received. He tended to be the one who did that first-day training, because the system was his. He'd done this enough times to have an idea of when to pause, when to nudge for questions, and when to plow forward.

He gave her a brief rundown of how the AI worked, and she nodded through the entire thing.

That was a good sign. He pulled up the data structure. "We have a fourteen-layer normalization." He paused and waited for her eyes to glaze over.

"Why?" she asked.

The simplicity of her query caught him off guard. Everyone else came back with an argument about how that was stupid or didn't make sense, or they simply stared at him blankly. He laid out the answer, complete with all the technical details.

"That makes sense. But typically, when I see a system that's created for flexibility, even the programmers struggle to extract information. How do you get around meaningless naming conventions and still keep things open ended?"

As the overview continued, she snapped back several more questions that implied she not only understood everything he was saying, but she also didn't have a desire to argue. Despite not wanting to like her, knowing one misstep while she was around could cost them financing, and telling himself she was nothing more than another cog, he liked how quickly she caught on. This kind of intelligence was sexier than the peek of lace from her thigh-high stockings each time she shifted in her seat.

Antonio hated to admit it, but so far she was impressive.

He didn't realize how much time had passed, until his messenger chimed through his speakers. It was the daily roundup, to see who wanted lunch. "I didn't mean to work you this hard. It's noon. We should take a break."

"If you don't mind, I'll stay at my desk and work through what we've gone over so far. I won't bill it back to Grant; I want to make sure I have a good grasp of what you're telling me."

Anyone else, and he'd wonder if the statement was either a way to kiss ass or some sort of passive-aggressive attempt at guilt. Nothing but sincerity shone in her eyes, and given how plainly she wore her emotions earlier, he believed she was genuine.

A sliver of regret wormed its way in, that he treated her poorly less than four hours ago. "Would you like company? We'll have something brought in and go over what we covered."

"Don't you need to catch up on work?"

"I do. But an hour's not enough time to find my focus. Let's get you taken care of, and then I'll get work done."

He asked one of the guys to pick something up for them, then continued to review with Emily until the food arrived. He stepped out of the room long enough to grab their lunch. When he returned, he was surprised at what he saw.

"Didn't expect that," Antonio said. He set her sandwich, chips, and drink in front of her, and took his to the other side of the desk.

"Expect what?"

"You still reviewing." He grabbed a fork. "You have five minutes free of the boss's watchful eye, and I figured you'd be checking your email."

"I wouldn't do that. We're working."

He raised his brows. "Every person I've met, no matter how dedicated they are to their job—and that includes me—checks their phone the moment they have a breather. I don't need a predictive algorithm to tell me that. It's just the way things are."

"Apparently you *do* need one. Unless you're blowing smoke about what yours is capable of, it would have told you, based on my previous behavior, that I wouldn't be looking at email when you got back. Or texts. Or anything like that."

"Don't pull that *I'm not addicted to my electronics* bullshit with me."

She laughed and grabbed a potato chip. "I never said I didn't check."

He ran the conversation through his head. "But you implied it pretty heavily."

"All right. I did do that. I looked when you left the room. From there, reality gets boring though. No new messages. No notifications on social media. I ran out of things to look at before you got back."

"You're exaggerating."

"I'm not. My life is that dull." She didn't look bothered by the conversation. Instead, amusement danced behind her eyes.

"Are you kidding? That sounds wonderful. I love the idea of not having a queue of pending notes because I kept my head down for an hour."

"You're full of crap." There was no malice in her words. "You'd go nuts if you found yourself without something to do. I mean, I'm guessing, but a guy like you in a high-profile job like this drives hard because you don't like to slow down."

Good point. Not that he was giving her the satisfaction of conceding. "I might; I might not. It's been a while since that was an option, and some days I do miss not being tethered. Back to it?"

"Doritos and education. Sounds perfect."

"I would have aced school if they offered that

kind of reward," he said.

Her shoulders relaxed, and some of the stress seemed to drain from her neck, so she didn't sit as stiffly. "Takeout as incentive for pop quizzes? Pizza for exams?"

"Not pizza. Not the way they make it here, anyway. I'm thinking a shot of Nyquil and an afternoon nap, for acing the final."

"Nyquil? Isn't that a bit…" She bit her bottom lip.

"A bit what?"

"Nothing."

He took a sip of his drink. "You were going to say *a bit high school*, weren't you? Poking fun at getting drunk off cough syrup?" This was nice. He was surprised but pleased with how easily the banter flowed.

"I was, but I realized that if you didn't grow up in the States, the joke might not mean the same thing culturally."

As pleasant as the teasing was, they did have work to do. "Dad and Mom did let us indulge a bit younger than is common here. Review time. Tell me the kinds of data sits at the tertiary level."

"Nice try. We didn't cover that. I'll make you a deal—*you* give *me* that information, and you can have my cookie."

"A bribe. Smart woman."

She shrugged. "I know the way to a man's heart. Pry open the ribcage."

"Ouch. Brutal." He expected her to say *through his stomach*, but that wasn't right either. The answer was definitely *his brain*. She was almost more invested in this conversation that Justin was.

Antonio hated the thought the moment he had it. Justin was burned out and answering to someone else's whim, but he wouldn't throw everything away. They were all trapped in this situation, and the only way out was through it.

CHAPTER FIVE

JUSTIN ITCHED TO CHECK IN with Antonio, to make sure things were running smoothly. He trusted Antonio to have a handle on it. That was one of the biggest reasons APPropiate Designs ran smoothly. But this retainer was an unknown variable, and Justin didn't like being without that information.

Appointments took him through lunch. A little after twelve thirty, Rebecca interrupted long enough to set a sandwich on his desk and tell him Antonio ordered out. That made Justin smile.

When his cellphone rang, he frowned at the familiar Italian country code on the screen and Antonio Sr.'s name. He answered. *"Buon pomeriggio."* More than a year in the country, and all this time with Antonio afterward, was enough to teach Justin basic words and greetings.

"No need for anything that formal." Tony chuckled. "I simply called to make sure you were doing all right."

"Everything's great, unless you know something I don't." He kept light laughter in his voice. It wasn't unusual for Justin to talk to the older man. Tony was like a mentor to Justin in many ways, and when Justin worked for him, they established a friendly relationship. Something about the tone and out-of-the-blue call still crawled over Justin's nerves. It might be he was on edge with the retainer in the office, but it felt more specific than that.

"It's late here, and you're busy. I won't take much of your time." Tony Sr.'s tone was clipped but pleasant. "I tried to get a hold of Antonio, but he's not answering."

"He's in new employee orientation. What can I do for you?" Justin suspected the answer was *nothing*, if this was a family thing.

"Has Antonio given you a firm resignation date, or is that still up in the air?"

Shock bled through Justin. At some point he'd known this day was coming, but over the years he pushed it to the back of his mind, until it held the same weight as an ancient curse no one actually believed but they still shared around the campfire to scare each other.

He grabbed his composure. He wouldn't commit to anything until he ran it by Antonio and they were on the same page. "We're negotiating. A transition like this takes time."

"Keep in mind none of us is getting younger. Tell Antonio I called?"

"I will. You have a good evening, sir."

Justin hung up and sent Antonio an instant message. *Can you break away?* Now seemed like the perfect time for a debrief.

He watched the telltale "…" of someone typing, as it flashed on screen for several minutes before the response arrived. *Sure. Your office?*

Yes.

Justin locked down his mind, to keep it from jumping to conclusions. Antonio would clear up the truth of the situation, and there was no point speculating.

Justin considered himself patient, but twenty minutes later, when he was still the only person in his office, his mood had shifted from *on edge but curious* to downright *sour*. As Justin picked up the phone, to find out what was going on, Antonio stepped into the room and closed the door behind him.

"Sorry about that," Antonio dropped into a seat.

"Is this a bad time?"

If Antonio had an issue with the sharp tone, it didn't show. "Now is fine. I had to get the new girl squared away while I was gone."

Right. The other thing Justin wanted to know about before this new distraction came in. "How's she working out?"

"She might actually be human." Antonio cracked a smile. "Talented. Intelligent. If she's not the best actor in the world, she's probably not here just to spite us. She could help us make up lost time."

A pang of something Justin couldn't identify knocked in his thoughts, and he stowed it. "In other words, she's doing more than reading developer notes."

"I've been giving her the official orientation. You're okay with that, aren't you?"

"Your department—you make the final call. And it's not why I wanted to talk."

Antonio raised his brows. "What's up?"

"Tony called me."

"All right…?"

"He asked if you'd given me a solid resignation date yet."

"*Fuck.*" Antonio pinched the bridge of his nose. "So much for my waiting until next month to discuss it with him."

Justin's next question should be, *What will it take to keep you here?* Or, *Do we actually need a transition plan?* "Why haven't you told him *no*?"

"He's family. My father."

"I understand." It was something Justin struggled to wrap his brain around. He didn't get along with his family and never believed anyone did until he saw Antonio with his parents. That kind of loyalty, simply because of blood, wasn't instinct to Justin.

"That's the stress speaking. What can I offer you to keep you here? I can't quite match his offer, with the whole *the family company is yours now* thing, but there's got to be something."

"We built this together. I don't *want* to leave. I'm working it out. Speaking of making things work—part of Emily's bribe to convince us she's not all bad is dinner on Grant. You should put in an appearance."

"Emily. You're already on a first-name basis?" This teasing was much better than floundering in the unknown of whether or not Antonio was staying in the States.

"I can't quite call her *The Retainer* for the next month."

"I don't see why not." Justin didn't believe anyone who made a living doing what this Ms.

Lowry did was all kindness and sunshine. She helped dismantle companies from the inside out. Who the fuck enjoyed that? It would be nice if *something* was unexpected in a pleasant way, but he didn't expect it.

*

EMILY REVIEWED HER NOTES from half a day of training with Antonio. Her head spun with everything she learned today, the whirring compounded by the highs and lows of her first day in the office.

She was grateful to work for Grant, especially on the retainer payroll. The small salary meant she didn't have to stress if there were lapses between her development contracts, and he was a good boss. However, walking into one of his jobs was always a game of balance. She had to exert enough confidence she wouldn't be stepped on, but not so much she came off as threatening.

When Antonio met her in the lobby, his rich accent slid over her skin like satin, teasing and drawing up images of her delicious Saturday night. The rush of fantasy and memory intensified when she remembered the Mr. Conroy she was supposed to meet was also a Justin. If *this* Justin was as hot as Saturday night's hook-up… *holy hell*, that would be hot.

Antonio helped her silence the delicious images by being an asshole, but then he had to turn around and be not only apologetic and kind, but also brilliant. And the fact his accent was both sexy and pretty much how her Saturday night fantasy sounded, didn't hurt.

She'd seen a lot of Silicon Valley startups over the years, and while there wasn't an exact science to predicting which would fail, there were some good indicators—and not the things most people looked for.

The décor at APPropriate Designs could belong to any office building. White walls, black stuffed chairs with basic trim, and gray carpet. However, Antonio and Conroy owned and occupied the entire seven-story building. That, combined with what she learned today about both the front-end product and the technology behind the scenes, made her wonder what she was doing here. They seemed to have their act together.

"Antonio." A male voice carried through her cubicle wall, sounding louder than its actual quiet hiss, thanks to the silence in the room. "I need you for a minute, for pro—"

"Yeah. My office in five minutes." A sharp edge lined Antonio's voice.

What was that about? A knock on metal caused her to spin toward her cube entrance. Justin— random world-traveler guy Justin from the bar— stood in front of her.

All her other thoughts evaporated.

The rise of his brows was the only indication that he recognized her. "I'm Justin Conroy. I'm sorry I couldn't meet with you this morning."

"Emily Lowry." She accepted the greeting and failed to ignore the rush of heat that traveled from his grip down her arm and over her body. She wanted to run. Hide. *Oh God.* Antonio *was* the guy from their shared fantasy, and he stood next to Justin, watching the exchange. The realization made her pulse race. She should probably say something. "Nice to meet you."

"Same. We have a lot to discuss about your next month here, and I understand you're free this evening. I'm looking forward to hearing what you and Grant have in store for us." Justin's cool tone never wavered, as he searched her face.

She forced a smile. "I'm happy to share. Do you mind if I steal a moment of your time? Now, if you're free." Not that talking to him alone would be a good idea in the future, but the tiny part of her brain that still worked insisted they clear the air *now*.

If Antonio noticed the tension, it didn't show. He leaned against a cubicle wall, one hand in his pocket and expression pleasant.

"Sounds great." Justin kept his voice low. "Fair warning, though. Antonio is my business partner. Whatever we discuss, he'll be privy to later."

Was he saying that for show, or was she about to have her personal life on display for a third party? "I understand. No secrets."

"We'll be right back. Take care of PP—make sure they deploy the beta tonight—and we'll all catch up in a few minutes," Justin told Antonio, then steered Emily toward an empty conference room, away from the developer area. He closed the door behind them.

"Really? *No* secrets?" The question slipped past her lips before she could stop it.

Justin turned to face her, calm expression vanishing beneath a clenched jaw and tight gaze.

"When it comes to business. There are a few details of how I spent my weekend that he doesn't know about."

"Details."

He shrugged. "Things I shouldn't have said that might make working conditions awkward. But don't think it's anything you can hold over my head."

"I hadn't even considered that." She didn't like the implied accusation. "I'd rather forget it happened."

"Was it that bad?"

"It was incredible." She snapped her mouth shut. His mouth twitched with an unformed smile, and her cheeks burned. "But I'd still rather… That is—it's between us? That's what you're saying?"

"Well… Yes and no. Some things can't be taken back."

The growing knot in her throat plummeted into her stomach. "Fuck." His words from the bar rushed back to her. Not the tantalizing story about the best friend, but what came before. *They're sending in a ruthless, heartless killer…* He'd been talking about her. "This is convenient for you, isn't it? I'm too embarrassed about the awkward situation to stay on, and you're free of judge and jury?"

"That would be a pleasant notion if I were delusional. Grant would send someone else, and the fire I'm floundering in would get hotter when I ran off *one of his best*. His words, by the way."

"Exactly." It was hard to keep the indignation in her voice when he took all the *oomf* out of her retort.

"Though, I'll be honest—I never pegged you

for a shark."

She bit the inside of her cheek, as more of her memories from the weekend flooded back. His fingers tracing over her skin. The conversation that convinced her to go home with him. All things she needed to disassociate from this contract. "I'm sure we have a to learn about each other. Professionally," she added quickly.

His smile looked as uncertain as her grip on keeping her cool. "We should keep this short. Antonio knows I picked up an attractive redhead, and he'll add one and one pretty fast. He wasn't privy to *any* details beyond that."

"Oh." The lightbulb went on in her head. "You don't want him to know what we talked about."

"Do you?"

Touché. Emily could picture that conversation with Antonio. *Yeah, Justin and I know each other. We fantasized about having sex with you. I mean, not that I knew it was you.* "I'm good with that arrangement."

"Everything all right in here?" Antonio cracked the door and stepped into the room. "No one's tearing anyone's head off?"

Emily looked between the two men. Best friends and business partners? Or more than Justin let on?

The curiosity was enough to make her pulse lick under her skin, igniting her senses and taunting her with images of Justin backing her against the conference room table and twisting his fingers in her hair and kissing her, while Antonio watched.

"Everything's shiny," Justin said.

This morning, Emily had been prepared for hostility. Her first job, Grant neglected to warn her what she was walking into—that most of the companies he invested in felt the same way about his retainers that Justin did. It caught her off-guard, and she fumbled her way through the week. But she finished the job.

Her second contract through Grant, she made the mistake of walking in all casual and friendly like, and they rolled over her. Third time around, she tried to project an air of owning the place, and no one would deal with her. The assignments weren't only about meeting development deadlines; they were also meant to settle waves between Grant and whatever company he sent his retainers into. If she didn't get this one right, Grant would drop her contract.

Which meant not fantasizing about being the Oreo filling in a co-founder sandwich cookie.

"You're all right?" Antonio was looking at her.

She made her smile as genuine and friendly as any smile had ever been. "Fantastic. I was just reciting my script. I'm not here to take over or ruin anyone's day. I'm only here to help. You know—all the things you heard this morning."

She wasn't letting Justin, or Antonio, or any other seductive, enticing executive take this job from her, for any reason.

CHAPTER SIX

"WOULD YOU LIKE TO SEE the dessert menu?" The waitress never took her eyes off Justin.

Which didn't surprise Antonio. She'd been hitting on Justin all night.

What struck Antonio as odd was that Justin wasn't flirting back. Instead, Justin's gaze flicked to Antonio and then Emily. "I think I'm all right. How about you two?"

The waitress set a booklet in front of Justin, and leaned in until her chest brushed his shoulder. "Are you sure? We've got a vanilla torte with cherry filling, and a drizzle of cream sauce. Tart and sweet, to keep things interesting."

"Sounds like the perfect dish to share." Emily watched the waitress with a pleasant smile, her tone as sweet as could be.

Justin furrowed his brow. "She's got a point. Sure. One of those."

The waitress scowled, but erased it before she looked at Antonio. "For you?" she asked.

"Just coffee for me." Antonio wasn't sure if he was more confused or entertained by how Justin and Emily shut the woman down.

"If she asked about your tattoos next, would you have a pre-spun story to go with one?" Emily looked at Justin. Her tone was light and teasing.

The question pushed Antonio's *curious* buttons. It wasn't the first comment she'd made along those lines tonight. Saying something distinctly specific given she'd spent a total of maybe ten minutes in the conference room with Justin. An explanation as to how she knew so much tugged at the back of Antonio's mind, but he couldn't quite grasp it.

Justin shook his head. "Sometimes people don't want elaborate tales. Those are best saved for someone who's interested."

Emily twirled her glass, ice rattling at the bottom, and looked at Antonio. "Where are you from? I hope it's all right to ask that. Your accent is Italian? From what part?"

The question was innocent enough. Small talk. A nice shift of pace. "Milan. Have you ever been?"

"I haven't." Emily tucked a strand of hair behind her ear. "But I've heard it's lovely. Should I add it to my list?"

"Your list?"

Emily hesitated. "I'm taking a trip after this contract. Or hoping to. You know how some people backpack across Europe?"

"Or South America." Which is what he and Justin did in their early twenties. It was how they met.

"Exactly." She smiled. It was a gorgeous expression that brightened her face and shone in her eyes. "I want to do the adult version of that. As in,

I'm-too-big-a-coward-to-do-it-without-a-safety-net. Should I add Milan to my list?"

"My answer will be biased. Never ask a native if you should visit their hometown. Ask someone who's seen it through a tourist's eyes." Antonio was more fond of vacationing in Rio Di Janeiro, but for personal reasons.

Justin leaned in. "You absolutely should. Milan in spring is gorgeous."

"You've been there too?" Awe lined Emily's voice. "Is that where you two met? I guess that's a stupid question. For all I know you ran into each other at some networking conference in L.A."

"We met in Brazil." Antonio was being sucked into her fascination. It had been a while since the world was that and amazing and vast to him, but she looked enthralled with the idea he and Justin had traveled.

Justin scrubbed his face. "Please don't tell her this story."

"You have to now." Emily looked amused.

The waitress returned with their dessert, and it sat untouched.

Antonio always hesitated to delve into the memories of how he and Justin met. It was a bittersweet moment. He'd gloss over the details and they'd move on. "A couple of friends introduced us."

She looked between them. "And that's an embarrassing story?"

Maybe he couldn't completely gloss over it. "It was a blind date. His friend read Justin wrong. She didn't realize Justin doesn't swing that way."

"Really?" Emily's eyes widened. Justin gave

her a look Antonio didn't understand and a frown crossed her face before vanishing. "I didn't know you were gay. That is, not that it matters. Or that I've spent a lot of time thinking about it." She dropped her face into her palm. "Oh my God, this conversation just became an HR nightmare." Her words were muffled. "I'm shutting up now."

The hint of flustered was as alluring as her confidence. Antonio liked the contrast; it made her feel even more real. "No one's going to Human Resources, unless you do. And I'm not gay. I'm more of a keep my options open kind of guy."

"Oh." She looked up. "So, um… the two of you meet in Brazil and *bam* instant friendship?"

Justin chuckled. "Exactly like that. If you remove the weeks of awkward fumbling and trying to find each other's boundaries, a lot like this conversation."

"Which tattoo is from Brazil?" Emily seemed determined to move on to a new topic.

Again, her question struck Antonio as oddly specific, given she and Justin only met a few hours ago.

"It's where I had my inspiration for APPropriate Designs, so it's an AI." If Justin thought Emily's insight was odd, it didn't show in any of his mannerisms.

The answer was misleadingly vague. It really didn't have anything to do with what Justin decided on in the end.

"As in artificial intelligence?" Emily asked. "Like Johnny Five from that old Short Circuit movie?"

"That's the one."

Antonio's phone vibrated in his pocket, and he ignored it. Whatever it was could wait a few minutes. "That was disturbingly specific." Especially since that specific tattoo was on Justin's right shoulder blade. "What am I missing?"

Pink spread across Emily's cheeks. "Nothing."

Justin grinned. "Not anymore, anyway. Saturday night, you missed the stunning redhead hiding several rows of teeth behind an incredible mask of sweetness and a sharp tongue."

Reality plowed into Antonio, and his world tilted. Emily was the woman Justin picked up? And now, not only was she working with them, but she and Justin were still flirting. What the fuck? Words escaped him. "This just got surreal. As in, bad plot kind of surreal."

Justin opened his mouth but was cut off by the shrillness of his phone. He answered it before the first ring finished. "Hey, Merc."

Mercy. The bizarre evening shifted aside in Antonio's head to make room for its neighbor, ill ease. Something had gone wrong with the Promiscuous Perks beta the developers deployed this evening. Wrong enough Mercy couldn't wait until morning to get it fixed. The code name was meant to be misleading so no one would guess it was Justin's education component.

"He's here with me." Justin looked at Antonio.

Antonio didn't expect him to say anything more specific. This was the project they weren't funded for, and the last thing they needed was Emily overhearing it was not only happening, but also going poorly.

"We're on it. Call you back in thirty minutes." Justin pocketed his phone and stood. He gave Emily a curt nod. "Ms. Lowry, pleasure to see you again." All the playfulness was gone from his voice, leaving a flat tone in its place. "We've got an emergency back at the office. I hope you'll excuse us."

Antonio shook her hand. "We'll talk tomorrow. Whatever the two of you have going on, I hope it doesn't interfere in the office." He'd give Justin more of an interrogation, starting with *what the fuck were you thinking?*

"Is there anything I can do to help?" she asked.

"We've got things under control." Antonio smiled, wishing he felt as certain as he sounded.

* * * *

JUSTIN WAS SUPPOSED TO HAVE put tasks like writing code behind him years ago, but he'd brushed off his skills when he and Antonio started doing double shifts to get PP ready for launch. Diving into the project was usually a surefire way to square away his thoughts and have them all make sense.

"Still getting scripting errors on the preview pane." Mercy's voice filtered through the speaker phone in Justin's office.

"Details?" Antonio had set his laptop up across from Justin.

Mercy read them the pertinent information. It was one of the things Justin liked about having her as an early adopter. She understood the back-end technology well enough to make troubleshooting easy. Or to at least take some of the more basic stress out of it.

"Were we wrong to push for deployment tonight?" Justin asked.

Antonio met his gaze. "They assured me we were set."

And either he or Antonio would have done a double-check any other day, but with Emily disrupting their schedules and forcing secrecy, they didn't have a chance to. Which brought Justin's thoughts full circle to the one thought he hadn't been able to shake all evening.

He coded, as half his mind took off in Emily's direction. He should have dialed back the conversation at dinner. Kept things polite, but professional. It was too easy to forget that when Emily started talking though. The same thing that drew him to her Saturday night shone through this evening. He was grateful she kept the details of their hookup to herself, though. Not that she seemed any more interested in spilling than Justin was.

And watching Emily was easier than admitting since Saturday night, he hadn't been able to get the shared fantasy out of his head. Every time he looked at Antonio, he saw more than the attractive man he shared business decisions and bar hopping trips with. He kept picturing Antonio's lips around his cock, or the two of them kissing. Fucking. Heat raced over Justin's skin, flaring to scalding.

"Holy fuck. What did you do?" Mercy's dismay dragged his attention back to the present.

"Nothing. Hang on." With a few keystrokes, he brought up the error logs, then mentally smacked himself making a simple error. He corrected the syntax and re-deployed. "Try it now."

Antonio raised his brows. "Are you here for this?" His voice was low enough Justin had to strain to hear the question.

"I'm fine." Justin's response came out sharper than he intended.

"Sure you are," Mercy said. "Listen, it's almost eleven here. Ian's waiting for me. Not that I don't miss the all-nighters, but… No, wait. I don't miss them. How long to roll me back to the old code?"

Justin forced down his frustration, until it burned in his lungs. "Twenty minutes."

"Awesome. Will you pick up?"

Justin exchanged frowns with Antonio but grabbed the receiver and took Mercy off speaker. "What's up?"

"I hate to bring this up, because I know the two of you are pouring everything into this and we're running a beta, but your quality is slipping. This isn't pre-production code. It never should have made it past QA."

"I'm aware." He didn't trust himself to say anything else. It would come out defensive or angry, and that was the wrong way to approach this. "Will you be set to try again over the weekend?"

"Will you?"

He snapped off a low growl. "One of us will send you an email when the old code's back up. G'night."

"She's pissed?" Antonio asked as soon as Justin hung up.

"What do you think?" There had to be better

ways to function. Mercy had a point; she didn't put in late hours these days—one of the perks of being her own boss. Andrew, their other friend from their bumming-around-the-world days, probably never worked past five. What were Justin and Antonio doing?

Making it past this one hurdle. That was it. Justin needed to keep telling himself that.

Antonio settled deeper in his chair. "I'm here all night if that's what it takes. Let's wrap this up before we have eyes on us tomorrow."

That was something to be grateful for—a reliable business partner and friend.

* * * *

AS EMILY APPROACHED THE APARTMENT she shared with Cynthia, her limbs begged for her to simply sit. In the middle of the floor would do fine. Her mind was overloaded.

She couldn't believe how poorly she behaved at dinner. Every other word that came out of her mouth was inappropriate. At the same time, she didn't actually regret any of it, despite feeling like she should.

Bright light greeted her when she pushed inside. Cynthia's brother, Paul, sat on the couch, watching something with explosions and violin music. He looked up the moment Emily walked into the room. "Hey."

"Are you only here for the night, or is this a long-term arrangement?" She wasn't in the mood to be social. She didn't mind Paul in small doses.

They'd known each other since they were kids. She didn't have the brain power to carry on a polite conversation right now. Besides, Paul usually visited when he was out of work and didn't have enough money to make rent with whoever had taken him in most recently. It always rubbed Emily the wrong way, regardless of how much she tried to be kind and look the other way for Cynthia's sake.

"I'm helping Cynthia with some front-end work, and I'm between jobs. We're going to spend a few days brainstorming in the same room."

"Awesome." Emily couldn't find any enthusiasm. She noticed a single rose in a vase, sitting on the coffee table. "Is Cynthia seeing someone?"

"It's for you." He grabbed it and almost tripped over a table leg, closing the distance between them. He righted himself and handed her the gift.

She looked between it and him. "Thanks?" She didn't know what to make of it.

"As a congratulations."

"For...?"

"I heard you're getting close to your goal of being able to see the world. I figured that was congratulation worthy."

That seemed like an odd reason for a flower. "I am. I just have to make it through this contract."

"You're brilliant; you'll make it happen." He guided her to the couch and tugged her to sit next to him. "Cynthia told me she stood you up on Saturday. We should all go celebrate this weekend instead."

Emily gave him a weak smile. "Sounds fantastic."

"It's a date. For tonight, you should take it easy. Sit and watch movies with me and unwind."

That sounded like a good idea. If she could lose herself in explosions, she could forget about the muddled day she had. She settled in.

When Paul took the spot next to her, his arm brushing hers, surprise jolted through her. She shook it aside. Dinner had her caught on the edge between wanting more of Saturday night and knowing it wasn't appropriate given her working conditions. There was no reason to take that out on Paul or misread a casual closeness.

The movie played on, but she couldn't concentrate. Normally, the high-budget special effects and cheesy one-liners grabbed her attention and let her zone out. Tonight, something nagged at the back of her mind, and she couldn't pin it down.

"Are you all right?" Paul asked.

"I'm fine."

"You look tense." He adjusted his position to sit sideways, one leg on the cushion and pressed against her thigh. He kneaded his fingers into her shoulders. "So many knots. Was this evening that bad?"

She forced herself to relax, despite the invisible spring coiling tighter inside with each new touch. "It was okay. My mind's all over the place. I'm good. Thank you."

"Of course." He took the hint and dropped his hands away, but kept his body shifted toward her.

It's because he's comfortable. It had nothing to do with her. The assurance didn't sit well. She ran their past through her mind, skipping along their every-day. Had he ever acted like this around her before? They shared things like hugs and high fives, but this didn't feel the same. There was an expectation behind it that she didn't care for, and couldn't tell if she was misreading.

"Do you want to watch something else?" His question pulled her back to the conversation.

"No. This is good."

"You seem distracted. Are you sure nothing's wrong?"

Yes. Jeez. Stop asking already. The mental shout echoed in her head, and she tempered the abrupt response. She needed to learn to better compartmentalize if work was going to be like this for the next month. She nodded.

"Okay. I'll drop it." He draped an arm around her shoulders.

She shot to her feet, confusion assaulting her. He looked at her, brow furrowed in confusion.

"On second thought, I'm super tired. Tonight must have hit me harder than I thought. I need some sleep." She spat the sentence out in a single breath.

"No worries. I hope you feel better in the morning."

She gave him a weak smile. "I'm sure I will." She headed to her room and shut the door behind her with a soft *snick*. She'd made that entire situation far more awkward than it needed to be. Once she had a little sleep and a clear head, she'd be able to reconcile that just because she'd slept with her boss—unknowingly, but still—didn't meant the rest of the world was hitting on her.

CHAPTER SEVEN

ANTONIO GLANCED AT EMILY and did a double-take at the tease of satin. She wore a green nightgown trimmed with lace. The brilliant emerald matched her eyes, and the black was a stunning contrast to her pale skin. "You two do this a lot?" she asked.

She stood next to him in the doorway, while Justin slept on one of his office couches. It was one of the few times Antonio had seen him recently without stress lining his face.

"We used to." He couldn't force his gaze to her face. Her breasts were pressed together and up, swelling with each breath, and her negligee barely covered her ass. As the blood rushed from his head and to his lower extremities, he struggled to find the brain power to speak. "I'd be happy if we never had to do it again, but it's worth it, if things pay off."

"What things?"

His mind caught up before his mouth ran too far, and he stopped himself from mentioning their side project. "You know what things." He kept his tone light and playful. "Same you're here for."

"Then you should have let me help." She

shifted her weight, giving him a generous view of cleavage. A trail of freckles ran along her collarbone, ending in a *V* at her neckline, as if the sun had planted each one.

He needed to distract her from the subject. That would put them on an equal playing field. "You and him." Antonio nodded at Justin's sleeping form. "How was it?" A tiny portion of him knew the question was inappropriate, but it made as much sense as Emily standing in the middle of the office in lingerie. What the hell—he was going with it.

"Hmm." She twisted her full lips, and his cock throbbed. "Are you asking how I was, or how he was? The answer to the latter—incredible. Everything you've dreamed of."

He'd dreamed of a lot. "What if I wanted the answer to the former as well?"

"You'd have to ask Justin."

Antonio dragged a finger along her jaw, to her chin, to lift her head. "I'd rather find out for myself."

When he brushed his mouth over hers, she whimpered. He dragged his tongue along her bottom lip, before catching the fleshy swell between his teeth. She tasted like coffee, and cherries drizzled with cream.

She dug her fingers into his chest and kissed back, hard and hungry, opening for his tongue. He glided a palm down her back and over her ass, drawing her close until her stomach pressed against his erection.

Emily broke away enough to ask, "What if he wakes up?"

"He can join us." That was a tantalizing

thought. Antonio guided her back toward the desk. Hands on her hips, he lifted her to sit on the polished mahogany, and slid between her legs. Every time she shifted or gasped, his nerve endings hummed in anticipation.

She hooked her feet around him and draped her arms over his shoulders, interlocking her fingers at the base of his neck. "You must think I'm easy," she said with a teasing glint in her eyes.

"I have a feeling you're quite picky, but I'm confident enough to think I'll make the cut."

She laughed. "*Arrogant*, you mean."

"Tomato, *pomodoro*." He worked an arm between them, lifted the edge of her gown, and slid under the elastic of her panties. His fingers glided easily between her folds, and she arched her back with a gasp, grinding into his touch. "You like that?" he asked.

"*Like* is an understatement." She squirmed against him.

He wanted to tease and play, but his dick dug into his jeans, begging for release and warning he wouldn't get a chance if he took his time. He wasn't sure what that meant, but he didn't have the desire to puzzle it out. Every time Emily moaned, his cock twitched. He zeroed in on the swollen nub between her legs. Her breathing grew more frantic, and when she dug her fingers into his arms, her nails stung his skin. *Christ*. This was delicious.

He nipped her earlobe. "Come for me, *passerotta*." He traced circles around her clit, tightening up and pressing harder in time with the thrust of her hips.

She tilted her head back, eyelids fluttering, as a delicious cry tore from her throat. He didn't let up until she shuddered away from his touch. How had they not woken up Justin? Antonio didn't know if he was relieved or disappointed.

Emily rested her forehead on Antonio's shoulder and gave a soft giggle. "We have company." Her mouth moved against his neck.

Behind him, leather creaked, and he heard the distinct sound of a zipper sliding down.

"I want you inside me, while he watches," Emily murmured as she fumbled with the button on Antonio's jeans.

Pain spiked through his neck, and he grunted. Agony stabbed his crotch. His eyes flew open, and Justin's office swam into view from a very different perspective than the one Antonio had seconds earlier. He sat up with a soft groan, stretching and rolling his neck, to get rid of the crick. The vivid dream wasn't as easy to wipe from his mind. He was rock hard, to the point it ached. Dream-Emily's voice lingered in his head, dancing with her taste and the heat of her soft skin.

He swung his legs around to plant his feet on the floor, and his erection roared in protest at being bent into such an awkward angle. He stood and adjusted himself.

He and Justin had finished up at about two in the morning. Rather than waste the time it would take to drive home, they each claimed a couch, to get a few hours of sleep. Late nights of coding, followed by a bit of tossing and turning, and a full day of work—it was a ridiculous thing to say at thirty, but he was getting too old for this shit.

The clock on the wall read five fifty. What an ungodly fucking hour. Justin was still asleep, brown hair brushing his eyes. Like in the dream, it was one of those rare moments when he looked peaceful. The scruff of a day's worth of beard darkened his chin. Antonio itched to run his fingers over the coarse stubble.

He needed to shake this off now, before the work day started. He adjusted himself as best he could, and untucked his shirt when he couldn't hide the bulge. Fortunately, no one would be in the office for a little while. There was a small gym on the main floor—a facility they built for employees. Until about six months ago, Antonio used the equipment on a daily basis. These days, he was more likely to use the spare change of clothes he kept on site for mornings like this.

He grabbed his gym bag from his locker and picked the private shower stall at the far end of the room. When he stripped out of his clothes, his dick sprang loose, grateful to finally be free of its prison. He turned on the water, stepped underneath the spray, and leaned his forehead against cool tile as the icy needles biting into his back shifted to warm, then nearly scalding.

He wrapped his hand around his shaft and stroked slowly. This was the only way he'd be able to focus today. In his mind, the intensity of the dream melted into a different, more familiar fantasy. One where Justin came looking for him. The shower door would creak open, and Justin would step into the small space, naked, his chest smooth and cock standing at attention.

The daydreams used to make it difficult for Antonio to look Justin in the eye. When he figured out diving into the images made it easier to get through the day, he surrendered.

He tightened his grip on his dick, increasing the pace as the pictures in his mind played out. Justin kissed him hard enough that teeth dug into lips. He yanked the short strands of Antonio's hair and tugged. Antonio didn't need more prompting. He kissed down the bare chest, dipping his tongue over curves of definition and pausing to tease and nip at a flat brown nipple. He mentally continued his journey, sinking to his knees as he went. Kissing Justin's pelvis before finally reaching his destination. He licked over the head of Justin's cock and was rewarded with a thrust of the hips, before he took the length into his mouth.

In his fantasy, Antonio sucked and licked. The taste of precum ghosted on his tongue. In real life, with the heat of the shower pounding into his back, he stroked his erection in time with the visions in his head. He lost track of time, as the daydream overlapped the real world. Justin tightened his grip on Antonio's hair, thrusting hard and desperate. He growled when he climaxed, spurting hot, salty fluid against the back of Antonio's throat.

Antonio came hard, shudders wracking his body as he squirted against the tile. Sticky white covered his hand. He kept jerking until he was raw and spent. His pulse hammered in his ears, and his heart scraped his ribs. He stood still for several minutes, using one hand to keep himself upright, while his shaky legs struggled to steady themselves. Once he was put together enough—mentally to think, and physically enough to stand—he finished his shower. With the pleasant traces of dream and fantasy hovering at the back of his thoughts but no longer clouding them, maybe he could get some work done.

It would be even better if the subjects of both decided they could get along, but he wasn't holding his breath.

* * * *

EMILY GRABBED A TOASTER PASTRY out of the box in the cupboard and made a note, using the pad on the fridge, that they needed more. "How did you get the dataset to scale for that many users and still return real-time results?"

"Industry secret. You're not the only genius in the house." Cynthia sat at the kitchen table, tablet to one side and coffee in front of her. She and Emily were discussing a breakthrough Cynthia had with her development and where to go next. "Seriously, though. If you have time this weekend, I'll show you. It's kind of a hack, but it works amazingly well. And don't think I didn't notice you changing the subject."

"Who? Me?" Emily laughed. "We were done with the previous conversation."

Cynthia raised an eyebrow. "Right. Let's gloss over the fact that your new contract is the guy you went home with, Saturday night. The sexy geeky guy with the bad pickup lines."

"Who hates what my job stands for and

understands professional boundaries as well as anyone." Emily stuck out her tongue. "Yes. Let's please not dwell on that." She took another bite of her food, just as her phone rang.

"Let the poor woman finish breakfast before you hound her," Cynthia yelled playfully at the chiming device.

Emily wished it was that easy to get a phone to shut up. Grant's name was on the screen, and she hurried to answer. "This is Emily." She tried to keep the hesitation from her voice, but some leaked in. Yesterday's potential conflict of interest, successfully suppressed after a night of sleep, rushed back to meet her full force. Not that Grant needed to know there'd been any hiccups. "What can I do for you?"

"I'm calling to check in and make sure everything went okay yesterday." Grant sounded cheerful. The request made sense. He did that with each new contract.

"It was fantastic." She winced at the overinflated enthusiasm in her voice. "I mean *fine*. Everything went fine."

"I'm glad to hear it. No friction at all?"

Not the kind he meant, but still enough to ignite a large pile of kindling. "Nothing more than normal. I handled it. Honestly, I'm not sure why they're struggling." Now she was overcompensating. Saying too much. "They even had issues with their beta last night, and Justin and Antonio personally oversaw cleanup." *Shut up, shut up, shut up.*

"They don't have any beta builds on the schedule." Concern leaked into Grant's voice.

"That's why you're there—to make sure they meet that deadline."

She knew that. *Wait.* Then what were they up to last night? "I must have misunderstood. Maybe it was an alpha. They were friendly with whomever they talked to. It might have been an informal test." She bit her lip, to keep from saying anymore. Part of the reason she was onsite was because Grant was worried they were doing other things informally as well. As in keeping some of their development off the books.

"You know, I haven't been here long enough to know their terminology. I'm sure I misunderstood. Whatever happened, I can tell they're on top of things."

"I suspect you're right. It's nothing. Have a wonderful day." Grant disconnected.

Emily set her phone on the kitchen counter and glared at it. She didn't throw Justin and Antonio under the bus, did she? Selling them out to Grant—even unintentionally—after one day seemed like the least likely way to earn their trust and convince them she was there for their benefit. She learned early in her first contract that everyone was happier as long as nothing went back to Grant unless it was going to impact meeting the deadline.

CHAPTER EIGHT

THE CONVERSATION WITH GRANT still played in Emily's head, as she crossed the office floor to her desk. Thinking about that was better than thinking about how things would go next time she talked to Justin. His name was enough to send flutters dancing across her skin. Each time he popped in her head, she called questions about the phone conversation to the forefront.

Had she given too much away, and sold APPropriate Designs out? *If there's nothing to give away, it doesn't matter what I said.* Her logic wasn't as reassuring as she wanted.

As she approached her desk, she saw the lights in Antonio's office were on. She smiled before she realized she was doing so. Sure enough, when she rounded the corner, she saw him. She set her stuff on her desk, except for one of the two cups of coffee she carried, and knocked on his open door.

"Hey." He looked up. Even with circles under his eyes and exhaustion lining his face, he was gorgeous.

What would have happened if she met him at the bar instead of Justin? She shook the thought aside and handed him the drink. "You didn't get to finish the coffee you ordered last night, so I brought you this." She had no idea why she ordered a second drink this morning, but it sounded like as good a reason as any.

He took a sip, before setting the cup aside. "Thank you. It's perfect."

"I don't know how you take it, but I figured after the long night you probably had, *extra shot of espresso* was a good start. I'm kind of surprised to see you here this early." The same thought that nagged her since yesterday whispered back. Why was she needed here? Justin and Antonio were dedicated to their jobs. Though she hadn't been here long, a day was usually enough to see some of the chinks in a company's operations. APPropriate Designs had hiccups, but nothing glaring.

"Sometimes I wonder why I bother going home at night." Antonio laughed. "If I set up a cot in the gym, I could move in and stop paying my mortgage."

"Did you get your crisis solved? Or are there any outstanding bugs I can help with? Something to dig into and get my feet wet?"

He shook his head. "Yes to the crisis. No to the rest. Thank you, though." He furrowed his brow, then waved to the chair across from him. "Will you come in and have a seat?"

"What's up?" The one contract she had before Grant's retainer that didn't go well was enough to instill a dread for those words. And it had accompanied pissing off the wrong person in management.

Antonio pinched the bridge of his nose.

"There's no delicate way to put this. I'm praying it doesn't backfire."

"Okay…?"

"I don't care what happened between you and Justin. The details aren't my business, and I'm glad he didn't share any. I'm not passing judgment. It doesn't change my opinion of either of you. You're consenting adults."

Not where she expected the discussion to go, but that didn't make it any less awkward.

"However, as the guy whose ass you're here to save, I need to know the events of Saturday night won't impact your work."

She let out a breath she didn't realize she was holding. If she'd built out a conversation like this in her head, her best-case scenario couldn't have gone much smoother. She looked him in the eye. "I promise it won't interfere."

"Dinner was a fluke, then? You're going to have to interact with him on a regular basis. And to ensure you don't think I'm picking on you, I asked him the same thing. He promised to behave."

She bit back the *he started it*, that wanted to force its way out. "I should have kept myself in check last night. Everything I told you about wanting to see you succeed is true. No one wins—not me or Grant or anyone—if this project falls apart."

"Thank you." Some of the lines vanished from around his eyes. "When my lead developer for this project gets in, I'll introduce you. You can start on the bug list and pull up anything that's a Priority Three that you're comfortable tackling. For the next couple of days, until you're both comfortable with your work, he'll review your fixes before they go to quality assurance."

"Are you sure you trust me to poke around in your code?" she teased. It felt odd being comfortable enough with him already to make a joke like that.

He didn't seem to mind. "If you plan on selling us out despite your repeated assurances to the contrary, tell me now, and I can make sure you only see the not-top-secret work." It was an oddly specific request, but she didn't know his sense of humor. He was being friendly and she was grateful for that.

"I'll do that."

She settled in to work, the conversation with Antonio flitting in the back of her mind like a happy hum. Her question from earlier drifted back. What if was him in the bar instead?

Would it have been better or worse if he was the man she went home with? Antonio *was* gorgeous, and that accent sent delicious tingles dancing over her skin. Justin had been right on both counts. Then again, the sex was amazing with Justin, and he wasn't the guy she had to look in the eye every day. If it was that good or better with Antonio, it might not be possible to stow the memories.

She shook it all aside. She shouldn't be lusting after either of them. There were countless other men out there, and she didn't know these two well enough to justify fixating on them. It was bad enough she'd—even unintentionally—slept with someone she had to report to but in a case like this, where she was supposed to be an objective outside opinion… If news of her hookup with Justin made it any further, she could kiss the retainer deal with Grant goodbye.

Which meant not having a pleasant nest egg for her plans to see the world. Worse, it'd screw up Emily's reputation. Possibly irreparably.

As the morning wore on, her surroundings grew louder. Snippets of conversation drifted in from everywhere, but most of it came from Antonio's office. She felt like there was a train platform behind her desk. How did he get any work done?

Wednesday morning, she remembered her earbuds. As with yesterday, Antonio's office light was on and his door open when she arrived. He wasn't at his desk, though. She reached her cubicle, and a giddy thread wove through her when she saw a cup of coffee on her desk.

There was a Post-It next to the cup, with a scrawling, handwritten note. *What can I say? I'm old fashioned.*

She wasn't certain of the note's meaning, but she had her assumptions. Most of them had to do with him feeling awkward a woman bought him a drink. She should be offended by the implication, right? She was progressive and independent. Instead, her smile grew when she took a sip, and sweet white chocolate mixed with espresso hit her tongue.

"I hope I guessed right." His seductive accent floated from behind her.

She used the blink it took her to face him as time to assemble a professional mask. "It's sweeter than I'm used to, but a little decadence and sin are nice once in a while." Did she really say that?

The twitch of the corners of his mouth implied he caught the hint of flirting and didn't mind. "Couldn't agree more. Holler if you need anything."

The rest of the day passed without incident, and she whispered a small *thank you* at another shift gone by without having to face Justin. Thursday morning there was no coffee, and the lights in Antonio's office were out. She couldn't ignore her disappointment, but reason barged in and pointed out it was for the best. She needed to concentrate more on the job and less on the scenery.

*

ANTONIO FELT AS THOUGH he'd been pulled in a million different directions at once, with no end on the horizon. The morning began with a breakfast meeting with a client that went long. Since then, he'd been ten minutes late to everything. He settled at his desk for the first time today, grateful for the chance to breathe. He had almost an hour to work through emails. That was nice.

His phone rang before he could get through the first message. *Figures.* The screen said it was his user-interface developer. Antonio grabbed the receiver. "Yes?"

"This focus group is running over. I'm going to be here today and tomorrow. Which means I won't meet my development deadline."

"Wait. What focus group?" Antonio didn't authorize that.

"The one for Promiscuous Perks. Justin set it up weeks ago."

Fuck. Leave it to Justin. Antonio gritted his teeth. "We'll take care of it. Thanks for letting me know." He hung up and dropped his head into his hands. He didn't have anyone with an open schedule and that skillset. A flash of red hair caught his attention, and inspiration struck.

"Emily, do you have a minute?" he called.

She locked her computer, then crossed the short distance to his office. "What's up?" Her relaxed posture and cheerful tone erased a layer of his stress. The view didn't hurt, either. Her jacket and slacks hugged her curves in all the right places, and she had an extra button undone on her blouse. If she bent over, the view wouldn't be as generous as in his dream, but the tease of what lay underneath might better.

He mentally cleared his throat. "You said the other day you've got experience with Android user interfaces and Java optimization."

"It's a hobby." She caught her bottom lip between her teeth, looking pleased with herself.

Christ, that was alluring. "I'd say odd *hobby*, but I'd be lying if I pretended wondering why didn't fascinate me. I need you on something more critical than bug fixes." He gestured for her to come around to his side of the desk and pointed at his screen. "My UI guy is tied up with a focus group. This is what you need to do."

When she stood this close, looking over his shoulder, the faint scent of jasmine drifted from her. It drilled into his thoughts and mingled with the dream he hadn't managed to shake two days later. "What's the picture of?" she asked.

She meant the image on his computer desktop. "Milan. My sister and I, last time I visited." The memory summoned traces of homesickness.

"It's gorgeous. You're lucky."

"Because I'm from Italy?" He glanced at her.

"Well, yes. That too. Though I suppose it's as exciting to you as San Francisco is to me. Big deal, right?"

It depended on whose eyes he saw the city through. Experiencing Milan with Justin for the first time had given Antonio an entirely new perspective. He didn't need to share that information, though. "It's got its beauties."

"I can only imagine. I meant lucky that you've traveled the world. The farthest I've been out of the country was when my best friend and I would take weekend trips to Mexico. I bet you have a million stories to tell."

Her awe reminded him of the wonder of setting out on his own, back then. His flight to Brazil. First time roaming a foreign country alone. "I've got a few. You talk like you'll never go. There's always the option."

"I guess. Work gets in the way. You know? The next job is waiting; the next paycheck is set aside for something."

He glanced at her again. The wistfulness on her face matched her voice. "I suppose you're right," he said.

"Anyway." She shook her head. "UI work?"

"Right. That."

As he spoke, she made notes, asked questions, and seemed to absorb everything he told her.

"Antonio." One of the developers interrupted. "I need your time." He was one of the people working on the other project. The team had been asked not to discuss it openly.

"I'll be by in a minute," Antonio said.

"I just need a *yes* or *no*. I can't move forward on Promiscuous Perks—"

"I said, I'll be there in a minute." Antonio cringed at the edge in his voice.

"Sure." The guy left so quickly, he might as well have vanished.

Emily looked between Antonio and the doorway. "What was that about?"

None of your business. He bit back the sharp retort. "Nothing." He spoke through clenched teeth. He gestured to his screen. "Back to UI requirements."

She frowned but let him dive back into his explanation of her new assignment.

Fifteen minutes later, she was back at her desk, working. He was grateful she didn't push the PP issue.

The rest of the day passed without incident. His meetings flowed smoothly, and by the time five closed in, he was ready to call it a day. Not that he could. He'd shift his attention to their side project for the next several hours before that was an option. But tomorrow was Friday, and after they redeployed Mercy's site on Saturday night, they could take Sunday off. Something to look forward to.

In the main office, he heard the various voices wishing each other a good night, and the shuffle of people leaving for the day.

"Promiscuous Perks." Emily interrupted. She stood in his doorway, watching him. "Is that what PP stands for?"

Fuck. She shouldn't care what it was. If he'd kept his cool earlier, there wouldn't be anything for her to question. He drummed his fingers on his desk and grasped the first answer that came to mind. One as close to the truth as possible without giving anything away. "We have a client who runs a string of porn websites. The developers think it's funny, because we're all a bunch of six year olds. They made up a nickname for his customization." He was a horrible liar. Worse, something gnawed behind his ribs for being dishonest with *her*.

"What does that have to do with the failed beta on Monday?" she asked.

"Monday night was a fluke. Nothing to worry about."

"Right. Because you didn't roll out a beta, because you have a tight deadline and you promised your board and investors you were dedicating all of your resources to meeting that schedule."

She was hitting closer to home than he cared for.

"Exactly." He tried to meet her gaze but couldn't. He settled for focusing on something behind her, and prayed she wouldn't notice.

"And if I go ask Justin, he'll feed me the same story about what PP stands for?"

Why wasn't she dropping this? "He'll tell you the same thing I did."

"Because in the amount of time it takes me to find his office on the top floor, you'll let him know I'm on my way and why?"

"Because he already knows."

Justin was a better liar than Antonio was. If she

decided to go up there, she'd run into a brick wall. Especially if she and Justin let themselves get as distracted as the last time they were in a room together. Antonio bit back a scowl at the thought.

She pursed her lips. "You can't do something that's going to threaten your stance with the board."

"I agree. We're not doing anything."

"No, you're not. We'll have the UI conversation when I'm done talking to Justin." She turned on her toe and headed toward the elevators.

Antonio thought about chasing her down, but a niggle of relief kept him in his chair. If she knew, there was no more need to hide this secret. No more waiting for the other shoe to drop and wondering when she'd find out and tell Grant.

He clenched his fist hard enough his knuckles ached. She was going to tell Grant. *Fuck.*

CHAPTER NINE

"MERCY'S TURNED YOUR NAME into an effective curse word," Andrew said.

Justin rolled his eyes at the phone, but he'd taken the call willingly and was grateful for the friendly distraction. "I thought you resigned from being her guard dog."

A note from Antonio popped on his monitor. *Incoming. I promise all she has is a name and a handful of assumptions*

Justin didn't need to ask for details. He could make assumptions of his own.

"I did." Andrew sounded like this was the least of his concerns. Then again, that was typical for him. "I'm the messenger. Nothing more. I don't care that you brought the entire site down."

"It's your site."

"It's data collection. *Oh no.* I might have to guess on my own which fetishes are trending next." Andrew owned Smut Central, one of the largest internet-porn distributors in the world.

Justin chuckled at the light sarcasm. It was one of the reasons they were testing PP with Andrew. The man had an instinct for what kinks were hot, and the goal was to see if PP's algorithms could match or even beat human experience. "If you're that blasé about my impending doom, thanks to Mercy's wrath, you called because…?" If Justin didn't cut to the chase, he'd get sucked into an hour-long conversation. Tempting but counterproductive.

"Yeah, yeah. You're a busy man with a busy life. This is a social call. One of Susan's classes is competing in San Francisco in a few weeks. She was wondering if those cute gay friends of mine are free for dinner."

"Her words?" It was an old joke. When Justin met Mercy in Brazil, she misunderstood his preferences and set him up with a friend of Andrew's. Who turned out to be Antonio. After the night Justin shared with Emily, though, Andrew's question tugged at a thought Justin didn't care to examine too closely.

"My words." Andrew said. "She actually bothers to remember people's names. It's a neat trick. Someday I'll get her to teach me. But I figured we'd drive into town for the day if you two are free."

The chance to catch up, unwind, and do something besides pound toward conflicting deadlines was tempting. "I can't say yet. This thing is devouring every free minute. I need an extra day in the week as it is."

A knock drew Justin's attention, and he looked up to see Emily standing in the doorway, lips pursed and cheeks flushed. Time to cut the conversation short. "If you're willing to pencil me in, I'll give you a definite *yes* or *no* next week," he said to Andrew.

"Will do. Do you think Antonio has five

minutes? Is he still around?"

Justin glanced at Emily again—the crossed arms and the furrow of her brow—then back at the message on his screen. "Odds are good. I'll send you over." Based on the clues, Antonio should welcome the distraction.

Justin blind transferred the call, then gave Emily his full attention. He wasn't sure how to approach her. The flirting they fell into on Monday probably wasn't appropriate. That didn't stop the swell of her lips and tapping of her foot from being alluring.

And she was still watching him with expectation.

He settled on, "I have a meeting in five minutes. What's up?"

"You have a meeting at five thirty-seven? You really do schedule your time down to the last minute."

"I do."

She stepped in the room and kicked the door shut behind her.

That was a bit odd and presumptive.

"Promiscuous Perks," she said.

Ice slid through his veins, but he shook it off. Antonio warned she had a name. Which also meant she now had a piece of lucrative information to use against Justin. Not that she needed to know that. "It's catchy." He kept his expression and tone neutral. "Are you thinking of taking what you learn here and competing with us?"

She lingered near the door. "Picture me pretending to be offended you think I'd break my non-disclosure and non-compete agreements. If I did that, I'd come up with a name you're not already using."

"Don't know what you're talking about. If Antonio hasn't given you access to the development timeline yet, make sure he does that. You'll see we're maxed out on man hours until we make this beta."

"The one you rolled out Monday night?"

He couldn't hide his wince. If all she had was assumptions, she'd put some pretty significant pieces together, to arrive at them. If he couldn't bury the truth, maybe he could sell her on the idea enough to buy her silence. It was a long shot, but the harder he pushed her away, the more curious she'd get. If she was at this point, after less than a week, it was time to try a new approach. A desperate play, but his reserves were drained. "Do you have time right now, or are you headed home?"

"It depends." She eyed him suspiciously.

He gestured to the table, on the opposite end of his office, and the chairs around it. He stood and approached his whiteboard. "I'll tell you what's going on."

She shifted her weight from one foot to the other, uncrossed her arms, then took a seat.

"I need you to use your imagination for a moment, if you will." The phrasing was an intentional reminder of Saturday night.

Her frown said she knew it. "All right."

"Picture an application that's been collecting buyer information from thousands of vendors for the last five years. Not in a nefarious, big-brother kind of way, but anonymously. The system doesn't care who bought what." He sketched as he talked. Shapes connected with lines. A data structure. "Every piece of data is a number, and it only cares what the patterns are across numbers."

"You mean… kind of like what APPropriate Designs does?"

"Exactly like that. The system is robust. Over the years, with the right people working on it, it's become an artificial intelligence that can guess who's moving into a stable relationship, based on how often they buy new windshield wipers." This was gross oversimplification at its finest, but if she caught on as quickly as Antonio said, she understood that.

She didn't look impressed. "I have an idea how the system works, yes."

"Perfect. You're still imagining, right?"

"Sure."

"Once a structure like that is in place, who's to say it has to be restricted to sales? If it can predict when someone is going to be in the market for diamonds, it should also be able to tell—based on grades, courses taken, the content of completed assignments, etcetera—whether or not someone will struggle in school."

She sat up straighter, and the glazed-over look vanished from her eyes. "Really." Curiosity replaced the boredom in her voice. "Could you go so far as to say if they're falling behind because they're bored, versus unable to keep up?"

"That's precisely what it does." This was too easy. True, it was his plan, but he didn't expect her to fold with a few words.

"It's brilliant. You've got this slated down the

road, for a future release after you meet this deadline?"

He mentally facepalmed. "This is Promiscuous Perks."

"Got it. Deceptive codename, to hide the fact you're working on something you're not funded for."

"Working off-hours. Why do you think we're always here late?"

"Except it's not limited to off hours, because one of your developers asked about it during the day." Her expression softened. "It's an amazing idea, and if it comes close to what I've seen, it'll be brilliant in execution. Make your deadline, get the board's sign-off, and then fit it into the schedule."

He wasn't going to lose his cool over this. She wasn't trying to be condescending; she simply didn't know the history. He tempered his response. "I understand what you're saying, and it's reasonable. Or it was, two and a half years ago. And then eighteen months ago. And then six months ago, when the shareholders told us the same thing each time. They don't think there's money in education. They keep vetoing us."

"Which sucks. I get it. But you're operating on someone else's capital. You don't get to tell them you're using it for one thing, and then apply it to something else."

"That's funny. I could have sworn your title was *Development Consultant*. I didn't realize you'd be involved in finance." He needed to watch himself. If he made this personal, he'd already lost.

When she clenched her jaw, a smudge of satisfaction flitted inside him. He wasn't the only one this was rubbing wrong.

Her smile looked strained—more teeth than joy. "My job is to figure out why you're not meeting your deadlines, and make sure you do. I've spent most of the week trying to uncover why it's a problem. Antonio runs a solid team. The company as a whole is put together well. There are none of the warning signs I see in most collapsing businesses."

"Because we're not in danger of crumbling."

"Unless you lose your funding, because—I don't know—someone can't keep their ego in check?"

"This isn't about vanity." His voice rose. He didn't care. "It's a solid fucking idea, and it's got far-reaching benefits."

She stomped to her feet, which put her a few inches away. "I'm not saying otherwise. But pursuing it this way? Risking everything for the people around you? That's your pride. There's a way to do these things, and this isn't it."

"If I did things the same way as everyone else, I'd have a net worth of nothing and be pitching my idea to any poor sod unfortunate enough to stand next to me in a line. Instead, I'm here. We built this because we're not in the habit of falling in line. We're pursuing PP to keep from losing that momentum. I won't be another face in a sea of forgettable apps. A flash in the pan. The guy everyone says *he used to be someone, but he couldn't adapt.* Fuck that. There's no point in doing this if I'm pursuing someone else's dream while mine collects dust in the hanger." He clipped off his words before he could say more. He hadn't meant to spill this much. To leave this much of himself on the table.

He'd leaned in until their noses almost touched. Emily watched him with wide eyes.

"What?" he snapped.

She licked her lips. The adrenaline and fury racing through his veins tugged at his cock. "I know now why I went home with you Saturday night." Her voice was quiet but as steady as her gaze that never left his face. "And for what it's worth, I don't have a counter."

"Don't." He dragged a thumb over her bottom lip.

She gasped. "Don't what?"

"Don't you dare choose now to be rational." He wouldn't have the wind sucked out of his sails.

"All right. I won't." She rose on her toes and kissed him. The caress of her mouth was so light, he felt the heat of her skin more than the brush of her lips.

He gripped the back of her neck, holding her in place, and kissed her back. Need roared through him. It danced on his fingertips and curled in his toes and singed his chest. Giving in to her was the worst fucking idea he'd had in ages. And the last thing he wanted was to stop.

CHAPTER TEN

THIS WAS A BAD, HORRIBLE, terrible idea. Career suicide. The equivalent of Emily lighting her resume on fire.

Justin pushed her jacket to the ground, pulled back the collar of her shirt, and bit her shoulder. The sharp sting drowned out her doubt.

"Let me help you a bit." He kissed up her neck, while he trailed his fingers down the front of her blouse. "This is the part where you say, *No. We shouldn't.*"

"Mmhmm." She tilted her head back as he dragged his mouth along her throat.

He reached her waist and undid the bottom button on her shirt. "That it was only supposed to be a one-time thing." He moved back up, undoing each button he encountered and brushing her bare stomach. "That it's not professional."

She was amused he vocalized her thoughts better than she could. It was hard to think when he was sucking a path down her chest, to the top of her breast, then gliding above the lace of her bra. "Then what do I say?" she asked.

"Well…" His words hummed against her skin,

and her nipples strained against fabric, wanting individual attention. He traveled his mouth back up to her jaw. "You don't say much of anything, because you can't talk when you're kissing me."

Good suggestion. She grasped the short strands of his dark hair and pulled his head up. When she kissed him again, tingles rolled over her. He rested a hand on her back, under her shirt, and pulled her close until her body molded to his. His palm was hot. It didn't matter how many arguments she came up with; she didn't want to break away. Tension flowed between them like electricity, raising the hairs on her arms and aching with need between her legs.

He let go, pulled back, and placed a finger on her lips. "You remind me you forgot to lock the door."

"That's actually a good one." She grasped his wrist. With a flick of her tongue, she drew his finger into her mouth, to trace a line over the pad. She dragged the digit over her bottom lip before letting go.

His groan settled deep inside her, as tantalizing as any physical contact. He met her gaze. "Antonio's the only other person left in the building."

That made her hesitate. Why? Because they used him in their fantasy, Saturday night?

Because she cared what Antonio thought of her. "That's still one person who could interrupt."

Justin's breath caressed her cheek when he whispered, "Be honest." He nipped her earlobe, then grabbed it between his teeth. "Are you terrified he'll find out, or turned on by the idea he might walk in on us?"

The way her pulse tore through her veins and her heart pounded to be free, she wasn't sure there was a difference. "I'm not answering that." Her reply was breathy.

"I'll alleviate your ambivalence." Justin undid her belt and slacks and pushed her pants to the ground. "He'll be busy for a while." He grasped her fingers and pulled her forward.

She stepped out of the clothing pooled around her feet, leaving her shoes behind. A flush of self-conscious warmth spread over her when she realized her shirt was open, leaving her exposed in bra and panties, while Justin was still fully clothed.

He raked his gaze over her, finally landing on her face. "Beautiful," he said with a smile. "Oh, and I have protection." He grabbed his wallet from his back pocket and pulled out a condom. "I promise this is only for one night. Our working relationship doesn't have to be impacted. It doesn't change my opinion of you."

"Which is good. I don't know if I could stand you thinking any less of me." She kept her tone playful, entertained by his disclaimer-like assurances.

He placed his hands on her hips and guided her, as he stepped backward toward one of the couches in the room. "You're frustrating as fuck." He kissed her. "I hate your reasons for being here." He dropped onto the leather cushions. "But don't think for a moment I don't respect you. Intellectually and professionally." He tugged her waist, prompting her to straddle his legs.

"How do you make that sound enticing?" She

draped her arms over his shoulders. He'd addressed most of her concerns, and despite the playful bullet list, she believed he meant every one. None of that made this a smart idea, but she wasn't going to turn back. There was no point in lying to herself about it.

"I'm that amazing." He slid his hands up her sides, to cup her breasts, then pinched her nipples through her bra.

She arched her back into the rough touch, grinding her mound against his erection, the hard length teasing her through clothing. She was wet enough the dampness would soak through soon.

He pressed his knuckles into the crotch of her panties, digging into her slit and rubbing against her clit in time to her rocking.

"*God*. I love that look. Mouth slightly parted, chest heaving—right when you're about come." His voice dropped an octave.

She couldn't manage more than a moan. She wavered on the edge of climax, riding a blade of pleasure but unable to tumble to the other side. He increased his pressure and speed, until stars danced behind her eyelids.

"Stop thinking," he murmured. "Let go."

The rest of her world swam out of focus, until his voice was the only thing she heard. His touch the only feeling. She dug her fingers into his shoulders, as orgasm tore through her, making her legs weak and her ears ring.

He eased back but didn't completely let up stroking. The sensations were too much, but she didn't want to pull away. She was vaguely aware of him tearing the condom from its package, dragging down his zipper—his fingers still pressing into her—and working his cock free to roll the rubber on.

He shoved her panties aside and dipped the bulbous head of his dick between her folds. "So wet. It makes me want to find out what else turns you on."

She wouldn't mind that. She should, but she wasn't supposed to be thinking.

He dragged his cock along her slit, spreading her juices. "I need to fuck you."

That sounded brilliant. She raised herself enough to let him in, and had to bite the inside of her cheek to keep a cry from escaping when he plunged inside her to the hilt, stretching her out and filling her up.

He set an increasing pace, digging his thumbs into her hips and rocking against her. Each thrust hit the same spot inside, coaxing her toward another peak. When her gasps and sighs grew louder, she clamped down on her tongue, to keep from making too much noise. The bitter taste of copper teased her taste buds, mingling with everything else. She clenched around him when she came again, squeezing his cock. Her head felt like it was filled with feathers.

His steady pounding shifted to hard and rough, skin slapping against skin. His groans became fractured grunts. The noise mingled with the unrelenting pressure, and when he peaked, it drew her orgasm to a dizzying height.

Their frantic rhythm slowed until the only sound in the room were the whir of a computer fan and their sharp attempts to catch their breath.

She buried her face in the crook of his neck,

struggling to find her voice. She was close enough to the ink decorating his skin that the vivid colors blurred and bled together in a dizzying array. His light touch on her shoulder made her giggle. "That tickles."

"Are you going to tell me?" he asked.

If she searched back through their conversation, she might find a point of reference, but she wasn't ready to turn her brain back on. "Hmm?"

"You said you knew why you went home with me." It figured he remembered that.

"My hell." She laughed. "You really are all ego."

"Not *all* of me." He thrust his hips, his semi-erect cock nudging her.

"All right. You're also scary smart, and passionate enough about what you love to sell it. Even if that thing is you."

"Now you're being mean."

Was she? "That wasn't my intention. I left the bar with you because you get this look in your eyes when you're being sincere. Like when you were talking about your tattoos."

He kissed her cheek. Such a tender gesture, compared to moments ago. "Don't let that get out. The last thing I need is for people to think I get all doe eyed when I talk about Dark Phoenix."

A snick filled the room. The door latched open, and she shot her head up. Time slowed to a crawl, as the door swung open and Antonio's voice carried through. "Next time you're going to pass me a half-hour time suck, warn me first." He paused in the doorway, gaze fixed on her and Justin.

A chill blanketed Emily, reminding her how little she wore.

Justin opened his mouth. "Ant—"

"You know what? I don't care," Antonio said. "It doesn't matter to me that you're fucking each other, but I need assurances it doesn't bleed into our work. Right now, I don't believe that. I'm going to close the door long enough for you to get dressed. I'll be here when you're both decent, and we'll all sit down and talk. Look each other in the eye. Discuss if this ends with me going back to Italy."

Emily's insides churned into a fine mush as he spoke, but the last bit of his statement knocked her thoughts off-kilter. Where the hell did that come from?

Before Antonio finished closing the door, Justin was prompting Emily to stand. She understood the urgency. There was no part of her that believed for a second she was—or should be—more important than their friendship. But the action still nagged her. Why couldn't there be a way to walk out of here right now—sneak back to her desk without being seen, grab her purse, and never come back?

At least after this conversation, she wouldn't be up all night wondering if Justin was going to call Grant and tell him to never send Emily back... for whatever reasons he'd give.

The thought wasn't as reassuring as she'd hope. She pulled on her slacks, buttoned her blouse, and grabbed her jacket from the floor. Justin had stripped off the condom and disposed of it. He stood near the door, waiting.

"You good?" he asked.

Not really. The anxiety clawing through her removed most of her mental capacity. Thankfully, it also blocked out her reaction to how incredible he looked with his hair mussed and his shirt untucked. She nodded.

Justin let Antonio back in the room. "Let's talk, starting with tabling the idea of you leaving and working our way out from there."

Emily sank into a chair by the table, hoping to keep her distance and wishing the weakness in her legs was caused by leftover euphoria, and not hedging nausea.

CHAPTER ELEVEN

ANTONIO SHOULD SIT, BUT the adrenaline coursing through him wouldn't allow it. Justin sat behind his desk, expression blank. Emily was on the other side of the room, looking like she wanted to crawl under the table and vanish.

Antonio felt bad about that.

"Your show, boss." Justin broke the silence.

Antonio looked at him. "Is it? Because the more time that passes, the more I feel like we're not actually business partners, and you're running a game I can't even comprehend." He shouldn't open with something this aggressive, but he needed to figure out what was going on with Justin. The relationship with Emily—or whatever the hell the two of them called it—was only a symptom. Sure, it bothered Antonio more than he was used to. More than Justin's engagement to Lia did. But it was because he hated watching Justin lose control.

This extended beyond tonight or the friction in the restaurant. It stretched into the company. Decisions Justin made. Priorities he set.

"Last time I checked, we were on the same page," Justin said. "If you have a problem with the way things are going, there've been plenty of chances before now to speak up."

"My problem isn't with *things*. It's with trying to figure out where your head is."

"Excuse me." Emily's voice was quiet.

Antonio was surprised she spoke up. She was the other half of what ate at him. His physical attraction to her wasn't what tripped him up, seeing her here tonight. Despite only working with her for a few days, he was starting to enjoy her company. Which made this feel like a betrayal on multiple levels.

He turned to face her.

She hesitated. "If the two of you are going to have it out in some sort of come-to-Jesus, you don't need me here."

"We do." Antonio studied her. "That's not limited to this moment in time. I mean that as a more sweeping statement. Speaking of—you were coming up here to talk about development projects. How did that become fucking on the couch? No. Wait. That's a detail I don't want." In a way, he did, but that kind of knowledge could be dangerous.

He looked at Justin. "And we shouldn't need her. We had this under control. Six months ago, developing PP on the down-low was doable. Now we're cutting too many corners and making mistakes. It's not all on you, but you're pushing hard, and you're going to do something stupid. Like screwing a contractor who has the power to bring this crashing down on us."

"You're right." Justin's reply caught Antonio off guard.

Antonio stared at him. "I'm sorry. Say it again?"

Justin smirked.

"I'm not actually that mighty," Emily said.

"No? If you called Grant right now and told him what you knew, what would happen?" Justin asked.

She shrugged. "I can guess, but I can't say. It's never come to that. I'm not sure how many more ways I can put this—I'm not here to see you fail. I look better if this project succeeds."

Antonio raked his fingers through his hair. The conversation was as undirected as his pacing. "Which brings us back to the couch. The lack of clothes. The why?"

"It was a negotiation," Justin said at the same time Emily said, "It was a lapse in judgment."

Justin slapped his palms on the desk. The *thunk* shook the floor, and Antonio covered Justin's hands, locking them in place. They stared each other down, and seconds ticked by.

"*Don't* get sidetracked," Antonio said with a growl.

Justin's nostrils flared, but he didn't pull or look away. Behind Antonio, leather creaked.

Seconds later, Emily moved into his peripheral vision. "I'm not sure what you're looking for. I meant what I told you—what he and I agreed on." She nodded at Justin. "It's just sex."

Antonio broke the staring match, to look at her. "You can see how the line blurs, especially when it happens again after the assurance is made. I want to know if we're going to have jobs after you talk to your employer."

"Funny. I have a similar concern about *you* talking to him." She quirked her mouth in a joyless smile.

"Neither one of us is calling him. It's none of his business who you sleep with." The irritation was gone from Justin's tone. "I did it because… It wasn't for blackmail. How's that? Hoping I'm not the only one." There was a hitch in the words. "Will you both sit down? Here, not on the other side of the room?"

Emily complied, and Antonio followed suit. He looked at her. "Your turn. Are you going to Grant with PP?"

Her wince summoned the irritation he'd tried to suppress since he walked in on them.

"Are you fucking kidding?" Justin's disbelief and annoyance echoed Antonio's.

"I already told you." She sounded apologetic. "I don't want to tell Grant anything, but ethically, I can't watch you spend investor money on this."

Justin sighed. "The company has been solvent for years. If you want to dig into our books for proof, we're funding PP without investor money."

"But PP is making us miss deadlines." Antonio hated to point that out in mixed company, but it wasn't a secret anymore.

Justin glared. "Whose side are you on?"

"Yours. Always yours." Antonio poured more emphasis into the assurance than he meant to, and he hurried to cover it. "It goes beyond pushing our people past their limits; our customers are starting to notice. If Mercy can't see past those fuckups, what happens when we give either beta to someone who doesn't know us? Doesn't trust us? Doesn't have the kind of coding experience she does, to help us troubleshoot? What happens when it brings the next site down?"

"I can't keep putting this off." Angry frustration propelled Justin's words.

Antonio didn't have a reassuring counter. "All the delays—the noes? They eat at me as much as they do you. But something has to give, before this all breaks."

Emily cleared her throat, drawing attention. "I still don't think I should be here for this, but since I am, may I make an observation?"

"Please, enlighten us." Justin's tone was half a step from sarcastic.

She rolled her eyes. "You're a stubborn jackass. Anyone ever tell you that?"

And the conversation was deteriorating again. "Could the two of you not, with the drifting off topic?"

"I'm done." Emily leaned in and rested her forearms on the desk. "But here's my point— unless you want board-approved contractors, you're under a hiring freeze until said board is happy with your work? What's stopping you from bringing in a third party, off the books? If you want this, and you're willing to foot the bill, pay them out of your own pocket. Even if you only get an extra ten hours a week, it has to be better than the fractured time you're pulling from your people now."

Justin shook his head. "I'm still waiting for your word that news about PP doesn't go back to Grant until it's ready."

"One more time, for those of you in the back."

She looked between them. "On the record, all I care about is that you meet your beta with a working product. If you're on track, there's nothing for me to tell Grant. Lie about being on schedule, do something like pull a UI developer for a two-day focus group they shouldn't be running—things like that, and you'll crash and burn at release time. We all fail if that happens." She furrowed her brow while she chewed her bottom lip. "And you should know Grant already suspects you're working on something else. He put the doubt in my head, not the other way around. You need to keep a lower profile."

This wasn't the best news, but given the circumstances, Antonio would take it. "Everything is out in the open now, and we're all on the same page? No more secrets?"

Emily looked at Justin, who raised his brows before turning to Antonio. "None," Justin said.

"Wonderful." Antonio wasn't in the mood to wonder if he should analyze that exchange. "We wasted half our night, but at least someone got laid and we got something accomplished." He turned to Em. "When you come in tomorrow, we'll be good?" He softened his tone. "No awkward pauses or not looking me in the eye?" It was going to be a long time before he let the image of her straddling Justin fade, but he didn't need that interfering with everyday life.

"No promises, but I'll try. Do you need anything else from me?" she said.

"No. Thank you."

"Ditto here," Justin chimed in.

"'Night. Both of you." She stood and crossed

the room, but paused in the doorway. "Sorry. One teensy, tiny thing."

Justin almost looked amused.

"What's that?" Antonio asked.

"PP is based on your standard engine, isn't it? Same data structure but enhanced algorithm?" The shyness was gone, and she stood a little taller.

"That's correct." Antonio was curious now.

She nodded toward Justin's desk. "That query doesn't return consumer results. It's calculating at the vendor level."

Antonio's eyes grew wide when he realized that one, Justin had been careless enough to leave a print out of PP code on his desk, and two, Emily was right. She must have read it upside-down and only seen two-thirds of it and absorbed it while talking to them. All without neither Justin nor Antonio noticing.

"How do you know we want consumer trends?" Justin snatched the printout and tucked it into a folder.

"I don't." Emily leaned her weight against the doorframe. "But anonymous vendor info filtered by user buying habits doesn't return the kind of data I've seen you chart."

Christ, she really was sexy. The code she was talking about had haunted Antonio for several days. His version worked, but it was too slow. Justin was a second set of eyes to help him optimize it. "How would you do it?" Antonio wanted to know. "That is, if you've got another five minutes."

She seemed to consider the question, then stepped back into the room. "What the hell. I'm not billing you right now anyway."

"I appreciate that," Justin said dryly.

Antonio braced himself to referee another argument.

Emily crossed the room and grabbed a whiteboard marker. "No comment."

*

TWO HOURS LATER, EMILY STOOD with her back to the wall, looking at Justin and Antonio. A series of diagrams and flowcharts decorated the board next to her. "Why not?" she asked.

Justin took the dry-erase pen from her, erased a few lines with the side of his hand, and connected different pieces. "The diagram says you need to go that way, but if you're not looking for middle information, you can bypass this layer and go straight to the source."

"Neat." She was impressed with the conversation. Justin hadn't let his skills lapse, despite being head of the company. When he and Antonio tossed proprietary terms around, she struggled to keep up. It was fascinating to watch. And enticing. Part of it might be thanks to the shared fantasy with Justin, which grew more vivid the longer she spent with both of them.

Justin glanced at his phone. "It's past eight. Didn't mean to keep you here this late. Since we're not paying you, at least let us buy you dinner."

"Which is his way of getting you to stay at least another hour, so we don't lose our momentum. For the record, it's a plan I support." Antonio stood and stretched, fingers interlocked and arms extended above his head. It elongated his torso, and muscle rippled under his shirt.

In her mind, she whistled. She could watch this for a while. Part of her insisted that wasn't appropriate, but a larger part pointed out she already crossed that line. If she scaled back to a little drooling, she was making progress. "I could eat."

Justin crossed the room to his desk, grabbed a menu from a drawer, and handed it to her. "Chinese food. What are you having?"

She scanned down the list. "Nothing too spicy."

"Had your fill earlier?" Justin asked, teasing in his voice.

"I don't want details." Despite Antonio's protest, he didn't sound upset. He watched Justin with an unreadable expression. It almost looked like adoration.

Which made sense, given what she'd seen of their friendship. If she read more into it, it was an inappropriate projection. She shook the thoughts aside, made her choice, and waited for Justin to call in their order. When he was done, she turned to Antonio. "Since the momentum is paused, may I ask you something?"

"Of course."

"Why would you go back to Italy? Why did Justin make it sound like more than a temporary arrangement?" Silence fell over the room, and two frowns met her curiosity. "Unless that's a bad question. Then forget I asked," she said.

"It's okay." Antonio's accent sounded heavier than normal. "It's something we try to pretend isn't looming. My family owns one of the largest technology companies in Italy, and my father wants to retire. He'd like me to take over, but Justin and I built APPropriate Designs… I'm torn, to say the least. Family obligation versus my desire to stay here." He looked at Justin with the same faint adoration as earlier.

"I get it." More than she wanted to. If Grant and the rest of the board were unhappy with the outcome of this project, the worst they'd do would be to buy out Justin and Antonio, essentially firing them with a sizable severance. It would leave Antonio free to go back home, but despite his expressed ambivalence, it was clear that wasn't what he wanted. Her good mood faltered, as she processed how much rode on success.

CHAPTER TWELVE

HOW DID EMILY LET HERSELF get sucked into this? She uncurled herself from the chair in Justin's office that she'd fallen asleep in. Someone had draped her jacket over her at some point during the night, and it tumbled to the ground as she sat up.

She should have left after dinner last night, but the conversation turned back to work and brainstorming and which Batman franchise of movies was the best. She did a quick scan of the room and found Justin asleep on one of the couches. Heat flooded her cheeks as memories of what else happened on that couch rushed back. She'd need to learn to control that reaction before she had to be in here with someone else again.

Did Antonio go home? She didn't blame him. She needed to do the same, shower, change, and get back here in time for her real shift.

She combed her fingers through her hair. Carrying her shoes, so they didn't clack against the tile, she took the stairs down two floors. It was barely six, but she didn't want to run into anyone while she still wore yesterday's clothes. The lights were out, as she padded toward her desk, the only illumination coming from streetlights that streamed through the windows and the dark gray of the sky, as the sun teased the skyline.

Her cellphone sat on her desk, and she swiped it out of habit. A handful of messages from Cynthia waited for her, starting at midnight and trickling every hour or two.

It's late. Making sure you're all right.

You're not home yet. You pick someone up again?

It's 3. It's Thursday. This isn't like you.

Reply and tell me you're alive.

Em, I swear to God, I'm calling the police if I don't hear from you soon.

The last one was from about five minutes ago. Emily sent back a quick reply. *I swear I'm all right. I'll be home in thirty and give you the short version.*

A reply came through before the light faded from her phone. *You'd better.*

Emily smiled at the concern and dropped the device in her purse. She turned and almost face-planted in Antonio's chest. A startled squeak escaped her. Her shoes fell to the ground. "Shit. Sorry." She settled her hand on her ribs, her heart hammering against her palm. "I didn't know anyone was here."

"I didn't mean to startle you." He put a few inches between them, a casual smile dancing on his lips. His hair clung damp and dark to his skin, and the faint scent of body wash teased her. "Justin and I have done this enough I'm in the habit of keeping a change of clothes on hand and using the showers in the gym downstairs. Both of us do that, actually."

"You're insane. You know that, don't you?"

she teased. Last night was fun, and working through problems was exhilarating, but she couldn't fathom how Justin and Antonio had kept up a schedule like this for six months. After one night, she wanted all the coffee and a short day so she could go home and get some real sleep.

He chuckled. "I've been called worse. I'd offer you something to wear, in case you wanted to do the same, but…" He trailed his gaze over her, and goosebumps rose everywhere his eyes traveled. "Size differences aside, all I have left is a pair of sweat shorts—it's been a long week—and your manager doesn't take casual Friday *quite* that far."

Maybe not, but he did justice to what he had. Instead of his standard dress shirt, tie, and slacks, he wore a T-shirt and jeans. She didn't know which style of dress was more alluring, but this one gave her a glimpse of something she'd never noticed before. Justin wasn't the only one with tattoos. A hint of what looked like scales peeked above the collar of Antonio's shirt, though it was difficult to make out details in the dark.

She forced her fingers to stay by her side, rather than reach up and trace the ink. "I appreciate the offer, but my roommate is panicked. I have to get home anyway."

"You're coming back, though." Despite his smile, seriousness bled into his statement. "No problems looking me in the eye?"

"I'm coming back. And no—I'm doing fine, thank you." In fact, if she didn't train her attention on his face, she'd be staring at the way his shirt hugged his torso and his jeans hung off his hips. Wondering what his ass looked like. His eyes were the safest place for her focus. She needed to stop. Sleeping with one was bad enough. Lusting after both… Well, it still didn't seem detrimental, but it would get distracting really fast.

Antonio stepped aside and gave a short bow as he gestured to the doors. "I'm glad to hear it. See you in an hour or two."

* * * *

AS A GENERAL RULE, MOMENTUM kept Justin going. It prevented him from overthinking, from talking himself out of good ideas, and from backing down. Emily stalled that. She made him pause long enough to question things, and that was dangerous.

It meant he was wasting large parts of his Friday morning staring at his personal finances and the various pieces of the company forecast, instead of catching up on work during his precious between-meeting time. The upside, if there was one in all of this, was that the task kept his mind from drifting back to the other conundrum he wanted to blame her for but couldn't.

He'd managed to ignore the nagging thought most of the week, telling himself that last weekend, using Antonio as a prop to turn up the heat and get laid was simply fun and games—a way to get the playful redhead to go home with him. Seeing her again made him doubt his motivations.

Talking to Tony Sr. was the first catalyst though. The reminder Antonio might not always be here tumbled pebbles loose in Justin's head that were attached to fear. He couldn't lose his business partner. His best friend.

She was wondering if those cute gay friends of mine… Andrew's words echoed in Justin's head. An ages-old taunt that Justin always shrugged off, because it was easier to do that than focus on Justin's shifting feelings that his attraction might be more than a simple appreciation for Antonio's handsome form.

When Antonio walked in on Justin and Emily, the ambivalence threatened to split Justin in two. A surge of desire to make fantasy a reality clashed with the nagging suspicion that Justin had crossed a line Antonio wouldn't forgive.

Justin shook the thoughts aside. Exhaustion and stress were screwing with his head, and he needed it clear, to move forward. He closed his eyes and counted down from ten, forcing out a distraction with each number. When he reached zero, he picked up the phone and dialed a familiar extension.

Antonio answered on the second ring. "Hey."

"What do you think?" Justin was referring to the email he just sent.

"It's going to be expensive."

Justin knew it. But Emily was right about a lot of things last night, including the need to break out PP from APPropriate Designs' payroll. "I don't expect you to foot any of the bill if you're not comfortable with it. This is my obsession. If you're still helping with the work, that's better than I can hope for."

"I'm in." Antonio didn't hesitate. "Do you have someone in mind?"

Same person he'd had on his mind for almost a week and shouldn't. "Take a guess."

"This is me assuming your choice is strictly for professional reasons. She's going to balk."

"Maybe. We won't know unless we ask." Justin had a valid list of why Emily was the best person to make this offer to, and Antonio could probably guess most of them. Besides, he was already on board. Justin would save the hard sell for Emily. "Ask her if she's free to join us for lunch. Wrap it in a pretty bow if you'd like. A *no hard feelings* kind of thing."

"No."

That caught Justin by surprise. "Why not?"

"If I do it, she's going to think I talked you into this," Antonio said.

"Who cares whose idea it was?"

"She does. Or rather, I would. I'd want to know whatever happened physically isn't the driving force for this decision, and that you aren't being coerced into asking for something that's questionable on this many levels. After everything she said last night, assume that she'll react in a similar way."

A foreign surge of jealousy gnawed at Justin's thoughts. How did Antonio already knew Emily well enough to say what he was with such certainty? "Point taken."

He hung up and dialed Emily without pause. Had to keep the momentum going.

"This is Emily." Hesitation lined her greeting.

"It's Justin. Do you have a moment?" Not that he expected her to say *no*. It was a perk of being the boss. Most people made time for him when he asked.

"I do."

"Are you free for lunch? I have a proposal I'd like to run by you." He winced. There were a lot of ways that could be interpreted, and as much fun as it might be to talk her into screwing in the coat closet of the restaurant, it wasn't on the agenda. "Rather, we do. Antonio and I. A business proposal."

Hesitation stretched over the line. "Can you give me a hint what it's about?" she said.

"I'd prefer we talk about it on our own time." With any luck, that would give her a hint, and if not, at least he was complying with her insistence from yesterday that they not conduct PP business on Grant's dime. It was partly stubbornness, but largely because she wasn't going to agree to anything unless the lines between the two aspects of the business stayed distinct.

"Do I have a choice?" she asked.

The question ground against his nerves and knocked him off the track. "Always." The reply held an edge he didn't intend.

"That came out wrong." Her voice dropped in volume. "I only meant… Boss asks for your time, it's unprofessional to say *no*. Not that I think you would… You know what? I'm going to stop talking now. Yes. I can make it."

"Great. Twelve thirty? We'll meet in the lobby."

"I'll be there." The line clicked off.

He placed the receiver back in its cradle and tried to make sense of the uneasiness left by the conversation. And then it hit him. He was bothered she had reservations about taking him at face value. That she didn't trust him. He didn't know which was worse—trying to decipher why it ate at him this deeply or not knowing how to change her perception.

125

CHAPTER THIRTEEN

EMILY TRACED THE HEM of the cloth napkin draped over her lap, focusing on the rough texture against her fingertips and trying to ignore the discomfort growing inside. She'd ordered the chef's special, but unless she got answers soon, she expected the food to taste like sawdust and sit in her stomach the same way.

On the car ride to the restaurant, Justin and Antonio kept the conversation light, trying to pull Emily in. She wasn't interested in talking about what her favorite movie was in high school; she wanted answers.

Under the table, Antonio nudged her knee with his. She looked up with a scowl, and he raised his brows. He turned to Justin. "If you don't ask her soon, she's going to threaten to walk back to the office." Even the way the word *threaten* rolled off Antonio's tongue and down her spine wasn't enough to lift her mood. That he recognized she was irritated helped, though.

"All right. I suppose we've spent enough time proving this isn't a work meeting," Justin said.

Huh? She tried to make sense of the statement

and failed.

Justin studied her for a moment. "I—we've been thinking about what you said last night. That if we want to put more hours behind PP, we consider hiring a contractor outside of the company structure."

He'd actually listened to her. She was pleased. "That's great. But why tell me? I meant what I said about keeping things to myself, but you're pushing your luck, looping me in on decisions like this."

"And we're about to push it a step further." Justin looked at Antonio. If they exchanged some kind of agreement or signal, she couldn't tell. He turned back to her. "We'd like you to consider taking a second contract. With us. Nothing extensive, mind you. I don't expect all-nighters or even your entire weekend. I'm hoping you'll give us maybe five or ten hours a week. Paid out of our pockets."

Her brain stuttered to a halt, returning a resource-overload error. "I think you missed the point of my suggestion. You're supposed to be avoiding conflicts of interest. While we're at it, I signed a non-compete agreement. As a retainer, I'm not allowed to take anything I learn to another contract and compete against one of Grant's investments."

"There's none of that going on here." Antonio picked up the pitch. "We made sure of it. None of these conversations happen while you're on the clock as a contractor. You're not using what you know to compete against us."

"Exactly." Justin dove in. Did they rehearse this? "In fact, you're doing your job, but one better. What is it you keep reminding us of? We finish the beta—everyone wins?"

Hell. She didn't like having her words turned against her. Worse, she hated that she couldn't come up with an argument. The offer wasn't right in spirit, if not in letter, but she couldn't find the right words to explain why. "Why do you want me?" She bit back a cringe at the choice of words and pushed on. "Make the offer to one of your developers. Someone who's already been on the project. Who knows your product in and out."

"Eh…" Justin dragged out the word. "The thing is they don't know they're not supposed to be working on PP We've asked them to keep it quiet and been vague about why, but that's standard for any of our new products. You're the only person we know of who's figured out we're bending a few rules."

"That doesn't make me any more likely to help you continue to do so." She didn't know how to make her point, and after what she saw last night, she wasn't sure how hard she wanted to argue. The technology they were working with was the kind of challenge she thrived on. It was similar to her reasons for helping Cynthia.

Justin leaned in, and his eyes softened. "I'm going to be straightforward—I know, don't die of shock—and put this all on the table. I'm desperate to finish this project, and you offered up a viable way for me to get it done without stepping on toes. We'll pay your full rate. You set your schedule."

Indecision warred inside. Saying *yes* was a bad idea. Probably a worse idea than screwing Justin last night. On the other hand, she wouldn't mind padding her savings with a little extra cash. That wasn't the big thing tipping her toward accepting. Sure, there was the learning opportunity, but Justin sold her with his pitch. She'd struggled in school. Wished on many occasions someone would notice she was bored. This was good experience. There were a dozen excuses to tell them *okay*. When it came down to it, she wanted to.

But she couldn't force the words out. "I don't know."

"You've got time to think about it." Antonio was kind.

Justin didn't look as accepting of the answer. "Until Monday. I wish I could give you longer." The undercurrent in his voice said he was reluctant to offer her that much. The heavy beat of an alt-rock song filtered from his direction, and he grabbed his phone from his jeans pocket. He glanced at the screen. "Have to take this. Be right back."

Justin walked away, and she turned to Antonio. His attention was focused in the direction Justin walked. She followed his gaze. Correction—he was specifically watching Justin. She knew the look on his face, too. She suspected she wore a similar one every time she stared at one of the men while they weren't looking.

The equation chugged away in her head, and even when it returned results, she took a minute to process. "Have you considered telling him?" The question escaped before her brain caught up. Justin was worried she'd tell Antonio they used his likeness on Saturday night, and had no idea Antonio might be happy to take her place.

*

EMILY'S VOICE NUDGED THE EDGES of Antonio's mind, and he realized he was staring. He dragged his gaze from Justin and faced her. "I'm sorry. What?" He managed to make sense of what she'd asked. "Telling who what?"

"Him." She nodded toward the corner Justin had disappeared around.

Antonio didn't care who knew he was bisexual, but this was one secret he didn't need destroying a friendship. Perhaps Emily meant something else. "I don't know what you're talking about. I tell him everything."

"Okay. My mistake." She picked up her water and took the longest sip she could without managing to drain the glass.

Silence stretched between them. Andrew hiding how he felt about Justin was as much a part of him as anything he knew. Andrew figured it out years ago, but it was one of the few things the man kept to himself. Antonio was grateful for that. He was also tired of holding back.

He didn't know Emily from a random stranger on the street, except for the glimpses of kindness and intelligence he'd seen. And her body. *Whew.* However, after last night's conversation, she didn't strike him as the kind of person who used sensitive information for personal gain. If he told her this, he'd get it off his chest, and she'd be gone in less than a month.

He measured his words before he spoke, hoping to strike a balance between vagueness and confession. "If you'd fallen for your best friend—someone you also had a business relationship with, who never showed the slightest inkling of interest in you *that way*—would you risk it all by saying something?"

"Is it any easier sitting next to him day after day, while he hooks up with people who aren't you?"

"Yes." Easier than losing him? Without question.

She set her glass down and shifted in her seat to look at him. "How?"

"He's still here. If I say something and lose him because of it, I won't even have the watching." He was saying too much, but it was easy with Emily. She studied him with curiosity and compassion instead of judgment. "It's not a flash-in-the-pan lust thing. I want him to be happy."

"I can tell." She turned her head away and tucked a strand of hair behind her ear, hiding her face with her hand.

He didn't know what else to say, and without her prompting, silence settled between them again. The clink of forks and knives on porcelain combined with quiet chatter around them, to take the place of conversation. Where was Justin? Or did Antonio need him gone a moment longer, to compose himself? No. The confession, even without a resolution, made him feel a bit lighter.

"Have you thought about…" Emily looked at him again, then shook her head. "Never mind."

"You do realize you can't lead with that and not finish the thought?" He should let her drop the topic. Why was he pushing her?

"Nothing. Rather, that is…" She fiddled with the edge of her napkin. "Maybe a less direct approach to feel him out? Not that it's any of my business."

Justin would be back any minute, and this was a ridiculous conversation to have. It gave Antonio a new kind of twisted hope, and he didn't want that. He resigned himself a long time ago to watching from afar and being content. "What do you mean? Pretend I'm dim and spell it out for me."

She furrowed her brow and twisted her mouth. "As in sharing? To feel him out, I mean. You go to the bar together a lot, don't you? Find a woman who's interested in experimenting, someone neither of you is attached to, and kind of use her to see if he might be interested in more?" She ducked her head. "I'm babbling. Don't listen to me. I can't believe I said that to you. I—" She snapped her jaw shut. "Sorry. Can we pretend I never brought up any of that?"

Probably not. The suggestion was more enticing than he expected. Abstract images coalesced in his mind, and the *woman who's interested* became Emily. Antonio pictured gliding his hands over her body. Kissing her, while Justin penetrated him from behind. The string of thoughts flowed over him, sparking his senses and stirring his cock. "I don't think it would work."

"Why not?"

"I don't want to get stuck in a situation where I'm second guessing what gestures do or don't mean." Like Justin kissing him hard and heavy. Or Antonio fucking Emily while she wrapped her lips around Justin's cock. Antonio swallowed a huge gulp of ice water, but it didn't relieve the heat flooding him.

"Similar to being in love with your best friend and keeping your distance for years and never daring to ask if he feels the same, but instead analyzing every single move he makes and wondering if maybe, possibly, there could be something there?"

Damn her for vocalizing his thoughts. "A bit like that, yeah."

"As I said, forget I brought it up."

The discussion faded from existence again. He smiled at the waitress and thanked her when she brought their food, but otherwise, neither he nor Emily said anything. Antonio was grateful for the pause in conversation. It gave him a chance to force down his arousal.

A few minutes later, Justin returned.

"Everything all right?" Antonio asked.

Justin took his seat, looking between Antonio and Emily. "I wondered the same thing. Did I miss something?"

"Nothing." Emily clipped off the word.

"Right." Justin caught Antonio's attention. "Mercy wants to know if we can deploy tomorrow morning. I told her *no problem*."

"Sounds good to me." Antonio was grateful for the shift in topics. Not that it swept Emily's suggestion from his mind.

Justin turned to Emily. "Speaking of tomorrow. No pressure, you still have until Monday, but if you're free this weekend, we've got work for you."

She frowned and let out a soft sigh. "I have to say *no*."

"Don't answer right away if you're not certain." Antonio had expected she'd waver but not outright refuse.

"I don't need more time. I can't. I know it's not technically a conflict of interest or a violation of my contract, but there are so many blurred lines. I don't want it to become an issue."

"Of course." Justin's tone went flat. "If you change your mind, we'll be at my place tomorrow. Probably starting at eight."

"Thanks, but no. I'm sure." She turned her focus to her food and picked at the vegetables.

There goes that idea.

CHAPTER FOURTEEN

THE DOORBELL RANG, and Justin moved to answer. He was surprised to see Emily on his porch. He opened the door wider and made a show of looking around behind her. When he turned back to her, she pursed her lips, but it didn't hide the hint of a smile.

"Do I dare ask what that was about?" she asked.

"Yesterday you were so sure your answer was *no*, I was looking for hidden cameras." If someone were to press him about where the playful mood came from, he'd be forced to admit he was happy to see her. Not only for the extra help she brought, but because it was her. Fortunately, no one was pressing. "What changed your mind?"

"I can't pass up the challenge."

Which was exactly what he'd hoped for. He stepped aside. "We work in the kitchen. You can set up your laptop in there."

"There's a condition." She stepped inside but didn't go further.

A crack formed in his mood. "All right?"

"I can't take any money for doing this."

"Then what's the point?"

She shrugged. "I asked myself that on repeat the entire drive over here. And last night, when I made the decision. I even dreamed about the answer. I guess, for personal reasons, the idea is fascinating. You've both sold me on how much it means to you to see this finished, and while it probably sounds odd to you, because we barely know each other, that matters. But I still can't reconcile drawing a paycheck with it not being a conflict of interest."

"If you do it for free, that makes it better?" Justin didn't understand. He didn't want her to back out, but making her work without getting paid hardly seemed fair.

"Not completely for free. You'll promise me that, when this whole thing is done and the board has seen how brilliant it is and signed off, and I'm out from under the contractual obligations, you'll find a way to make it up to me."

He should accept her offer and leave it at that. Why wasn't he? "That could be a long-term gamble."

"I can't explain my reasons any better than I have. Not because I'm trying to keep something from you, but I don't know if I understand them myself. If you'd still like my help, leave it at that?"

"We're working in the kitchen." He couldn't ask for a better explanation, when he didn't completely understand his motivations. It wasn't fair to ask her to own up to something he wasn't willing to do the same with.

* * * *

MANY HOURS LATER, AS the sun dipped behind

the horizon, they had wrapped things up for the day. The deployment went smoothly, and Justin felt more confident about the PP project than he had in months.

"Help me understand why you've got this obsession with Batman." Emily sat on one end of his sectional, feet tucked beneath her, looking as if she'd always been a part of the scenery.

Antonio lounged a few feet away, arm draped over the back of the couch. "He's always been like that."

"It's not an obsession." Justin sat in the chair across from them, enjoying the evening and the company, including the lighthearted ribbing. "I don't understand the appeal of the guy. His super power is money. And being emo. I can do that."

"You mean you don't already?" Emily stuck out her tongue. "Or are you jealous because he has the emo bit down, and you're simply not any good at moping?"

"He's really not. He's all about the moving on and getting things done," Antonio said.

Emily seemed to ponder this. "Batman gets things done. Is it the utility belt? The car?"

Justin had no idea how they ended up here, but it was a reminder of why he enjoyed her company the night they met. He could be himself tonight, and that was wonderful. "I'm not jealous. In real life, even Bruce Wayne would have to answer to investors. And seriously? Fuck that."

"Okay, okay, okay." Emily held up her hands. "Tangent. I heard the most ridiculous story Thursday afternoon."

"Was it when you were riding him on the

couch?" Antonio asked. "Because if he told you that was first time he'd done that there, it might be true."

Pink dotted her cheeks, and she ducked her head. Entirely too alluring. "No, it— Wait. Really? Two leather couches, and you've never…?" She looked at Justin.

"Contrary to—I was going to say *popular belief*, but I don't talk to a lot of people about my sex life, so—*your* belief, I'm not some kind of manwhore. No, I never had sex in my office before two days ago." Justin kept the teasing in his voice.

Antonio scooted forward in his seat. "Is this the tangent? Or was there more to the original statement?" he asked Emily.

Emily furrowed her brow, and then smiled. "Yes, there was more. He"—she nodded at Antonio—"told me you call the project Promiscuous Perks because you have a client who's got a porn website, and it's kind of a joke. Why do you really call it that?"

"He told you the truth. You haven't figured out yet that Antonio is shit at lying?"

"I'm not— All right. I am." Antonio grinned.

Emily fiddled with a loose strand of hair, watching her lap for a moment before she spoke. "Pardon my naiveté, but what kind of rewards program does a porn site use? And how did that partnership even happen?"

"Technically, their advertising firm is our client, but it's the same kind of rewards as any other site." It didn't matter that they'd been working with Andrew for five years; Justin still had an urge to giggle like a child when it came to discussing sex and business. He didn't have an issue with it, but the six-year-old inside liked the innuendo and implication. "Buy so many subscriptions, get one free. He's more of a data-gathering spot for us though. We go back a long way with the owner, and he's got a human knack for predicting the same things our engine does. He lets us test our algorithms against him."

Emily raised her brows. "Wow. Selling sex has never sounded so dry. You buried the lede, though. You and he go way back? Who's he? How far back?"

Though she helped them with the deployment today, she knew she was working on R&T servers—Mercy's company. They never gave her Andrew's information, because it wasn't needed for what they were doing.

"Here's a thirty-second history of us," Antonio said. "We met in Brazil, while we were backpacking around South America. Another one of the guys we knew went on to found a tiny little startup called Smut Central."

"In other words, when you say *porn site*, you mean a series of the largest in the world? And you know this guy? Did either of you star in one of his movies?" Emily's eyes were wide, and the pink on her cheeks darker than before.

Antonio shook his head. "Now you disappoint. That's the question everyone asks when they find out."

"Together?" Emily tacked onto the end.

If Justin were drinking something, he'd have spit it out. Out of the corner of his eye, he saw Antonio's jaw drop. Did Emily really say that?

"We'd more or less gone our separate ways by

the time he got things rolling, and we didn't meet up with him again until years later. So no. Not separately and not together." Justin's impulse was to go with a vehement denial, but he bit that back. A tiny bit of his mind insisted it was to let Emily think the topic wasn't a big deal.

Another bit of him argued, asking if that was the real reason he let her keep talking. If the fantasy was good, how would the reality be? Emily was obviously willing, and the atmosphere was laid back tonight. Would Antonio—

Justin shook away the question. Antonio might like both men and women, but that didn't mean he was up for something like this. There were too many reasons it was a bad idea.

But why couldn't Justin think of any?

"It's probably a good thing he'd moved on before then," Antonio said. "We were young and impulsive, and if he'd asked in the right way… Well, it might not look good to have that kind of footage floating out there on the internet."

Justin's mind tripped over the words and stumbled to catch up. A fast denial flew to his tongue, and he choked it down. This situation was getting surreal. Justin wasn't sure he minded.

"You're telling me, if this guy had said, *be in my porn movie together*, you might have agreed?" Emily's eyes were bright, the green catching the overhead light and shimmering with mischief.

Knowing what he did about Emily, Justin could guess where this was going. "I might have. If the question was more like, *be in my movie together with this attractive woman*." The moment the words were out, he hesitated. Was he pushing things too far?

Emily wore a tiny smirk, and Antonio looked more curious than anything. An excellent sign.

"The things they do in those videos don't translate well to real life." Despite the words, Antonio's tone was light, rather than dismissive.

Emily rolled her eyes. "I know. It takes six hours to film a single blow job, and everything is posed for camera angles. Spoil sport."

"Hear him out." Heat raced over Justin's skin, teasing with possibilities. He wasn't ready for this to end yet.

"Thank you." Antonio grinned. "I'm not talking about that. Sure, that destroys some of the fun of watching the movies, but the positions themselves don't equate to enjoyable sex."

"You know from personal experience?" Emily sounded amused.

"Yes. I consider myself a life student of physics and human anatomy." Antonio gestured to the spot in front of him. "Stand up."

Emily hesitated.

Antonio motioned again. "I promise—no biting, unless you beg."

The words sent a fresh wave of memories tumbling through Justin's head. Of undressing Emily a piece of clothing at a time, then leaving teeth marks on her shoulder. The images were tinged with flares of jealousy, intensifying them. That was weird. He didn't have that kind of attachment to Emily, even if the sex was good.

She stood.

Antonio grasped her fingers. "This is a practical

demonstration." He pulled her toward him and patted his thigh. "You'll need to be closer."

Emily straddled his legs, and Antonio gripped her hips.

When did the two of them become so comfortable with each other? The question struck Justin. He nudged it aside, in favor of the now. Besides, he had an idea where this was going, and he wouldn't spoil the fun by overthinking things.

Momentum.

"Perfect." Gravel snaked into Antonio's voice. "Here's the issue with something like a porn threesome. You've got the woman in the middle, like-so. Hopefully enjoying herself as much as the man is."

"She is." Emily draped her arms over Antonio's shoulders.

Fuck. This was too much, and they hadn't moved past playing. Justin's cock strained against his jeans, and his pulse screamed through his veins, insisting he become part of the scene. He stood and closed the distance between him and them, but didn't make contact.

"Guy number two comes along and wants to join in the fun." Antonio met his gaze and nodded. "Unless he's hung like a yard stick, the angles don't work."

Justin pressed against Emily's back for emphasis. She let out one of the whimpers that drove him wild and leaned into him, never letting go of Antonio. "See, that's such a guy thing to assume," she said.

"How do you figure?" Justin struggled to hang

onto enough brain power to have this conversation. He wanted to slide his hands under her shirt and up her sides, to cup her breasts.

"I say *threesome*, and the two of you automatically gravitate toward penetration. Even in the implausible fantasy of internet videos, there are other ways to get off."

"Enlighten us." Justin brushed her hair off her neck, dragging his nails along her skin. He was having a hard time thinking about anything but how vivid Emily's imagination could be.

Logic tried to point out that he and Antonio had never done something like this before. It had the potential to change everything between them. Justin argued with himself that no one was complaining, plus they shared the rest of their lives; there was no harm in letting this conversation go where it would.

Was there?

CHAPTER FIFTEEN

WHEN EMILY SEGUED INTO THREESOMES, Antonio was ready to shut things down and change the subject. Her question from lunch yesterday—*have you considered sharing, to feel him out?*—taunted him most of the night. That didn't mean he wanted to risk anything by exploring the option.

Within a few sentences, however, it was clear Justin wasn't balking. Rather, he was actively participating.

Now, with Emily's warm weight in Antonio's lap, and Justin close enough to touch, Antonio was harder than he ever remembered being. She had to feel that. The seam of his jeans pressed into his cock under her weight.

Logical reminders like *don't sleep with the contractor* fell on deaf thoughts. It hadn't stopped anyone yet, and with reality this near and vivid, Antonio's daydreams suddenly felt two-dimensional.

Emily shifted against him, and he tightened his grip involuntarily, digging into her hips. She drew a finger along his collar. He knew without looking she was tracing the edges of his tattoo.

"What is it? And what was I saying?" she asked.

"It's easier to show than tell." He stripped off his T-shirt. He was tired of dancing around the *will we, won't we?*

She trailed along the Chinese dragon, where it wrapped up his bicep, then finished near his collarbone. "It's gorgeous."

Her feather-light touch sped over his body, fueled by Justin's attentive gaze. Justin knotted his fingers in her hair. "He gets that a lot." He tugged her head back and lowered his mouth to her neck. She gasped and gripped Antonio's arm. The sharp sting tugged at his nerves, lighting his senses on fire.

While Justin made her squirm, Antonio glided his hands up her sides, pushing her clothes out of the way. Every time she adjusted in his lap, she ground against his erection, obliterating his thoughts. "As for what you were saying…" He pulled her shirt over her head, then kissed along the top of her breasts. "I believe you accused us of lacking imagination."

"Not quite my words." Despite the clench of her hands on his biceps, her bra fell away.

"But it was your meaning." Antonio slid the straps down her arms, exposing her breasts. Her skin was pale and smooth like porcelain, free of freckles below the neckline. He might have misplaced dreams of happily-ever-after with Justin, but Antonio's attraction to Emily was distinct and unique; she was temptation airbrushed with lust. He lowered his head to a swollen pink nipple, and drew it into his mouth, to suck and nibble.

From the corner of his eye, he saw Justin kissing her neck.

"I take it all back." She spoke between gasps.

"And whatever else I need to say, for you to keep going." Her grinding against him shifted to a steady rocking, as she rode him. The heat of her mound seared him, despite the clothing in the way, and his cock begged to be let loose. To slide inside her. Her moans became more punctuated, as her pace increased.

He dropped his hands back to her hips and held hard, to keep her from moving. "Not yet, *passerotta*." He clenched his jaw when the endearment slipped out, but he didn't want to take it back.

Justin eased up as well, and Emily met Antonio's gaze. Her flush covered her cheeks and neck, and her chest heaved from exertion. *Intoxicating*.

Justin reached over her shoulder to grasp her hand and prompted her to stand. The sudden loss of warmth and weight should have been a relief, but pressure still strained against Antonio's zipper.

"God, I like watching you." Justin undid the button on Emily's jeans.

She slapped his hands away. "No. You don't get to stay dressed this time, while everyone else strips down."

"That was once," Justin said.

"Fifty percent. Not great odds." Emily nodded at his chest. "Shirt off."

Antonio should be jealous of the playful, intimate exchange. Instead, it added to his arousal. Justin obeyed Emily's command, and Antonio bit the inside of his cheek, to keep a groan from escaping. He'd seen his friend shirtless on numerous occasions, but the mood changed the experience. He felt like he was taking in Justin's toned upper body, wrapped with an eclectic assortment of ink, for the first time.

Antonio was barely aware of undoing his jeans and working himself free. The release sent shudders over him, followed by a second wave when he wrapped his hand loosely around his shaft.

"Better?" Justin asked.

Emily nodded.

"Good." Justin pushed off the rest of her clothes.

Christ, that view from behind… The curve of her back where it met her ass was a delicious sight.

Justin reached for her, and she stepped back, out of reach. She whirled to face Antonio, giving him a perfect view of what he'd craved to see when he walked in on them. Reality was much better than fantasy.

A playful smile dancing on her lips, she glanced at his crotch, then knelt on the couch next to him. "I want to help." She kissed a lazy zig-zag pattern down his chest, then over his wrist, before moving his hand out of the way. She flicked her tongue over his bulbous head, and pleasure surged through him, tingling as far down as his toes.

When she slid her mouth down his length, he twisted his fingers in her red locks. He wanted to tilt his head back and fall into the sensation of her soft lips against his dick and her tongue circling his length. He was intensely aware they had company, though. When he forced himself to look at Justin, he was surprised to see him watching the scene, enraptured.

A hungry smile spread across Justin's face when he caught Antonio's gaze.

Justin shed the rest of his clothing. When his cock sprang free, standing at attention, Antonio's thoughts short-circuited. He couldn't look away. Justin rolled on a condom and stepped up behind Emily. He glided a hand down her ass and, and the sound she made carried through Antonio's shaft, humming and teasing.

When Justin entered Emily, she whimpered and increased her attentions on Antonio. The combination of sights, sounds, and sensations tightened in his balls, and he almost came. He didn't want this to be over yet. He bit back climax, in favor of diving into the experience. Working one hand down Emily's chest, he moved the fingers of his other hand between her legs. *Fuck.* She was slippery. Which was the perfect excuse to slide from teasing her clit to caressing Justin's sac.

Her breathing grew shallow again, and Antonio focused more attention on her sex, stroking and coaxing the swollen button. She slowed her sucking but didn't pull back when she came, her cries muffled.

Antonio risked another glance at Justin, whose eyes were closed and his face screwed up. Justin pounded harder against Emily, his grunts coming in staccato bursts. When Emily resumed her fevered attentions on Antonio's cock, the intensity caused him to hiss between clenched teeth. Part of him slid into his own mind, drowning in the stimulation, but he was also wondering what it would feel like to be in her place, bent over, with Justin thrusting inside him from behind.

Fantasy and reality melted into a vivid haze. Justin's thrusting and growls said he was close. He shuddered when he climaxed.

"*Passerotta,* please." Antonio tried to pull Emily away. Instead, she gripped the base of his shaft, and stroked in time to the bob of her head. It was all too much. Antonio couldn't hold back. He came hard, hitting the back of her throat and filling her mouth. Her touch became dizzying, and then bordered on painful, but he didn't want to pull away. Finally, ecstasy wracked his body, and he slumped back against the cushions, spent.

She sat up. The only word he could think of, for the look her face, was *impish*.

"*Fuck.* You get hotter each time. I don't know how that's possible." Justin grasped her hand and tugged her to her feet.

She wobbled for a moment, but he helped steady her. He kissed her hard, their bodies pressed together. Antonio couldn't hold back the guttural noise that tore from his chest at the sight of Justin tasting him on Emily's lips. Want mingled with the sharp tang of envy, though he wasn't sure anymore who it was directed at or which role he'd rather fill. He cleared his throat when the kiss lasted for several seconds. "Someone else is in the room." His throat was dry, and his words cracked.

Emily pulled from Justin's grip and turned to face Antonio. "No one gets left out." She rested her hands on the back of the couch, on either side of him, and dipped her head in to press her mouth to his. He nipped at her lips, and their tongues danced a twisty two-step.

She squealed and broke away when Justin grabbed her by the waist, dropped onto the couch next to Antonio, and pulled her down with him. She settled, resting against Justin and placing her feet in Antonio's lap. A pleasant silence settled over the room, interrupted only by the hum of electronics.

"So"—Justin's voice was a sharp crack in the still—"does this mean we're having another one of those *talks* where everyone promises this is only physical and it doesn't impact work?"

Antonio was sick of those conversations. He metered his response. "I think we're all on the same page." He had a feeling they weren't. Not even close.

If Justin caught the lie, he didn't say anything.

Antonio had enjoyed everything about the interlude. There were no regrets. But in that short span, he'd gone from denying anything could happen with Justin, to getting enough of a taste that he wanted more. Something told him *more* wasn't an option, but neither was putting the genie back in the bottle. It was official—Antonio was seriously fucked.

*

EMILY DRIFTED ON THE EDGE of consciousness, when her world shifted. She forced herself awake enough to see Antonio untangle himself from the pile the three of them made. She couldn't drag her attention from his back and the ripple of muscle when he stretched. Without a glance behind, he padded from the room. She tried to be careful getting up, to not disturb Justin, but it didn't seem to matter. Once he was out, he stayed that way until he was ready to wake up, and unlike Antonio, he didn't strike her as a morning person.

She plucked her clothes from the ground, tugged on her jeans and T-shirt, and followed Antonio.

She found him in the kitchen, moving around as if he'd always been there, filling the coffee maker with water and then grounds, and setting it to brew.

As water hissed and heated, he turned to face her. "I thought you were kidding at lunch. When you were talking about how to feel the situation out." His voice was quiet in the early morning still.

Did he think she'd set him up? The notion he saw her as deceptive gnawed at her. "I didn't plan that."

"You were inspired."

"Are you upset?" Kinky sex and games was one thing, but she didn't want to push him away. Even though technically, they only worked together, she cared what he thought.

He smiled and shook his head. "Not even close. Thank you. I'm a bit fucked, but that's on me. Besides, you were incredible."

The compliment brought back images of last night, complete with whispers of touch, sound, and smell. Heat flooded her face. "You too. That is… everything you said—me too. Or rather…" Hell. She was awkward. "I should get home. Change. Shower."

"You got quiet after. Are you okay still? We're good?" he asked.

"I promise." Ignoring the fact that she wanted

to close the distance between them. Trail her fingers over his bare chest. Steal a good morning kiss. He wasn't hers, though.

He seemed to relax. "We're taking the day off. We got a lot more done yesterday than we planned, thanks to your help. You should go home and enjoy what little weekend you have left."

"Yeah. Definitely." She'd enjoy it here fine, but it felt like ages since she saw Cynthia. "See you tomorrow." She really wanted a goodbye kiss, but that way lay trouble. Instead, she walked to the front door with him, grabbed her keys and purse, and was on her way.

She was lucky for lighter-than-normal traffic on the drive home. It was an excuse for her mind to wander and replay the highlights of the night before. Being pressed between two men, stuck in the middle of intensity and adoration—that was the kind of thing she could sell for hundreds an ounce if it could be bottled.

It was barely seven when she arrived home. She let herself in quietly, not wanting to wake up Cynthia. It didn't matter; her roommate sat at the bar in the kitchen, a mug in front of her and a scowl on her face.

Concern filled Emily. "Are you all right?"

"Are you?" Cynthia's voice held an edge.

Because she was out all night again. "I'm fine. Sorry if I worried you."

"We were supposed to go out and celebrate your new job last night. Paul said the two of you talked about it, but Saturday night rolled around and *bam,* no Emily."

Emily cringed. "I'm sorry." The apology felt flat. "We never set a time, and then…" She sighed. "It slipped my mind. I didn't mean to stand you up."

"I guess I get that." Some of the irritation seemed to fade from Cynthia's voice. "You know, it's funny. A week ago, you balked at the idea you'd ever do something like pick up a guy in a bar, and now you've been out three of the last seven nights. You meet someone new?"

"Well…" Emily wasn't in the mood to share details or even hints. It felt too intimate to lay out bare.

"Justin again?"

"Maybe."

Cynthia pushed her mug aside and leaned in. "You know that's the most supremely bad idea in the history of bad ideas."

"I do. It's just that…" What? Emily fumbled for the words to finish her sentence.

"As long as you know what you're doing."

Emily wasn't so sure. "I never thought I'd say this, but I guarantee there's nothing more to it than sex." The reality of the assurance sank in her gut like a stone. It was obvious Justin adored Antonio as much as Antonio did him. She was a prop. Not that she minded the fun. Now was a good time to cement in her head that was all it was.

"It's my ghost date." Paul's chipper tone cut through the quiet mood. He strolled into the kitchen and draped an arm around Emily's shoulders.

The gesture crawled over her skin like a million pinpricks. She swallowed the response. No reason to overreact. She gave him a quick squeeze, then ducked from under his arm. "Any coffee left?"

"Help yourself." Cynthia nodded at the pot. "Paul can tell you his amazing news."

"Okay?" Emily poured herself a drink, added cream and sugar, and stayed on the opposite end of the kitchen.

He grinned. "I got a job. I'm being brought on as a retainer at the same investment firm as you."

"Which means the asshole will only be underfoot for a few more weeks, until he gets his first check." Cynthia's tone was light and playful.

"That's awesome." A strange uneasiness climbed through Emily, but she couldn't name its cause. She shoved it aside and focused on her happiness. "It's a great place to be. Congratulations."

He beamed brightly. "Thank you. Do I get a congratulatory hug?"

The request struck her as odd. "Sure." She set her mug down and held her arms open as he embraced her. He held on a little longer than he needed to. Or she was imagining it. Maybe she was letting this thing with Justin and Antonio become more personal than she wanted to admit. Time to get over that.

Still, acid churned in her gut when she squeezed Paul back, then had to nudge him to back away.

CHAPTER SIXTEEN

JUSTIN DIDN'T EXPECT TO get into the evening as much as he had. The first night he was with Emily, when they shared the fantasy of Antonio joining them, Justin told himself a big part of the turn on was hearing her talk dirty and glimpsing that flash of her kink not obvious on the surface.

Last night he told himself it was about Emily. She wanted to play and seized the chance when she saw it. As he was drawn deeper into the scene, watching her with Antonio and being a part of the moment, her comment about the intimacy clicked. It was Monday morning now, and feathers of being with both of them lingered in his mind.

Everything else aside, he was grateful things weren't awkward with Antonio. A heat-of-the-moment fling wasn't worth losing his best friend over. Then again, if they didn't meet this deadline, Justin would lose him anyway, when Antonio went back to Italy to take over the family business.

Which meant he needed to pull his head out of the clouds and get back to work. Starting with ensuring their contractor wasn't freaked out or intimidated by the weekend. He could place a phone call to either Antonio or Emily, but he needed to look her in the eye and make sure she was okay with everything too.

Antonio wasn't in his office when Justin approached, but the murmur of voices drifted toward him. He rounded the corner to Emily's cubicle and paused, curious. She sat in front of her computer. Antonio stood behind her, hand on the back of her chair, side of his palm against her back and head bent low so they could talk without their voices carrying. Neither of them looked up at Justin's arrival, but he was close enough to hear the conversation.

"Call the tracking API from your ETL using the CLR. They're labeled according to function." Antonio pointed at her screen.

Emily shook her head. "It won't compile on my local server. I don't think it's my configuration; I've mirrored the sandbox."

Justin raised his brows. Despite appearances, they were talking shop. Not that the casual passerby would know that. "Do you have a minute?" he asked.

Emily jumped in her seat, then whirled.

Antonio spun as well. "Sure." He strode into his office, and Justin followed and kicked the door shut behind them.

"That wasn't exactly keeping a low profile." Justin winced at the sharpness of his own voice.

"We're discussing work."

Justin's concerns were purely in the company's best interest. "But that wasn't what it looked like."

"I'll be more careful in the future."

Was Justin overreacting? No. This was the worst possible time to question himself. Everything had to go smoothly now, and that included any and all outward appearances looking exactly as they should.

The rest of the week passed without major incidents. Everyone was too busy keeping their heads down and working, for much else to happen. When the weekend rolled around, they were a few days behind, but they'd made up a lot of lost time.

* * * *

EMILY JOINED THEM AT JUSTIN'S house on Saturday, and they dove back into PP work. They didn't accomplish as much as when he'd had multiple developers on the project, but it was headway, and as long as he saw forward momentum, he could accept it taking longer than he hoped.

The three worked late into the night. Status quo for him and Antonio, but he worried Emily hadn't realized what she was signing on for.

"Are you ready to let us start paying you?" Justin asked. It was nearly three in the morning, and it took the last of his focus to speak without slurring.

Emily shook her head, then stopped and pressed her palm to her forehead, blinking. "Nope. I meant what I said." Her words were chipper and flowed out in a jumble.

"You both need sleep." Antonio's eyelids drooped, and he didn't look like he fared much better in the exhaustion department. He stood and reached for Emily's hand. "Come on. I'll show you where the guest bedroom is."

"Then where will you sleep?" She gripped her

fingers and let him pull her to her feet.

"Here." Antonio gestured to the couch.

"That's not fair. I don't want to steal your bed." Despite the tiredness in her movements and her giddy tone, a clarity lay underneath.

"Technically it's not *my* bed. It's Justin's."

She grinned. "That's brilliant."

Justin stared at her, trying to make sense of a series of mental tangents he couldn't see or fathom. "What is? Me having a bed?"

"Yes and no. We'll all sleep in your bed. That way, no one has to sleep alone, and no one has to sleep on the couch." Her logic was ridiculous.

"Makes sense to me," Antonio said.

Maybe Justin didn't have the brain power to process.

No. He was pretty sure there was a flaw in the decision, but he didn't have the desire to argue. "All right."

When he woke up the next morning, Emily lay facing him, Antonio behind her with an arm draped over her hip. Her shirt had crept up her stomach in the middle of the night, and the shoulder fallen down, leaving temptation on display.

Justin trailed a finger lightly along her bra strap, not processing how intimate the gesture was until her eyes fluttered open and she grabbed his wrist.

"That tickles." Despite the words, there was no protest in her voice.

Could they do what they'd done last weekend, and share? Have fun, all three of them? "Would you rather I was doing something else?"

She stretched, which from Justin's prone angle

looked like she pressed back into a now very awake Antonio at the same time. "What did you have in mind?" she asked. "Remembering I learn best in a hands-on environment."

"I'm sure we can figure something out." Antonio glided his hand under the elastic of her panties, and she sighed.

While Justin didn't think two times made a habit, he was willing to take the risk.

* * * *

THE NEXT WEEK AND A HALF passed the same way—weekdays filled with plowing toward the deadline, another weekend mixed with PP work, and both spiced by a healthy dose of play. By some unspoken rule, sex never happened without all three of them, as far as Justin knew. It was working. He didn't have any complaints.

They were going to meet their beta cutoff date with a working product. PP was a few weeks delayed, but it would be ready to wow the board shortly after.

One thing nagged at Justin, and the closer their dates loomed, the harder it was to ignore. No one mentioned it, but when this was all over, Emily would move on to another project. The three of them didn't have any sort of a romantic relationship, but without the guise of coming together for work, Justin didn't think it was right to suggest she show up as a booty call. In fact, the notion left a foul taste in his mouth.

His phone rang, and he answered it, lost in

thought. "This is Justin."

"Hey." A familiar female voice tickled his memory. "It's Lia. How have you been?"

His ex-fiancée. Every muscle in his body tensed. "Fine." He tried to keep his voice pleasant.

"I'm glad to hear it. I was wondering—can I see you?"

* * * *

"WHERE'S THE OLD MAN?" Andrew asked.

Antonio had never understood the nickname for Justin, but that was probably because he was closer in age to him than they were to Andrew. "This is the first night we've had off in a few weeks, so he had to run some errands. He'll be by in an hour or two." He didn't know why he held back the full story. It might be because he couldn't help his concern over what it meant that Justin was having coffee with Lia.

Andrew and his fiancée, Susan, were seated in Antonio's living room. Antonio was happy to see the couple, but it still took some getting used to. Andrew was the last person Antonio expected to settle down, and Susan was as much Andrew's opposite as was possible. She was light to his darkness and optimism to his cynicism.

Antonio had never seen Andrew happier.

"That means we can gossip like school girls until he gets here." Andrew smirked. "Tell me how it's going. How are you two?"

Antonio wanted to feign irritation at the comical tone, but the attitude made him smile. Andrew's support and friendship when Antonio was younger were among the key reasons Antonio was able to admit to himself that he was bisexual. That also meant Andrew was the only other person besides Emily—and Susan soon, if she wasn't already up-to-date on the situation—who knew how Antonio felt about Justin. "We're… good." Shit. Why did he hesitate?

Andrew raised his brows. "Which sounds different than the stock answer of *same as always*."

"It's been a long few weeks," Antonio said.

"I've heard. Not sure what that has to do with the conversation. What's changed?"

"We met this woman." Antonio wouldn't tell this to anyone else, but despite Andrew's tendency toward storytelling, he was trustworthy and could keep a secret.

Susan sat up a little straighter. "As in both of you?"

"Don't give her any ideas." Andrew's voice held a warning tone. "But what she said. Since when is there a *we* between you two, when it comes to women?"

Antonio cringed. "That came out wrong. Justin met this woman, who turned out to be our new contractor, and things got complicated. She likes to be *shared*? I don't have a better way to put it."

"People really do that? He"—Susan nodded at Andrew—"insists that's movie magic and fantasy."

"And you believe him?" Antonio had a hard time swallowing that Andrew pulled off a comment like that with a straight face.

She smiled and leaned her head against Andrew's shoulder. "No. But I told him I did, because it's flattering he's vocal about keeping me to himself."

The ease with which the couple showed their affection for each other pinged a jealous chord in Antonio that he couldn't ignore. He wanted something like that.

Andrew growled. "Don't tell people that. I have a reputation." He turned back to Antonio. "Seriously, though. I'm trying to make sense of this. You meet this woman who doesn't mind being the filling on a meat sandwich, and she's sticking around, but you're still hung up on him."

"Yes and no."

"Not the vehement reassurance of *I'll always love him* that I expected. What gives?"

Antonio had been kicking this around in his head for the last couple of weeks, the questions growing more each day. It was both a relief and a shock to have someone he could talk about it with. "I haven't had this much fun in a long time. Not relationship wise. I don't know that she's the answer or the reason, but it's enough to make me wonder if I've been hung up on Justin for so long, I've forgotten how to enjoy myself."

"Ten years, you've never said a word to him. Not that it's my place to decide for you, but yeah, that sounds a bit like spinning your wheels."

"You're a Scrooge." Susan elbowed Andrew.

He rolled his eyes, then pulled her into his lap. She squealed but didn't try to break free. "Scrooge hates Christmas. *I* think love is for saps and losers."

"Which does that make you?" she asked.

"A sap. Definitely." Andrew kissed her.

Susan shifted to face Antonio. "I don't know you two nearly as well as Andrew does, but if you'd like my opinion…"

"I would." Antonio suspected she'd offer a more genuine and straightforward answer than he'd find anywhere else.

"The few times I've seen the two of you together, the connection is pretty obvious. Don't listen to Mr. Jaded here. Stop stalling. Tell Justin how you feel. I think you'll be pleasantly surprised."

The advice was exactly what Antonio wanted to hear, but it didn't help ease his indecision. He had no idea what to do.

CHAPTER SEVENTEEN

THIS WAS THE FIRST TIME since Emily entered the corporate workforce that she wasn't looking forward to Friday. She tried to ignore the creeping surrender inside, but it wouldn't be silenced. She stood in her bedroom, grabbing and discarding every T-shirt she owned. When did casual Friday become this difficult to dress for?

The struggle had raged since before she stepped into the shower. She wanted to leave an impression and wear something cute and flirty. But she didn't want to be obvious to anyone who didn't know she was sleeping with the company's founders. Then again, technically she wasn't anymore, because Wednesday night they wrapped up her work on PP, they were taking the weekend off, and her regular contract would be up before the end of next week.

Which was the real reason her mind refused to stay on a focused track. What she had with Justin and Antonio was nothing more than sex. There was no discussion around it beyond consent and whatever playful banter happened during the fact. She reminded herself it was because there was nothing to say. She didn't see either of the men keeping silent if they had thoughts on the matter. She was the only one who was going to have a hard time letting go of two men she barely knew, who were obviously in love with each other, even if one wouldn't admit it.

Yeah, she was psyching herself out over something that would never be. Now seemed like as good a time as any to screw her head on straight and start acting rational. *Fuck it.* She grabbed the first shirt from the top of the *reject* pile and paired it with her most comfortable jeans.

She moved into the kitchen and dropped a bagel into the toaster. Coffee was probably a bad idea, with her already on edge. The caffeine might send her brain clawing out of her skull, in an effort to discover a different answer than she'd already provided.

"Hey, stranger." Paul's greeting startled her, and she whirled.

"Hey, yourself."

He crossed the room and stopped less than a foot away. "I'm glad I caught you. Do you have a few minutes?" His words sounded stilted. Almost uneasy.

"Sure, but not more than that. Work and all." She hoped she didn't come off as rude. The vibes he radiated amped her anxiety—as if it wasn't already cranked to the max—and she didn't understand why.

"Right. With the sexy boss?" Paul leaned his shoulder against the fridge.

The posture almost blocked her in the corner. "I suppose. What's up?"

"I need to tell you something, and I don't think I've been going about it the right way."

Behind her, the toaster popped, making her

jump. She wanted to reach back and grab her breakfast, mostly to give the gnawing in her gut a different source to chew on. "What's up?" Great. She was so off kilter, she was repeating herself.

He glided a palm down her arm, raising goosebumps of disdain as he passed, then intertwined his fingers with hers. "I know you see me as the guy you grew up with, but I want to find out what it takes to mean more to you."

"I— What?" It was a dimwitted response. She understood exactly what he meant. The words clicked with every misgiving she had since he showed up almost a month ago, confirming suspicions she hadn't been able to give a name to. Apparently, she still struggled with the concept.

"I like you, Emily. A lot. I have, for a long time. I'm wondering if you'd give *us* a chance. I don't expect you to dive into anything head first, but we could start with dinner—the two of us alone—and see where things went from there."

That sounded simple enough. It was a sweet request, and the way he stared at their linked fingers, rather than looking her in the eye, was shy and endearing. Seeing what could be with Paul made more sense than lusting after two men she couldn't have. She and Paul had a little in common. He'd be a way to move on and experience a healthy relationship.

"Emily?" Concern filled his voice. "You still with me?"

He expected an answer. She grasped at the *I'd like that*, that was the right reply. "I'm sorry. I can't," came out instead. "I don't feel that way about you."

Unlike the confusion in her head, the words made sense. It was nice something did.

"No?" He tightened his grip on her fingers until they ached. "How can you be so sure? You haven't given it a chance."

"I don't have to justify myself. Can we talk about this later? I need to get to the office." She tried to work her hand free, subtly at first, but then with more force.

He straightened up and slammed his palm against the fridge. It impacted with a loud *slap*. "I'd like to talk about it now, so I don't have to wonder how many other guys you're fucking every time you leave the house."

"I'm not sleeping with a roster of men. Not that it's any of your business." Acid burned in Emily's throat. How was Cynthia sleeping through this?

"Why him and not me? What makes this Justin guy so special?" He angled his body, blocking her escape.

She'd never told Cynthia about Antonio. Until now, she wondered why not. Paul's question might have sparked some deeper spiral of questions in Emily's head if she weren't focused on how quickly the situation deteriorated. "Nothing." She tried to convince herself as well as Paul. "He's a guy. That's it. Nothing special. Nothing different. Nothing I'm hung up on."

"Then why won't you give me a chance?"

Was she talking to a brick wall? "I told you. I don't feel it."

"We'll fuck a couple of times, and then maybe you'll feel it." He squeezed her hand harder.

She jerked from his grasp and shouldered him aside. "We won't." She didn't dare look back as she grabbed her purse and keys and left the house. By the time she reached her car, she shook so bad, she dropped the keys on the sidewalk. She sank into the driver's seat, and the adrenaline settled into her empty gut. *What the hell was that?*

Emily needed to get out of here. She backed the car out of its spot, and made it around the corner before she had to pull over or risk steering herself off the road. It took several minutes of counting to ten and then four-hundred and fifty, before her pulse calmed enough that she could grip the steering wheel again. She grabbed her phone and sent Cynthia a quick text. *We need to talk. Call me when you get up.* She had no idea how to approach the subject, but she had to say something.

In the meantime, Emily needed to get to the office. It was still early, and that meant silence and a chance to hide out in the cafeteria until she collected her thoughts. She reached work without any more freakouts. As she was walking inside, Cynthia called.

"Morning." Emily didn't have the energy to act chipper. Cynthia would understand.

"What did you do?"

Or not. Defensiveness spiked inside Emily. "Excuse me?"

"Sorry. That came out wrong. Paul is furious. Said you were in a foul mood when you got up. That you barely spoke to him in the kitchen, and you shoved him in your rush to get out the door. What's going on?"

"He told you that?" Emily almost choked on her

disbelief.

"It didn't sound like you, but you've been working hard lately." Sympathy bled into Cynthia's words. "What really happened?"

"He—" What? Didn't force himself on her. He got a little aggressive and rude. "He told me he liked me." *Wow. That was weak.*

"Which, if you hadn't been so busy screwing around for the last month, you would have noticed. I'm sorry. I don't mean it that way. He's really upset. Did that warrant you being bitchy?"

"But backing me into a corner, twisting my hand so hard I thought my fingers might break, and telling me if we fucked *maybe* I'd learn to love him, warranted more than a casual, *No thanks. Have a nice day.*"

"That's not his story."

"Of course it's not." Was Emily overreacting? No. The confrontation with Paul was anything but innocent.

"Then you're calling my brother a liar?"

"Are you saying I am, instead?" Emily didn't want this to turn into a childish argument, but she was too frazzled to think through a better response.

Cynthia sighed. "No. It's not that. Listen… Come back to the apartment, and we'll talk about it. All three of us. It was a misunderstanding."

Except that it wasn't. Emily knew what she'd been subjected to. "I have to work." She disconnected and set her phone to silent, before dropping it in her purse. Now she had something new to obsess over. The thought wasn't reassuring.

*

ANTONIO TRIED NOT TO CARE that Justin stood them up last night. Told himself it was annoying because Andrew and Susan were only in town for the day. Insisted he didn't care the cause was Lia.

He didn't believe his own bullshit.

As he headed toward the office elevators, he caught a movement out of the corner of his eye. Emily sat at one of the cafeteria tables on the patio, back to him and head in her hands. Might as well say *hello*.

She didn't look up when he pushed outside.

"Billing extra hours?" he teased.

She spun in her seat, expression blank. "I'm sorry—what?" Concern spread through him as he looked at her. Creases lined her forehead, and the edges of her eyes were puffy and red. Had she been crying?

"Are you all right?"

She gave him a weak smile. "I'm fine. The long hours became such a habit, I think my body is rejecting the full night of sleep I got."

He hid his cringe at the reminder that those long hours had come to an end. "You'll have to get back in the habit."

"I suppose so." Her expression drooped further.

"Really, what's going on?" It had to be more than the work. She looked miserable.

"Nothing. I'll be fine with a little extra coffee."

"If you're sure." What was he going to do? Bully her until she gave him the answer he wanted? "Take your time. I'll see you upstairs?"

"Yeah. I'll be there soon."

He hated to walk away with her in this state, but if she wasn't sharing, there was nothing to be done for it. He made his way to his office and forced himself to dive into work. Emily settled at her desk about fifteen minutes later. No glance in his direction or acknowledgment of any kind.

He managed to shift his concern aside, so he could accomplish his tasks, but it hovered in the peripheral of his thoughts, never vanishing completely. When anyone interacted with her, she was polite but clipped the conversation. She stayed at her desk during lunch, nibbling on vending machine chips and soda, but that was typical for half his team.

As the clock crept up on five, Justin sent him a message. *I need to cancel tonight. Sorry for the late notice.*

Antonio scowled at the note. The two of them were going to celebrate meeting their deadline. *Did something come up?*

Nothing work related. Dinner with Lia. Turns out I missed her more than I realized.

Totally understand. Have fun. Antonio was glad the conversation was remote, so Justin couldn't see the way he glowered at the screen. He was irritated with being stood up, but it did give him an excuse. He sent Emily a note. *Do you have a minute?*

On my way out.

It was five on a Friday. That made sense. *Thirty seconds then.*

Through the doorway, he saw her shoulders slump. She stood and strolled into his office. He nodded at the door, and she shut it.

"I know I don't have any right to press, but it's clear something's wrong." He kept his tone gentle and sympathetic, to not aggravate whatever this was. "I'm grilling tonight, and I've got an extra steak if you want to keep me company. No obligation to talk, though the offer is there." Was he asking her out? No. This was the concerned gesture of a friend.

"You said *I* not *we*."

He shrugged. "I got stood up. Hence the extra steak."

She looked up, her smile looking more genuine than it had all day. "That sounds nice."

"I'm not firing up the grill for a few hours, so I'll give you my address, and you can head over when you're ready."

She turned her gaze to her shuffling feet. "Would you mind if I followed you over now? Or, rather, when you leave for the day? Is that all right?"

"Absolutely." It was more than all right. It made his pulse skip in a way he didn't expect. "In fact, I'm ready to go now."

The corners of her eyes pulled up, as more of the tension lifted from her face. She let out a half-sigh, half-chuckle. "Sounds perfect."

Joy nudged Antonio's thoughts, at the realization he was the cause of that. He'd do an awful lot to keep her smiling. *Where did that come from*? He and Emily had a friendship, at best. A shared connection he'd only felt with a handful of other people, but still friendship.

He didn't know which was worse—that he was trying so hard to convince himself it was true, or that he didn't believe it.

CHAPTER EIGHTEEN

"YOU'RE TELLING ME you have this gorgeous home and you never spend any time here?" Awe filled Emily's voice. She stood in Antonio's foyer, gaze drifting around the living room. It was nice to see her more calm than an hour ago.

Antonio laughed. "I only miss it when I think about it." He gestured toward the plush furniture. "Have a seat. Can I get you a beer or anything?"

"*No.*" The word landed sharply between them, and she frowned. "The last thing I need right now is alcohol sucking me back into the pit."

The verbal confirmation something was bothering her brought his curiosity back. "This is the last time I'll ask. Tell me to fuck off if you don't want to talk about it," he said. "What's wrong?"

She sank onto his loveseat and nodded at the spot next to her. "You're hovering. It's awkward."

"My apologies." He kept as much space between them as was possible without looking forced, given the confined spot.

Silence settled over them, and he bit his tongue to keep from saying anything. He promised not to ask again, but he was worried, if he changed the subject, she might not open up. It was clear she needed to get something off her mind.

"It's really nothing. I meant that." She fiddled with a thin spot on her jeans, dragging her nail over the loose threads. "I'll tell you, and you'll agree."

He had a feeling it went deeper than that. "Okay."

"My roommate's brother is staying with us. He does that sometimes, when money is tight and he can't find a contract. I've known them both forever. She's my best friend. Apparently he wants… He got a little aggressive this morning is all. Nothing more than that." Her insistence ran together. "But she's taking his side, and home feels a little alienating right now. Anyway." Emily looked up, smile so thin it stretched over her teeth. "It'll pass in a few days, once I've had some time to mope."

As she told the story, Antonio's anger heated from simmering to boiling. His imagination filled in the details she glossed over. "That doesn't sound like nothing." He forced himself to not speak through clenched teeth.

"It really isn't a deal. It's so far from being one that it's not on the same planet." She sank back against the cushions and scrubbed her face. "That's what I've been telling myself all morning. It's not like he touched me or tried to force himself on me. Problem is I'm not having any of my own crap."

The assurance was enough to help him put a lid on his response. Showing her his fury wouldn't help, but it was clear she was talking herself down when she was justified in being upset. "Stop trying to convince yourself you were in the wrong. No one deserves to be treated like that." *Especially you.* The surge of protectiveness caught him off guard. He wanted to pull her into his lap, wrap her up, and keep her safe. The feeling was foreign and impossible to shake.

She also didn't need him being grabby.

"Thank you for that." She seemed to relax a little.

"For the truth? Always. What can I do to help?"

"Distract me. We can talk about anything but this morning."

"Did you have another topic in mind?" If he were the one to choose, he'd want to know what happened when she was done with her contract. Would she move on and never see them again? Was there the potential for something more, without the confines of work bearing down on them? Now wasn't the time to press for details like that, though.

She looked around the room. "I don't know. Um… Why a dragon tattoo?"

"It matches Justin's phoenix." Easy answer but hardly a conversation starter.

"Really?" She scrunched up her face. "He told me— Never mind."

"That it was Dark Phoenix? Like in the XMen comics? It's true. The original was." Maybe there was a story here after all. He never talked about things in this way, because it meant delving into how he felt about Justin, and he didn't want that showing in front of the wrong people. With Emily, he wasn't concerned. "A year or two after we met, I was ready to head back home. Obligation and the family business waited, and I thought I was done seeing the world.

"My dad's company hires a lot of foreign contractors. Not as in overseas work, but people who do exactly what I had. Twenty-somethings backpacking around the world. He hires people from everywhere and never expects them to say more than six months to a year. It gives the company new vision and direction, and keeps things from getting stale. I didn't want to leave Justin behind, so I landed him a job, to convince him to come back to Italy with me, and crossed my fingers he'd be one of the few who stayed."

"Instead, somewhere along the way, he sold you on this idea and convinced you to come back to the States with him?" She shifted her position so one foot was tucked under the other knee, and she faced him, leg pressing against his thigh.

"Pretty much. Not that he had to work hard, to sell me. It's a good idea—one I still believe in—and I would have followed him even if he wanted to sell snake oil." It felt odd to admit that aloud, but it was a relief. He trailed his finger over the back of her knuckles, only half-aware of the gesture.

She turned her palm up, sighing when he brushed along the lines of her hand. "That doesn't explain the tattoo."

"When we got to Italy, we were handed a big project. Most of the junior developers didn't get things like that, but I was the boss's son, and I wanted a challenge. We nailed it. There was a synchronicity there that I didn't expect. Like yin and yang. In fact, that was the comment I made to him. He had a habit of commemorating milestones with ink, and said we should pick the same thing because neither of us could have done it alone. He'd been wanting to touch up the phoenix for a while, so that was what we decided on." Telling the story dragged up feelings Antonio hadn't touched in years. That original spark he felt for Justin—an intensity that had changed with time but was as strong as back then.

Maybe Susan was right; he was a fool to give up on Justin. He looked at Emily, and bright green eyes stared back. Then again, Andrew had seen the pining from the outside for a decade, and cynic or not, he had a good point too. Antonio might be missing out on a lot by nursing a crush that would never go anywhere.

He moved his hand to Emily's cheek, keeping his touch so light he felt heat more than skin. "It's probably the wrong time to ask this," he said.

"If it's not about my morning, it's the perfect time."

He drew his fingers along her ear, and she fluttered her lashes. When he cupped her face, she leaned into his palm. *Christ.* He wanted to kiss her without pretense. To find out if there was more potential here than a little kinky fucking around. "What happens when your contract is up?"

"I should be more careful next time I say, *anything else is fine*." She gave a choked laugh.

"You don't want to talk about it."

"Exactly the opposite." She gazed at him. "I want to toss it out in the open, hash the entire thing out, and get answers. But I don't know what to say."

"How about we start with this?" He dipped his head and brushed his lips over hers. She whimpered and leaned into the kiss. His pulse kick-started so loud, it hammered in his ears. How was such a simple gesture turning him on?

She rested her hand on his chest and pushed him away. "Stop."

"I'm sorry. After what you've been through, that was thoughtless of me."

"It's not that." She gave a bitter chuckle. "Though that you noticed and you care makes me feel stupid for what I'm about to say."

He watched her, not wanting to interrupt.

"I can't do whatever this is with you."

"Because of Justin." Antonio should have seen that coming. She'd always been in this for Justin.

"Yes, but I suspect I don't mean it the same way you do." She didn't break the contact between them, which meant she had him at arm's length, the warmth of her palm threatening to burn through his T-shirt. "I didn't realize it until you were telling your story, a few minutes ago. I get along with you better than almost anyone I know. It's easy with you. Things click. I don't know where the two of you will wind up, but it's real apparent how much you adore him. If I have to choose between being a rebound girl and seeing what kind of friendship we could have, I'm not choosing *rebound girl*."

Her words settled deep, knocking loose an avalanche he couldn't process all at once. But she had a good point. "You're right; that's not what I was thinking. Keeping that in mind, I'll ask again. What happens when your contract is up?" It was unfair of him to push the question on her twice, when he couldn't vocalize what he wanted.

She seemed to be thinking more clearly than him, though. "In a perfect world, where I get to write things out and they happen exactly like I say?" she asked. "We still hang out, but we stop keeping it a secret. We learn more about each other. We see what happens next."

She made it sound so simple. Could it be that straightforward?

* * * *

JUSTIN SAT ACROSS FROM LIA in the restaurant, doing his damnedest to hear every word she said. When she called and said she wanted to meet, he agreed out of politeness. However, yesterday over coffee, things were wonderful. She was bubbly, he was drawn into the conversation, and the entire thing reminded him why he proposed to her.

He didn't have to schedule dinner for tonight, and he felt bad about bailing on Antonio at the last minute. That was the plan, though. Justin saw how Antonio and Emily interacted day to day. Intimacy radiated from them when they did simple things, like talking about directory structure. Whatever the three of them had done sex-wise needed to end. Justin hoped he could spend some more time with Lia, if he stepped aside tonight. Make things really work this time, the way they should have six months ago.

If Antonio was smart, he'd snag the free evening and spend some time with Emily.

The gnawing behind Justin's ribs every time he thought about Antonio and Emily together was reflex. A fake bond formed because of the physical one. It would fade quickly, and he'd have the life back that he should have had.

"And then I told her lemons aren't going to grow out of that old Subaru unless you swap the gasoline for diesel," Lia said.

Justin stared at her, forcing the words through his head, to make sense of them. Nope. It was gibberish. "I'm sorry—lemons?"

"You were good for almost an entire day." Her laugh sounded tired. "Would you rather be somewhere else?"

"No. This is the only place I want to be. Here. With you. I promise." He knew as he said it that the words were false. He reached across the table and grasped her fingers. "That's a lie. I'm sorry. I loved you. Maybe I still do, but we're better off without each other."

Her chin quivered and tears welled in her eyes.

"*Shit*. Lia, hon, I didn't mean—"

"It's okay." Her voice cracked. "I… Did it hurt when I did this to you?"

"Yes." But it hadn't. Not like this. He felt rejected. He was pissed off and confused. But he never once mourned her leaving. It took him this long to figure out he never quite loved her? There was no reason to be that blunt with her. "I'm glad you called, and I'm happy to see you're doing well. You and me? It's a bad idea."

The rest of the meal passed in awkward silence. He paid the bill, walked her to her car, and gave her the most tentative hug he remembered giving someone.

Justin drove to Antonio's house out of habit. When he saw Emily's car parked out front, his mind ground to a halt. It figured; his half-assed fucking plan had one thing go right. Seeing the familiar sedan in the driveway hurt as much as telling Lia there was no chance for them. That made no sense, but realizing it was a far cry from being able to stop the painful throb of his heart. The pain didn't even do him the courtesy of explaining itself.

CHAPTER NINETEEN

JUSTIN SHOULD TURN AND go home. A tiny spark of his mind—one the rest insisted was delusional—told him he was making some pretty broad assumptions The thought was enough to prompt him to send Antonio a quick text. *My evening freed up. You doing anything?*

A reply buzzed through, seconds later. *Hanging out. Emily says hi. You coming over?*

The simple note washed away the cloud hanging over Justin's head. *Already here.* He shut off his car and headed inside. He and Antonio had keys to each other's houses since they bought the properties. As Justin stepped through the front door, he saw Emily leaned against Antonio, his arm around her shoulders. Justin stalled, unable to process his reaction.

Emily looked up and grinned, and his mind was clear again. She held out her hand. "Perfect timing. Come join us."

"What are we doing?" Despite his sort-of attempt to set the two up, Justin was grateful to walk into the welcoming and innocent-looking scene. He didn't know where she expected him to sit, though.

The loveseat was only meant for two.

She tugged his arm and shifted as he sat, somehow making the arrangement work. "Distracting me," she said.

"From what?"

"If we tell you, it's not distracting." Antonio's posture wasn't as casual as Emily's. A tension coiled in the way he moved, and faint lines marred his face.

Justin would ask about it later. The overall mood in the room was light, and he wasn't going to spoil that. "How does this *distracting* work?"

"First of all, she promised not to vanish into oblivion when her contract is up." Antonio sounded calm.

"Oblivion?" Justin tried to look incredulous. "That sounds like a difficult place to get to. You're sure you're not agreeing for convenience's sake?"

Emily screwed her face up in thought. "Maybe. A little bit. Seriously, though. I told him, I'm addicted to your company, so I don't want to sever ties."

"I'm great with that." And he was. "But that took about a minute to tell me, so now what?"

"Hmm… Now you tell me—why Brazil?" Emily said.

Fuck. He hadn't thought about his reasons in ages. It had been even longer since he shared any bit of the story. "Antonio already knows. I don't want to bore him." Why was Justin hesitating to share something so simple?

Because it wasn't simple; it was personal. Even if he glossed parts over, he had to reach deep inside for the words. Did he want this woman seeing those hints?

Antonio met his gaze. "I never mind hearing it again. If you want to keep it to yourself, say so. Don't use me as an excuse."

"All right." Justin pushed out the doubt. No reason to make a bigger deal out of this than it was. "It was because of my grandpa."

"Thank God." Emily sounded relieved.

Justin raised his brows in question.

She gave him an impish smirk. "I thought you were going to say it was because a random mugger killed your parents and left you alone as a poor but hyper-wealthy orphan."

"Sorry my origin story isn't as glamorous as Batman's." When did the ribbing become so comfortable?

"I'm glad." She sounded sincere. "I want to hear your story, not a comic book exaggeration. What about your grandpa?"

"He fought in Korea." Dredging up the tale summoned a muddled swarm of emotion. Happy memories, mingled with grief and everything in-between. "I didn't know it until I was twenty-one, because he never talked about it. I pushed through college, to graduate early, and I was back home, trying to figure out what to do with my life. The internship offers were lined up, or I could get my M.B.A. It was all collapsing in on me, demanding I decide *now*, and I couldn't handle the stress. I snapped at everyone who tried to talk to me. My parents shrugged it off as me being a moody, hormonal asshole."

"Who? You?" Affection and sympathy

peppered Emily's question.

It helped ground him in the present, rather than sinking into the kaleidoscope of the past. "I know; it's hard to believe. Grandpa saw something they didn't. He pulled me aside one day, and that was when he told me about Korea. He looked so haunted, but there was also a glimmer in his eyes I'd never seen before. Ghosts of exhilaration. He said he'd enlisted to see the world. He didn't want to die only having seen a tiny corner of Las Vegas. And he saw so much, both horrible and glorious. I asked him if the terror outweighed the wonder. He was dismayed I'd even suggest it. He told me he hated the horrible things he'd seen, but he wouldn't surrender the grand experience of it all to get rid of a few scars. The next day, I burned the offer letters and MBA program applications, emptied my bank account, and bought a one-way ticket to Brazil."

There was enough of a rush associated with that moment in his life that it filled him again, flowing through his veins.

Emily looked fascinated, but so did Antonio, despite having heard the story before.

"Why Brazil?" she wanted to know.

"It was Carnaval, and I figured that was a good starting point."

"So many times I've imagined what that would be like—leaving it all behind and heading into a country you'd never been to, in order to taste something new. It sounds incredible."

His parents had been furious, but he never regretted the decision. "It was amazing."

"I kind of wish I'd done something like that

while I still had the chance." Emily looked wistful.

His reply stuck in his throat with a concern that telling her to pursue the dream might mean never seeing her again. He was being ridiculous. "The opportunity is always there."

"I guess."

Her uncertainty was more reassuring than it should be. God, he was such a hypocrite.

* * * *

EMILY WAS GRATEFUL CYNTHIA and Paul's cars were gone when she went home on Saturday morning for a change of clothes. She'd have to deal with them both, but she was riding the high of last night and didn't want to ruin it. There was no sex. Instead, the three of them talked until early in the morning.

Antonio invited her back, promising there was no work involved, and she accepted without hesitation.

She hurried through her shower. When she emerged, she hesitated at the bathroom door, straining to hear other sounds in the house. Still empty. Perfect. As she finished getting ready, her phone chimed with a new email. She scanned the message from Grant, plucking out the highlights. He wanted her to skip the APPropriate Designs offices on Monday morning and meet with him instead.

It would the perfect time to let him know they'd meet their deadline without issue. She sent back a quick but professional version of *I'll be there* and headed for the door. It swung open as she reached for the handle, and her heart jumped into her throat.

"Jeez. You startled me." Cynthia stepped into the apartment.

Emily gave a nervous laugh. "Same."

Cynthia looked at her purse and shoes. "Are you leaving or getting home?"

"I'm on my way out." Could Emily sidestep an uncomfortable conversation? Or better, maybe they'd forget anything happened. A perfect answer, as long as she avoided Paul until he moved out.

"Do you have a little bit?" Cynthia stepped aside, despite her question. "A couple minutes. I want to make sure we're all right."

That was about as non-aggressive an approach as Emily could imagine. "Sure. I can stick around for a few."

"Good." Cynthia sounded relieved. "I was worried you wouldn't talk to me for a while, after yesterday."

"I thought about not, but we have too much history."

"Exactly. All three of us do."

Discomfort scraped through Emily like nails on a chalkboard. "That's true…"

"Then hear Paul out?"

Emily clenched her teeth. "I already did that. We didn't have the same perspective, and he didn't want to listen to my side." She tried to keep the irritation from her voice. Cynthia wasn't being obtuse on purpose; she was looking out for her brother.

"You need to give him a chance. The two of you have a lot in common." Cynthia's voice took on an edge. "He's a good guy, and he's always adored you."

"Which is sweet and fine and good, but I'm not interested in him romantically."

"You'll throw away someone that good for an asshole who sleeps with his employees? The bozo you met at the bar?" The kindness vanished from Cynthia's voice.

The contrast to last night, Antonio and Justin's acceptance of *I'm not making any commitments right now* smacked Emily about the cerebral cortex. "*Throw away*? Paul and I didn't have anything. I didn't even know he was interested until recently. Why are you blaming me for not feeling the same?"

"Because I don't think you're trying."

Emily growled. "I don't think you're in a good frame of mind to have this conversation. Call me when you're ready to be rational." The hurt and fury spilling inside made it easy to ignore anything Cynthia said, as Emily walked out the door. Once they had cooler heads, maybe they could talk through this. Right now, she was seconds from saying something she might regret later.

* * * *

EMILY FELT LIKE HER EMOTIONS had been hosed down, hand-wrung, and hung out to dry. She spent Saturday and Sunday at Antonio's house. She didn't call it *hiding,* but that was what it was. The argument with Cynthia left her frazzled, and she had no idea how to approach reconciliation. When this morning rolled around, the Mondayness of it crept through her. There was nothing to be done for it. She had to go home, to get ready for her meeting with Grant.

She sneaked into her own house. Her heart leaped every time something creaked. Before Saturday morning, she'd have considered this overreacting, but if Cynthia wasn't going to be reasonable, Emily needed time to think through what she'd say.

Fortunately, the doors to both Cynthia's room and the guest room stayed closed while Emily got ready for work.

Now she sat in the lobby of Grant's investment firm, waiting to see him. Fortunately, this was one encounter she didn't have to worry about. When it came down to the wire, Justin, Antonio, and their team had pulled off a tremendous comeback, and their beta would be ready on time. The thought made her smile, not only because she'd been more successful on this contract than any in the past, but also because it made her happy to see them succeed.

"Ms. Lowry? Mr. Lent is ready now. You can go on back," the receptionist said.

Emily smiled and thanked her, and followed the familiar path to his office. Grant was behind his desk when she stepped into the room. There was a woman already seated across from him. He nodded at the empty chair. "Thank you for making time in your schedule today." His tone was clipped. That wasn't like him. Maybe he was infected with Mondayness too. "This is Melinda from Human Resources."

Weird, but okay. "It's not a problem." It wasn't as if she was going to tell him, *No, I'm busy.* She knew how this would go. They'd make small talk for a few minutes, then he'd ask about APPropriate Designs, and she'd give him the great details.

"I'm hearing some troubling things about your current contract."

Her blood turned to ice in her veins, and a chill ran down her spine. "I'm sorry to hear that. Everything's running smoothly, as far as I know."

"Quality of work is not my concern. You're competent. That's why I hired you."

"May I ask what you've heard?" The creeping uneasiness under her skin told her she didn't want the answer, but she'd rather hear it now than drag it out any longer.

He sighed. "This is a bit difficult to say. I've been told you're not acting appropriately in this position. That there may be some misconduct with a member of upper management."

The bottom fell out of Emily's stomach, and she searched for a response.

"Basically"—Melinda spoke up—"our policies prohibit fraternization with colleagues as well as with any employer you're assigned to."

Emily gripped the arms of her seat, to keep from wobbling, as disbelief stole her thoughts, making her dizzy. "May I ask where you heard this?" It was a stupid question. Justin didn't tell them, and neither did Antonio. She had no doubt. Cynthia was the only other person who knew, and three days ago, Emily would have sworn Cynthia would never say anything either.

Realization sank in. Unless Cynthia told Paul.

"You may not ask," Grant said. "The issue isn't

where the rumor came from, but rather whether it's true. Have you gotten involved with Justin Conroy?"

The lie stuck in her throat a moment longer than it should, to sound believable, but she forced herself to say *no* anyway.

"I see." He didn't look like he believed her.

Melinda handed her a folder. "Regardless, a situation like this puts undue pressure on everyone involved. I'm afraid, at this time, we have to terminate your current contract and your retainer. You'll need to sign the enclosed paperwork, to get your final check."

"But I didn't—" What? She'd done exactly what they said and more. And they weren't even calling her on the lie.

Melinda gave her a tight-lipped smile. "If you've got concerns with our decision, I can put you in touch with our legal team regarding our policies. I assure you, if this goes to arbitration or something more severe, details will come out if there are any. If there's nothing to find, I'd understand your contesting things."

Emily wanted to call her every foul name under the sun, for the language that effectively backed Emily into a corner. "I'd rather not deal with that kind of headache." She already dreaded having to face the fallout if these rumors got out. True or not, this kind of information would keep her from getting work at a number of places.

She'd been so stupid. How did she manage to justify such an irrational decision?

The answer teased her, floating at the edge of her mind, but she shot it down without examination.

It didn't matter. She fucked up, and it was time for damage control.

CHAPTER TWENTY

ANTONIO GLANCED AT HIS PHONE when it rang, and ambivalence filled him when he saw his father's picture on the screen. It was the only dark spot in their recent accomplishments. He had to tell Dad he wasn't coming home to run the family business. It would be better to share the news now than wait until he was in Milan. His father would be furious, but with any luck, Antonio's telling him now would mean Dad's anger passed before Antonio visited in a week or so.

Knowing all of that didn't stop him from pressing *Decline*. Guilt wormed its way into him. He'd never missed a call from his family before. *Tomorrow*. After the board meeting, when everything was tied up and the company was officially out of the woods, Antonio would tell him.

He frowned at his phone when the notification light flashed for new voice mail, and tried to ignore the remorse spreading inside him.

He forced himself to turn back to work. What had been doing? Oh. Wondering why Emily never showed up. She had the meeting this morning with Grant, but he expected her in after. They agreed she wouldn't tell them anything about her discussion with Grant, but what was keeping her from letting Antonio know she was running late?

His desk phone rang, displaying Justin's name. Antonio hit the speaker button. "Yeah."

"Lunch. Now. Cancel whatever you're doing. Be in my office in two minutes." Justin's voice was tight.

Antonio wanted to ask what was up, but he had a feeling he'd have an answer if Justin was going to talk. "I'll be right there."

Antonio found Justin pacing in the middle of the room. He barely glanced up when Antonio entered.

"What's going on?" Antonio felt fidgety simply from watching the display.

"They fired Emily."

"Jesus Christ." Antonio sank into a nearby chair, as he processed the words. "Did she call you? Grant? Do you know why?"

Justin gave a warped chuckle. "As a matter of fact… Grant had what he believed was significant reason to believe she was sleeping with me. Not his words, but definitely his meaning."

"Only you?" Antonio couldn't find a more intelligent question. Why hadn't any of them expected this? Because no one got caught when they did things like this. Stupid assumption. Not that this would have changed his desires or actions.

"Because you'd want to make it worse by having both of our names on the list? You were never mentioned."

That wasn't comforting. Next steps. If Justin

was freaking out, they had to figure out what to do. "Have you talked to her?" Antonio asked.

"No. I tried. I called her and left a message." Justin dragged his fingers through hair that already stuck up at multiple angles.

"What happens next? To us? You? APPropriate Designs?"

"She worked for Grant, so he could fire her. We don't have fraternization policies, so he can't touch me." Justin didn't sound relieved. "The board could still vote to let me go. It didn't come up, but since we're meeting with them tomorrow…"

He didn't have to finish the thought. One of the worst things about their board of directors was Grant's group held three seats, Justin and Antonio only two. Which meant, if it came down to a vote, odds were low it would end in Justin's favor.

No. Justin couldn't go. It was bad enough Emily had been fired. Antonio wasn't losing the only other person he did this for. Justin was as big a wreck as Antonio had ever seen him. His gaze darted around the room, and he never stopped moving. He must be dealing with everything Antonio was, plus the guilt of being the other party named in Emily's *crime*.

Though Antonio had plenty of complicity and regret there, too.

Antonio needed them both thinking straight. He stood and stepped in Justin's path.

Justin tried to step around him, but Antonio blocked the way again.

He grabbed Justin's arm. "Look at me."

"*What?*" Justin jerked his head up and focused on Antonio.

"Calm the fuck down."

"Are you serious?" Justin laughed. The attitude was distinctly un-Justin. Was it because Emily was involved, or was there more to it? That gnawed at Antonio. "Where do we start?" Justin asked. "What do we focus on first? How are we supposed to move forward without answers? When the fuck do we get to run our own company, instead of having to plan around their whims?"

Antonio had several replies, but he didn't think Justin would hear any of them in this state of mind. He searched Justin's eyes, as if an answer might reflect back at him.

There was nothing there that hadn't always been. Same pale-blue color. Same nose. Several days' worth of dark scruff on his chin—evidence he hadn't shaved since last week. That tempting mouth set in a hard line.

Antonio wasn't aware of tilting his head closer until the frustration in Justin's eyes melted to shock, and Antonio's lips brushed his.

His heart ground to a halt when Justin froze. What the hell was Antonio thinking?

Then Justin gripped the back of Antonio's head and kissed back hard.

Antonio swallowed a whimper and dove into the crush of teeth against lips and tongues clashing.

Justin let go and stepped back with a gasp. Terror and arousal whirled around Antonio.

"What was that?" Justin asked.

"A distraction." It was more true than Antonio expected. A delicious, forbidden, fuck-with-his-head-for-weeks distraction.

"That was one hell of a distraction. Better than rehashing our pasts."

Antonio steeled himself. "I've got more."

"I'd take anything that helped me step back and look at this differently, but if you're offering more of *that*, I'm in."

Antonio's heart soared. It wasn't a confession of love, but there was time. Baby steps. He dropped his hand to the front of Justin's slacks and traced the outline of his shaft. "I've got better, too."

Justin jerked into his palm. "I'm the novice here, but don't let that slow you down."

"Slow   it   is."   Antonio   intentionally misinterpreted the words. He caressed Justin though fabric, cupping and teasing him.

"You're a bastard." Justin spoke through gritted teeth.

Antonio liked this light level of control. "Yeah. I am." He unzipped Justin's pants, glided his hand under his boxers, and gripped his cock. The hot skin against Antonio's palm seared his thoughts and desire raced through his veins. "You don't like the teasing?"

"It's pretty decent." Groans punctuated Justin's reply.

Antonio used his body to nudge Justin back, never changing the pace of his pumping. "Sit," he said.

Justin complied.

Antonio knelt between Justin's legs and flicked his tongue out over the bulbous head in front of him, licking off a drop of precum. The salty taste on his tongue and the warm pulsing in his hand blew his imagination out of the water.

He took Justin in his mouth, and growled when Justin hissed with pleasure. If Antonio edged off at the right times, could he drag this moment out for a while? He was willing to try. He caressed Justin's sac, as he sucked and stroked his cock. Justin thrust his hips, grinding in time to the attention.

"Are you hard?" Justin asked.

Antonio pulled back long enough to say, "As a rock."

"Show me." Justin's tone left no room for argument.

Antonio stood and unzipped his slacks. Justin's gaze scorched his skin everywhere it fell. When Antonio worked his dick free, Justin grabbed his own loosely, never taking his eyes from Antonio's crotch.

"I want to watch you jerk off." Gravel ran through Justin's voice. "Sit down and go slow."

Antonio complied without question. He dropped into a nearby seat and worked the length of his rod.

"Run your thumb over the head," Justin ordered.

Antonio sank into the words. It took what little focus he had, not to speed up. He didn't know which aroused him more—watching Justin mimic his movements, or that his self-care was turning Justin on.

Antonio pumped faster with each passing minute. Living this moment, one he'd fantasized about for so long, made it impossible to hold back.

"God. This is fucking intense, watching you." Justin's voice had dropped an octave, and his words were raw. "I want to see you come. Sticky and wet."

The request—command?—was enough to push Antonio over the edge. His eyelids fluttered, and he tilted his head back, sinking into the orgasm, as bright lights danced in front of his eyes.

He heard Justin's groans. They were as vivid as any time the two of them shared with Emily, and—Christ—they were better than a daydream. Antonio looked up to see Justin climax, coating his hand with jizz and not stopping until he was spent.

Antonio sank back into his seat, spent. For a few minutes, the only sound in the room was of them trying to catch their breath. He didn't dare look at Justin. What was he supposed to say after something like that? As much as he wouldn't mind cuddling, it didn't seem appropriate.

"That was incredible." Justin's words shattered the silence and Antonio's creeping doubt. His voice was closer than Antonio expected. "Exactly what I needed and wanted."

Antonio watched Justin kneel next to him, box of tissues in hand. Justin cleaned Antonio's cock gently, squeezing enough to tantalize without hurting. Pleasant chills raced down Antonio's spine with each touch.

Justin stood and tossed the tissues away, as Antonio did up his slacks.

"Can you think now?" Antonio asked.

"Better than in ages. That was like magic. We're good, aren't we? You and me?"

Better than ever. "We're great," Antonio said aloud.

Justin grinned. "Then let's plot out what we're

saying to the board tomorrow."

This wasn't quite as clear an ending as Antonio wanted. It lacked any sort of closure or commitment, but it was a good starting point. As long as things were stable with Justin, he was happy.

A new thought flitted into Antonio's head. He wished Emily weren't gone. Odd thing to think of, after living one of his ultimate dreams. But it made sense he was concerned about her.

Then why did the random thought fill him with apprehension and leave him conflicted?

CHAPTER TWENTY-ONE

EMILY DIDN'T CARE IF she ran into Cynthia or Paul. As she stormed back into the apartment, she itched for a confrontation. A face to take her frustration out on, since she'd held back in Grant's office.

As with earlier in the morning, the other doors were closed. The silence in the familiar space helped Emily bring her racing thoughts under control. Maybe it was better this way. She didn't need to pick a fight in this frame of mind; she needed to go somewhere she could calm down. Find her center enough to listen to Justin's and Antonio's messages. Figure out what came next.

She didn't know why, but she grabbed a couple changes of clothes and threw them in a duffle bag. Almost a month of spending half her nights someplace else, and she hadn't had an overnight bag before now.

"Didn't expect to see you home in the middle of the day." Cynthia's voice behind her startled her. "Are you going somewhere?"

Emily zipped her bag and turned to the doorway. "I don't have a job anymore. I suppose I can be anywhere I want in the middle of the day."

"I didn't think your contract was up yet."

"It wasn't." Emily let her irritation creep into her voice. "They let me go because someone told them I was sleeping with the boss."

"I'm sorry." Cynthia was geniune. "But… you were."

The reaction sank into the churning pit that was Emily's gut, stirring the discomfort. She didn't expect the sympathy to come with a qualifier. "I know that. And obviously it wasn't the smartest thing I could have done. I'd rather have dealt with it myself, than have one of you tell my employer."

Cynthia crossed her arms. "It sucks. I agree. But what makes you think it was one of us?"

"Because no one else knew." Emily wasn't in the mood to go on the defensive. She knew what she had and hadn't done, and didn't need it throw back in her face. Compassion would be good.

"Besides the man you were screwing."

"Mistake. I get it." A chanting in the back of Emily's skull wasn't so sure, and that bothered her. "But I didn't expect either of you—people I trust—to sell me out." As she spoke the words, she realized that was why this hurt as much as it did. Yes, she'd made a bad decision, but going over her head and telling her boss violated her trust, and she didn't understand why. "I wasn't using the opportunity to get any special privileges. It wasn't impacting my judgment in the office."

"It was impacting other things," Cynthia said. "But I don't think anyone meant to hurt you. I'm guessing Paul did this for you."

"In that case, it's all fine. What should I do next?" Emily let anger bleed into her questeion. "Go to Paul? Thank him profusely for possibly destroying my career? Beg him to take me, love me, make sure I was his happy little homemaker? Be content with a man I don't feel that way about?"

"That's not what I'm saying." Cynthia spoke through clenched teeth.

"No. You're sticking up for your brother, because he's family. Because you care that much about him that you're blind to his flaws. I understand that. I'd do the same for you. Defend you until the ends of the earth, even if you made a mistake, which we all do. I'd stand by your side. Once upon a time, I thought you'd do the same for me. Paul cornered me in the kitchen and tried to feel me up against my will, because he's got a crush on me. Your response? *I* misunderstood. I needed you to keep a tiny secret. One that didn't impact you at all, and you couldn't do that. And I'm the one who's wrong for being upset?"

The guest bedroom door creaked open, and Paul stepped into the hallway, stretching. "Why are you two yelling?"

"Just a minor misunderstanding." Cynthia spoke through clenched teeth.

The implication that this wasn't important… The lack of sympathy… Paul staring at her breasts, despite the heated situation…

Something snapped inside Emily. "I'm done here. I don't mean today, but overall. Find someone else to share the rent with." This was rash. She had nowhere to go and couldn't afford a place on her own. Especially without a job.

She didn't care.

"If you leave, you can't…" Cynthia frowned, and her voice cracked. "You don't get access to the project anymore." The words came out like a childish taunt.

In the back of Emily's mind, she knew Cynthia was fumbling, but Emily couldn't do this. Too much hurt already. She let out a half-laugh, half-sob. "What the hell does that have to do with anything? Why would you even bring that up? I don't care about your stupid dating app." When Cynthia frowned, Emily felt a smug bit of victory. It was misplaced, but she didn't care. "In fact, that's fine. You lock me out. You don't own my intellectual property. If you launch with my back end in place, I will fuck you from here to New York, to keep you from using what I built."

"Because you're a selfish, petty bitch, who did something she can't own up to?" Paul asked.

Emily would have slapped him, but he might like that. She shouldered her bag and shoved past them both. "I'm done. I won't talk to brick walls."

She stormed to her car, blinking back the tears that stung her eyelids. What was she supposed to do now?

Her phone rang, startling her. It was Antonio. She couldn't talk to him She wasn't in the right frame of mind to talk to anyone. She turned the device off and shoved it as far into her purse as she could. She cranked the stereo, and headed in a random direction.

* * * *

JUSTIN COULDN'T FIND HIS FOCUS. He stood in front of the board, in the investment firm offices, talking through scripted lines. He didn't hear what he said. Meeting Antonio's gaze jumbled his thoughts further. The other men in the room wore impassive masks, which was unnerving. Justin settled for staring at the screen and his presentation as much as possible.

Emily hadn't returned their calls. What happened with Antonio yesterday still occupied most of Justin's mind. The same rationale accompanied it, repeating on a loop. *It was just sex. A way to get our heads back on straight.* It didn't sound right, and no matter how Justin poked at the thought, he couldn't figure out why not or decipher the reality.

He reached the end of his presentation. "As you can see, we're on track, and we'll release on time and under budget."

"Good to hear." Grant's tone was as flat as his expression. "It's heartening to see you've pulled this off, despite the hiccup. I knew you could."

Justin clenched his jaw, to keep from responding. He didn't like hearing Emily referred to as a hiccup, and if Grant knew they could do it, she wouldn't have been there to begin with. "We couldn't have done it without the contractor help."

Grant frowned. "I heard. Did you have anything else?"

"Yes." Justin had been waiting for this opportunity. He *would* pull something positive out of this affair. "Now that we're moving into the next phase of deployment, I'd like to start shifting some of my staff's time to working on an education piece." He had figures and preliminary previews of the functionality. Not nearly what they'd developed, but enough to tempt the board.

"No," Grant said.

Justin swallowed a growl. "You haven't heard me out."

"We've heard this before. It's not a profitable component. We've already voted it down. The discussion will not be reopened. Do you have anything for us besides education?"

"Yes." When the idea occurred to him last night, he told himself it was ludicrous. Not worth considering. But it didn't leave him alone, and now it was the only right answer. "I'm tendering my resignation. I'll stay on long enough to transition to my replacement, and be available for consulting after. You'll have my official signed notice by this afternoon."

The room erupted in a wave of people talking over each other. Justin didn't process any of it. The only thing he was aware of was Antonio staring at him, lips pursed and lines creasing his forehead.

The next hour and a half was chaos, with the other members begging, threatening, and trying to bribe Justin.

This isn't the way to negotiate.

If you want a change in benefits instead, say so.

He shot it all down. It didn't matter at this point if they caved and gave him permission to build education—which they didn't. He was tired of bending to their will. It was the antithesis of everything he'd built the company for.

The situation might be amusing, but Antonio never said a word, and that filled Justin with a low hum of dread.

The meeting adjourned, and Justin walked out with the satisfaction that at least one thing had gone his way. He was free. The realization was more liberating than he'd expect. Antonio kept pace with him but didn't speak. They reached Justin's car and climbed inside.

"Lunch?" Justin asked.

Nothing.

"Korean barbecue?"

No response.

Justin pointed the car in the direction of their favorite barbecue place. They drove in silence for several minutes, but it chewed on his nerves. "Are you going to talk to me?"

"Would you listen if I said anything?"

That was a start. "Of course I would."

"Are you certain?"

"I said so, didn't I?" Justin didn't like the hostility radiating in his direction. Sure, his announcement came out of left field, but Antonio would be slotted as his replacement, and it wasn't as though Justin was going anywhere. Not even into the office, after a couple of weeks. "What's on your mind?"

"*My* mind? No. The better question is what the fuck are *you* doing? Is this because of Emily? Something else? Make me understand."

Justin gripped the steering wheel until his knuckles ached. "The only part of this that has to do with her is she reminded me who I am and how I got here."

"Or, for those of us who aren't in your head, she dragged that damned story out of you and let you relive the thrill of running away, like you did ten years ago."

Was that what Antonio thought of him? The revelation hurt more than Justin thought possible. "I'm not running away," he shouted. He swallowed at the sound of the childish words and pulled into the restaurant parking lot. He shut off the engine and twisted in his seat, to face his friend. "Ten years ago, I stopped letting other people's expectations drive my path, and I made a decision. That's what happened today, too. Why are you pissed off? Now you get to stay in the U.S. With me gone, you'll be tagged for the CEO spot, and even if you decide to stay in your current position, you're still a stakeholder. You'll contract with my new firm to sell me the backend tech, and I'll build PP into what it should be."

"You think that's what this is about?" Antonio stared at him in disbelief. "Me keeping my job, so I don't have to go back home?"

"Yes." Though, now, Justin wasn't so certain.

"This isn't about the fucking company. This has *never* been about the company."

"I don't understand."

"Jesus Christ." Antonio scrubbed his face. "This is about you. Sure, I'm proud of what we built with APPropriate Designs, but only because we did it together. Did you think everything with Emily was because I was feeling kinky and wanted to experiment?"

The question tugged at the thoughts Justin had been ignoring since yesterday, but he refused to let them loose. "Kind of. Yeah."

"Is that what you think yesterday was?" A sliver of hurt leaked into Antonio's voice.

Justin tried to pretend he didn't hear it. He had that answer. It had been taunting him since their shared moment. "Yesterday was sex. Like you said, we've been doing some kinky shit lately. I was stressed—you helped me wrap my head around it."

"You say *I'm* a horrible liar. You're full of shit. That wasn't *just sex*." Antonio's voice grew in volume with each new sentence. "I don't know how you don't see this, but it's my fault for assuming you would. For not saying anything. Yesterday, collaborating with you on APPropriate Designs— *everything* is because I love you. I have since Brazil, and—Christ—sometimes you make me feel like an idiot for not letting it go. But there it is. And I could stay friends. I'd be fine with that. But you're throwing everything away, and it's not all yours to dispose of, and I can't watch you do this."

Justin's thoughts stalled. He didn't know how to process the confession.

I love you. Antonio's voice echoed in his head. Justin struggled for a response. "I'm not... I don't... I'm sorry. You're my best friend. Partner in crime. I never could have done any of this without you. But I don't feel that way." Because he wasn't attracted to me. So he couldn't love Antonio, could he?

Antonio stared at him, nostrils flared and lips drawn in a thin line. He shook his head. "Fuck you." He climbed from the car and slammed the door behind him.

Justin should go after him. He didn't have anything different to say, but he should figure it out. He couldn't move. His hands were glued to the steering wheel and his legs locked in place. What had he done?

CHAPTER TWENTY-TWO

ANTONIO DIDN'T KNOW IF he was relieved or simply and overwhelmingly hurt that Justin didn't try to stop him from leaving. It was better this way. Now he knew Justin didn't feel the same, and this way, he avoided any attempts to gloss it over or pretend their universe hadn't imploded.

Antonio called for an Uber. He said maybe five words to the driver on the ride home. Once he got inside, he sank onto the sofa and stared at the wall. He couldn't find the energy to turn on the T.V. or stereo. Deciding what to do meant using his brain, and if he did that, he'd have to think about things.

Like his family.

And Justin.

And how his heart felt like it had been pushed through a sausage grinder.

He should call the office. Let them know he wouldn't be back in that afternoon. Then again, did it matter? The thought was fatalistic, but he couldn't make it go away. He needed to climb out of his own head before he drowned in here. He could call Andrew, but he wasn't in the mood to be told to man up and make this work. He could call Mercy, but she'd always been more Justin's friend.

Did he really not have any other close friends in this country?

His phone rang, and he grabbed for it out of instinct and gratitude for the distraction. He wouldn't answer if it was Justin. Hurt that it wasn't him rushed back in, but it was tempered with relief at seeing Emily's name on the screen. "*Ciao?*" He winced, as the Italian slipped out. He was so out of sorts, he'd reverted to his native tongue.

"Hey." Emily's greeting was sad, but it was still a salve on Antonio's fractured mind. "Are you all right?"

"Did you call to ask me that?"

She gave a light laugh. "No. I'm returning your calls from yesterday, but you sound a little... not all right."

"I've been better. I've been worse." Was that true? He never remembered anything hurting this much. "But I called yesterday because I heard the news and was worried about you. How are *you*?"

"Same as you." Amusement mingled with the strains of sorrow.

This was perfect. He'd much rather spend time with her, maybe even brighten her day, than suffocate in his self-pity. "Are you busy right now? Do you want to have coffee?"

"I can't take you away from work." She hesitated on the word *work*.

"You're not. I promise. Where and how soon can I meet you?" He needed her to choose the spot. Any place Antonio knew would be tainted with memories of Justin.

She chuckled. It was faint, but it was an amazing sound. "I didn't say *yes*."

"You were going to."

"I was. There's a place downtown on Market Street. They make an amazing Spanish latte. If I say half an hour, does that give you enough time?"

"That's perfect. I'll see you there."

It didn't take Antonio as long to find the place as he expected, and he walked in fifteen minutes early. Emily already sat at a table near the back of the room, laptop out and a mostly empty mug next to her. He crossed the dining area to meet her, and she stood as he got closer. He swept her up in a hug, joy flooding him when she squeezed back tight.

She buried her face in his shoulder. "I didn't know if you'd be alone."

He hated how much the statement dug under his skin. "Possibly for a long time. Is that the latte you mentioned?"

She nodded. "My fourth. I should probably switch to something lower octane." She pulled back, to look him in the eye. "You drop a statement like that and expect I'll let you gloss over it?"

"I kind of hoped. I'll be right back." He squeezed her fingers then made his way to the counter. He ordered her an Italian soda—resisting the urge to roll his eyes at the name—and got a coffee for himself. When he returned to the table, he set her drink in front of her and made himself comfortable in the other chair.

She fiddled with her straw. "I'm guessing I shouldn't ask how your morning went."

"If I tell you clusterfuck meets Hellraiser, does

that give you an idea?"

She twisted her mouth in a half-smile. "It makes me a curious little monkey. Are you okay to share details?"

He didn't know if she meant professionally or personally, and he wasn't sure it mattered. "High level. What about you? You got tossed in the shit pond too."

"But you already know my details. Fired for sleeping with the boss. Apparently sold out by my best friend's spiteful brother. She took his side, and if that continues we may never speak again. See? Nothing new."

Most of it was, but he understood the desire to gloss over and make light of the situation. "It's funny. Your story's got a lot of the same details as mine. Boss quit. I told him he was an asshole for it but I loved him anyway. He doesn't feel the same, and now we may never speak again."

"I'm so sorry."

He didn't want her pity. "Me too. But I'm not ready to process yet. Give me a few days, and when it really sinks in, I'll call you sobbing and beg you to bring over beer and ice cream."

"Together? You're on your own. But I'll be there for the sinking-in bit."

"I know you will." It was amazing how much that meant, which led him to another realization. "You were right about one thing. Well, several, but one in particular."

"What's that?" She looked curious.

"You would have been a rebound girl if you hadn't stopped me the other night. You deserve better than that."

Her sad expression deepened, and she slid her hand under his. "Seems like we both got a bit fucked over."

"It really does."

"What now?" she asked.

It was the last question he was qualified to answer.

*

JUSTIN COULDN'T BELIEVE HOW much of him felt bruised and battered—his heart, his mind, his soul. It wasn't like when he and Lia broke up. He didn't know what to do. How to approach Antonio. How to go back to being his friend after what transpired.

When left Lia left, the shock had faded under his drive to build PP regardless of what the board said. The next morning—*bam*. He had a distraction. That wasn't working this time. Tuesday bled into Wednesday, Thursday, and Friday, leaving them a smear in his mind.

Antonio wouldn't talk to him. He worked with his office door closed, and business correspondence came in single-word replies, with any personal questions ignored.

Friday afternoon, Justin received word from Grant. The board had made its decision on his replacement, and transition wouldn't be necessary. When Justin reminded Grant he was still a member of the board, he was informed buyout paperwork was being drawn up and he'd have it by Monday morning.

The news should have bothered him. Instead, it was a relief. He hated not knowing if Antonio would take his place or where their friendship stood, but he felt lighter than in ages, that he was no longer beholden to someone else's vision for his company.

Friday night, he hit up the bar. He wasn't really in the mood to drink, and he definitely didn't want to hook up, but the background noise kept him tethered to the outside world.

He was nursing the same beer he'd had for the last hour, when a flash of color caught his eye. A familiar redhead sat alone near the pool tables. She didn't see him; her attention was on her phone.

He pulled out the chair next to Emily, and she looked up, startled.

"Buy you a drink, my lovely siren?" he asked.

She smiled. That seemed like a good sign. "You can't afford what I'm having."

"No? What are you drinking that a hearty buyout check can't buy?"

"A hardcore escape from reality." Pain cut through the teasing in her voice.

"That's where you're wrong. Every single bottle on that wall will get you that." He nodded at the glass shelves behind the bar.

"Until the morning after. Then the *now* rushes back, polluted with regret." Was she talking about them?

"Do you regret it?"

She looked at him, green eyes thoughtful. "If by *it* you mean you and me, No. I probably should. That seems like the smart thing to do, but I don't. Aren't you going to ask me if I'm here to land a shark, or if I'm the predator?"

"That didn't work out so well for me last time. I *am* curious why you're here."

"I'm not sure. Same reason as you?" She shrugged.

That didn't help much. "To pretend you're drinking, but really be a miserable body in a chair?"

Her smile grew. "Sounds about right. I don't know. I guess maybe part of me hoped, if I returned to where it all started, I could do that one thing differently, to make it all right."

"If you meet future-me while you're here, will you ask him what I'm supposed to do next?" Justin hadn't meant to let his uncertainty slip out.

"Talk to Antonio."

Justin eyed her warily. How much did she know? "I'm not the one refusing to talk."

"Never said you were. You want a different answer? Do what you wanted to do. License the tech from APPropriate Designs and make PP happen."

He'd never phrased it to her like that. "He got to you first."

"*Got to me* makes it sound sinister. He took my call. You didn't."

Jealousy spiked inside. Were they fucking? The thought gouged holes in his chest. Wondering if there was more made the wounds throb. "I haven't been quite myself for a few days."

"Welcome to the club. Talk to him."

"You know." Justin studied her. "You knew before. How long?"

She ducked her head and fiddled with the

napkin under her glass. "How he felt? I figured it out pretty early on. It wasn't my secret to share, though."

The invisible divots behind his ribs pulsed in protest. How did she see something he missed for years? "That's what's at the heart of this, isn't it? Too many secrets. And you can tell me to talk to him as many times as you want; he still won't have anything to do with me."

She frayed the edges of her napkin, shredding tiny triangles and building a pile. Silence settled between them.

Suddenly Justin wasn't so enamored with the background noise. "How's the job hunt going?"

She scowled. "That's a mood killer. Um… Not well? I can't say why no one is returning my calls, but I've got a pretty solid guess in some cases. I've never had this kind of trouble landing interviews before."

"You're still looking, then?"

"You put those pieces together all on your own?" She twisted her mouth and her expression relaxed.

It was perfect. The idea helped Justin ignore the churning mess inside. "Come work for me."

"I'm not sure anyone told you, but you don't have a job either. Or a company." She knew *everything* that happened.

"I have a plan, though. Or a plan to make a plan." The rush was fading, his frustration floating back in. That wasn't right. This was a way to regain control. He had to follow the momentum. "Are you two sleeping together?" No. Wrong question. He needed to get away from thoughts of Antonio.

"Not that it's any of your business, but no."

Thank God. "You're right. I shouldn't have asked."

"I should go." She pushed back from the table and stood. "I'll think about the job."

"Answer the phone next time I call?" It was the best he could manage.

"I will. And for the record, I nag him to call you as much as I did you to reach out to him."

"And?" The relief inside grew.

"Has he called you?"

No. "I don't know what to say to him." Justin's mood was on a high-speed roller coaster, and the bottom had dropped out again.

"The truth."

"I don't know what that is."

She bent at the waist and kissed him on the cheek. "I can't help you there. Call me. And him."

God damn it.

CHAPTER TWENTY-THREE

EMILY WANTED TO CHUCK her laptop out the window. She'd only been looking for work for a week, and it was already driving her nuts. Considering she only had enough savings to live in the extended-stay hotel for another two months, and that didn't include new hardware purchases, destroying her computer in frustration was probably a bad idea.

She settled for putting the computer next to her, where she sat cross-legged on the bed, falling sideways, and screaming at the top of her lungs into her pillow.

Frustration temporarily vented, she rolled onto her back. For as long as she'd been contracting, she'd never gone without work for more than a week or two. Silicon Valley was a wealth of startups and shutdowns, and there was always contract work for an experienced developer.

She was on her second Monday of unemployment, and she couldn't get headhunters to return her calls. Lining up interviews? That was a universe she couldn't even see from where she sat.

If she believed it was a thing, she'd wonder if

she'd been blacklisted. The thought was ridiculous; that didn't really happen.

Antonio would bring her back without hesitation—he said as much—but he was still under a hiring freeze until their new CEO was announced. He'd been told there was one, but not given a name. Even if it were an option, though, she couldn't go back to APPropriate Designs. Her employment agreement with Grant forbade her from returning within six months to any company he'd placed her with as a contractor.

The job search wasn't getting her anywhere. If she hit *Refresh* on her email one more time, she might break her F5 key.

She sat up and pulled her computer back into her lap. Maybe there was something new on the tech blogs that would point her in a direction. Some startup that didn't care who she was—only that she had experience.

She was only two or three headlines into scanning her RSS feed, when her brain stalled.

Trouble in PParadise for APPropriate Designs?

She scowled at the headline. Someone thought they were being clever.

Technology giant and rewards provider extraordinaire, APPropriate Designs, announced today their founding members had been bought out. Justin Conroy and Antonio Bianchi are no longer with the company.

The official statement from the board of directors is that the company needed to move in a new direction. However, rumors say the CEO, Justin

Conroy, got in trouble for fraternizing with a contractor.

She slammed the lid shut on her laptop. *Fucking tabloid trash gossip-mill tech blogs.* Why was she following this one, anyway?

The content of the article sank in, as she stared at the wall, and a throb started behind her ribs. That meant Antonio was out too. As of yesterday, he had no idea. Hell. This sucked.

Her phone buzzed with a text from Cynthia.

I'm seeing the news. I'm so sorry. I didn't mean what I said. You don't deserve this.

Emily growled at the screen and deleted the message. Fuck that. She wasn't in the mood for pity. If Cynthia didn't care a week ago, it hardly seemed genuine now.

I'm seeing the news. An afterimage of the text was seared in Emily's thoughts. It never mentioned her by name, but how many people were talking about it? Enough it stood out to Cynthia.

Justin's offer looked better every day. Except he didn't have a plan, and it would take him a few months to get the ball rolling. If she budgeted, she could hold out that long. Something made her hesitate to accept his offer, and she couldn't say what.

He was sincere—she believed that. Despite it being a half-assed suggestion in the middle of a noisy bar, he'd meant it. He was competent, skilled, and had a brilliant platform.

She wasn't getting anywhere with her thoughts spinning in circles. She should call Antonio and make sure he was coping with this news okay. The idea settled in with a realization. She couldn't tell Justin *yes*, because she didn't want to be seen as taking sides. If the men stayed on the outs, would she be caught in the middle?

And if that happened, and someone forced her to choose one or the other, would she do it? Could she?

Her phone rang, and she scrambled to answer the unfamiliar number. "This is Emily Lowry."

"Hi, Emily. This is Terry from Tech Consult Source. I found your resume online."

She whispered a silent prayer to every god and demon who might be listening. "That's great. What can I do for you?"

"I have a client who's looking for someone with user interface and database skills, for a temp-to-hire position. It looks like you've got a lot of what they want. Can you tell me about your most recent job?" His tone was pleasant.

This was a nice change. She'd turned interviewing into an art form. This call would be no problem. "Certainly. I've got both the skill sets you mentioned, with several years' experience in each." She launched into a brief, keyword-filled description of what she'd done with Justin and Antonio.

"That's fantastic." Terry sounded genuine. "It says here that was APPropriate Designs. They're a client of ours, but they're not doing much hiring lately. I'm curious how you got in the door."

The question sounded like pleasant small talk. She suspected it was more ominous. "I wasn't on their payroll. I was hired by the investment firm who owns controlling shares."

"I see. And your contract with them ended before or after their CEO resigned?"

Her gut sank. "I believe both happened at the same time." She could lie and tell him she didn't know anything about it. Insist things came to a close when they should have. But if they did any sort of reference check on her, they'd get a different timeline from Grant.

Terry was silent for a moment. "Well, thank you for taking the time to speak with me. I don't think this position is a good match for your qualifications after all, but I'll keep your name on file, in case that changes."

She wanted to scream that *he* called *her*. With a job. That he already said she was qualified for. And—God damn it—why was he making assumptions?

Instead she said, "I understand. Thank you for your time." She disconnected, tossed the phone aside, and flopped back on her bed. The harder she fought to ignore the despair creeping over her like a black fog, the denser the feeling got.

*

TROUBLE IN PPARADISE FOR APPROPRIATE DESIGNS?

Antonio's anger increased more with each sentence he read in the blog post, as he processed what the vague statements meant. *Justin Conroy and Antonio Bianchi are no longer with the company.*

Which struck Antonio as odd, because he sat at his desk, taking a break from working on the development schedule. He was composing an email to the blogger, asking for a correction, when someone knocked on his office door.

"Crosstown courier dropped this off for you." The receptionist handed him a thick envelope, then left.

The return address was Grant's investment firm. Antonio's anxiety spiked, as he tore open the envelope and slid out the contents. A letter sat on top of it all, printed on a familiar embossed letterhead. He clenched his fist more tightly as he read. His knuckles ached by the end.

It was a buyout offer and severance package, with a request he sign and return both by the end of the week. If he needed a lawyer to look it over, he had to submit notification in writing before end of day Tuesday.

This was bullshit. Antonio might not like the way Justin handled his own resignation, and he might not be interested in running the company alone, but he didn't have any intention of ditching and running.

He dialed Grant's office, irritation ticking through him as he waited for the older man to pick up.

"Antonio. I'm glad you called, and I'm sorry about the news. I meant to tell you before the press releases hit. I have no idea how that information leaked early."

That was one hell of a shitty apology. "I don't care how the news got out. I want to know why it exists. Justin resigned for himself. I didn't have anything to do with that."

Grant sighed. It was a long, drawn-out noise

that made Antonio feel he was about to be talked to like a child. "The board feels APPropriate Designs needs a new face." Yup. There was that condescension. "We're concerned, given that the two of you always acted in tandem, that your staying on with Justin gone will cause rifts."

"What does that mean? *Rifts.* That doesn't make any sense."

"I'm not sure how to better phrase it." Grant's tone was kind, to the point of being insulting. "You've always governed together, and while he resigned, we understand there's some resentment still. We don't need that spilling into everyday business on your part."

Antonio didn't know how to argue against statements like that. "I'm not Justin."

"The decision is made. Have your lawyer contact our Legal department if there are questions about your contract." Grant disconnected.

Antonio stared at the phone in disbelief. Justin cost him his job. Antonio hated to cast blame, but he couldn't think of any other way to look at it. He leaned back in his chair, the energy draining from him, washed away by powerlessness.

He could fight this. Alternately, his name wasn't in the headlines, so finding another job would be easy enough. Especially with his qualifications. He could retire at the age of thirty-three—the buyout amount was enough for him to live a carefree life of boredom. Or start an incubator and fund other app ideas.

None of that sounded appealing. This experience had soured him. He didn't have Justin. He missed his home and his family.

Only one solution appealed to him. He was flying back to Italy this weekend, for his father's birthday. It was the perfect opportunity for a change of scenery. He grabbed his cell phone and dialed his sister.

"*Il mio fratellino.*" Her cheerful greeting nudged aside some of his dread.

"Hey. You busy?" He slipped into Italian without pause. The sounds rolling off his tongue tasted like the sweetest comfort food.

"I'm plotting world domination. Same old stuff. But it'll wait. What's up?"

"I need a favor. I don't know if it's possible to finish before I arrive, but I'm hoping."

"Well? Spit it out."

He steeled himself. "I need you to find me an apartment. Long term. I'm moving back home. But don't tell Mom and Dad. I want to surprise them."

Her squeal of happiness threatened to split his eardrums. "Are you serious?"

"Deadly."

"One bedroom? Two? Is your boyfriend coming with you?"

He wanted to pretend he didn't know what she meant. Had he been that obvious with Justin? "Two bedrooms. I don't need a lot of room, but find me a nice loft if you can."

"I'm on it. And I'm glad you're coming back."

"Me too." In a bitter, melancholy kind of way, but he was still glad. "I've got some other calls to make. Talk to you soon?"

"I'm looking forward to it."

After he disconnected with her, he pulled up his plane-ticket reservations and changed his flight to one way, while he waited on hold for a real-estate agent. Someone he could talk to about listing his house.

Maybe be was being a bit rash, but it worked for Justin. Might as well give it a shot. And if Antonio was lucky, somewhere along the way it would stop aching like a knife through the heart every time Justin's name crossed his mind.

CHAPTER TWENTY-FOUR

Justin rolled his eyes at the pretentious article title, but as he read, annoyance turned to shock and then anger. Why wasn't Antonio taking over the job as CEO? Was he going to be this spiteful about the entire thing?

It wasn't supposed to go this way. True, Justin didn't know what to say to Antonio and hadn't talked to him in a week, but that would blow over. They'd figure things out, establish new lines, and right their friendship. His chest pinged at the word, and he ignored the nagging sensation. If Antonio wasn't accepting the CEO position, did that mean…?

Justin refused to assume. He needed answers. He dialed Antonio's number, wincing each time the phone rang in his ear, and disconnecting when it went to voicemail. In-person visit it was, then.

Antonio's office was empty. Justin snagged one of the developers, who told him Antonio left for the day. At noon, on a Monday? That didn't make sense.

He could second-guess where in town he'd find Antonio, but one thing was certain. If he wasn't at home, he would be sooner or later. Justin would wait there.

By the time Justin reached his destination, he was fidgeting so much, he thought he might crawl out of his skin. He didn't like not having answers.

Fortunately, Antonio's car was in the driveway. Justin forced himself to walk to the front door, rather than sprint, and knocked.

The Antonio who answered had dark circles under his eyes and wore a scowl. "I almost ignored you." Instead of inviting him in, he leaned against the doorframe with his arms crossed, blocking the entrance.

"At least I know the not answering my calls was intentional." Justin wasn't sure how to lead into this conversation. "Why did you turn down the CEO job?"

"Excuse me?"

Now that he'd asked the question, Justin's out-of-control thoughts tumbled forward. "You can't walk away from this. How is that right, after you gave me so much shit about up and quitting?"

"Okay. Let's ignore the elephant in the room and address your concerns." Sarcasm dripped from Antonio's voice. "I didn't turn down any job. They never offered it. I found out I was being let go thanks to a press release and a poorly timed buyout offer.

"I— What?" That didn't make any sense.

"You heard me. The board doesn't think I'm capable of acting without your influence, so they pushed me out. You walk away because you're a whimsical jackass, and everyone pays the price."

The words stung, and Justin didn't have a retort.

"But you're perfectly competent."

"Why are you here?" Antonio asked. "To demand answers I don't have about a decision I didn't make? If so, the conversation is done."

Justin's mind stumbled at the wash of hostility. This sucked, and it was mostly on him. "I'm not sure why I'm here. I miss you. I want our friendship back."

Antonio gave a bitter laugh. "I'm still missing the apology in everything you've said. The part where you're sorry you made decisions about our company, without consulting me. Where you realize your actions have consequences."

"I'm here to fix things."

"You're right. This is my fault."

"That's not what I mean." Justin raked his fingers through his hair in frustration. "Can we talk inside?"

For a moment, he thought Antonio was going to say *no*, but Antonio stepped aside and let him in. They stood in the foyer, facing each other, tension pulsing through the room.

"I don't feel *that way* about you." Bile rose in Justin's throat at the taste of the words. "That doesn't mean I want you out of my life. I need you."

Antonio winced. "Please don't say that. Not that way. I can't. I'm sorry. Maybe someday in the future, I can reconcile the ridiculous fantasy I built in my head with reality, but right now I'm trying, and I can't find that point. That's probably not fair to you, because you're right—I can't force you to feel something you don't. But the same goes for me. I can't turn it off, and now that it's out there, I don't know how to put the feeling away again. I need to get away. Not because you don't feel the same way about me, but because you threw everything away. It's a careless disregard and it involved both of us, and I can't let you do that to me again That's not friendship, it's selfish. I need to get away."

Justin had been selfish. He saw that now, but he didn't know how to make it right. *I need to get away.* It could be a casual statement. The equivalent of *give me some time*. The rawness clawing at Justin's throat didn't let him believe it was so simple. "You're being literal."

"I am. I'm going back to Italy. I made arrangements this morning."

"No. You can't." Panic welled inside Justin. He didn't like this feeling at all. "You have to stay. I can… I don't know. Learn to make us work?"

Antonio stared at him, disbelief and hurt in his eyes. "Make what work? A love you don't want? Out of pity? Desperation? No thank you. I'd never want such a thing. I can't believe you think that's a viable alternative."

"I don't know what else to say." Justin wasn't used to being at a loss.

"You've said enough."

* * * *

EMILY SAT IN HER CAR in the coffee shop parking lot, staring at the *New Voicemail* bar on her phone. The message was from Cynthia, and Emily didn't know if she wanted to listen or not. She needed to make a decision soon, because she was supposed to meet Antonio inside. He called her last night, confirmed the news about him being laid off, and said he wanted to talk to her about something but wouldn't give any hints. He asked if she was free Tuesday morning.

She was. And Tuesday afternoon, and based on her lackluster job search, every moment from now until eternity. How long until this stripped-raw feeling of desperation passed? She deleted the message from Cynthia and headed inside.

Antonio was waiting at their table, a drink in front of him and a second in front of the empty seat across from him. The gesture stripped away a layer of her frustration. He stood as she approached, and swept her into a hug. The gesture had become natural over the past week, and it lifted her spirits another notch.

She wasn't certain, but it seemed like he held on longer this time. Or that was her, squeezing more than normal, needing this line to stay tethered. He released her, and they sat.

She sipped her coffee. He even got that right. "How are you doing?" she asked.

He shrugged. "Better than I should be. Not as good as I'd like to be."

"That's an improvement. Any specific reason, or is this an overall sense of good will?"

He chuckled, and the pleasant sound rolled over and through her. Combined with his smile, it would be a temptation under happier circumstances. "There's a specific reason. I'm moving home. To Italy."

"Oh." The bottom dropped out of her world.

Funny—she thought it had disappeared days ago. She and Antonio had barely known each other more than a month, but he was already one of her closest friends, and one of the few friends she had left.

"And I want you to go with me," he said.

Her bottomless world rolled on its side, and her thoughts jumbled into chaos. "*Oh.*"

"Rather, I'd like you to think about it. I've got a job for you. I'll have an apartment. I don't expect any sort of romance, though I wouldn't rule it out in the future, and you've always wanted to see the world."

The idea was brilliant. It was temptation wrapped in terror. "I don't know."

"I didn't expect you to answer right away." His sad smile implied he'd hoped.

"I'm not saying *no*." She didn't think she could if she wanted. The problem was she couldn't find a *yes*, either. "How long do I have before you need an answer?"

"I'm leaving at the end of the week. It would be nice to have you by my side, but it's an open-ended offer. Decide tomorrow or six months from now."

They talked about anything and everything, staying through the lunch crowd and for hours after the rush-hour crowd cleared up. His offer lingered at the forefront of her thoughts the entire time.

For every *con* argument she came up with, a *pro* countered.

She'd be walking away from the life she'd always had and into the uncertain. Then again, there was no reason she had to stay if it didn't work.

What if she got there and found herself

stranded? She'd hop a plane back home. Or to another state, where her reputation wasn't tarnished.

She didn't know Antonio that well, despite the trust they'd built. Then again, she thought she knew Cynthia better than anyone, and look how that turned out.

He walked her to her car at the end of the evening, squeezed her hand as he said *goodbye*, and sent her on her way. He could be her ultimate Prince Charming. Except for the whole him-being-hung-up-on-another-guy thing.

Back at her motel, she tried to focus on getting something done. When that didn't happen, she changed into the shorts and cami she slept in, climbed into bed early, and turned on the TV.

It droned on in the background, but Antonio's offer had her attention. The clock crept past midnight then 1 a.m. Exhaustion gnawed at her limbs and senses, but sleep refused to come.

It was nearly two when her phone buzzed. She grabbed it and pulled up a new message from Justin.

Can we meet up?

She typed out an answer without thought. *I'm up now, or tomorrow is fine.* She included her room information. The rational part of her mind told her that might not be her smartest decision, but at least it was a decision. Something she didn't have to fret over until all hours of the morning.

Twenty minutes later, there was a knock. She let Justin in. He looked as tired as she felt, but his blue eyes and scruff of beard were sexy as hell.

Before the door finished closing behind him, he cupped her face between his palms and crushed his mouth to hers. She whimpered against his lips. She grasped his T-shirt in both fists and held on for all she was worth. He backed her against the wall, sliding one hand to the back of her neck and holding her head captive. As he dipped his tongue into her mouth she tasted hints of coffee and mint, but no alcohol.

The intensity stole her breath and her thoughts, leaving her with the fear that letting go meant fluttering into oblivion and hanging on would burn her from the inside out.

He let go with a gasp and stepped back several feet.

As the cool air rushed around her, she was grateful one of them had hold of their senses.

"That's not why I came over here. I swear." His voice was hoarse.

God. This fervor with him was a new level of terror. "I get it." She stepped around him and settled into the chair by her desk, not trusting herself on the bed. "What's up?" A safe question. She hoped.

He stayed near the entrance. "I wanted to ask if you thought about my job offer. You were supposed to see the message in the morning, hem and haw about it, and then agree to meet face to face, so I could read your reactions and plead appropriately."

His question overlapped and contrasted with Antonio's. If the indecision was bad before, she was fucked now. This was the crossroads she'd feared— having to choose one or the other. She could side with safety and comfort and everything sweet, or opt for a heat and passion that would flare hot and burn out fast.

On the surface, that wasn't what either man was asking. This was about work. She didn't believe that, though. It didn't matter what their intentions were; she doubted she could stay away from Justin any more than he could her.

"Emily?" He studied her, and concern hung in his voice.

What was she going to say? "I'm flattered you want me back, working with you." As the answer hit her tongue, she didn't question the decision. "You'll do amazing things with Promiscuous Perks, or whatever you decide to call it, but I've got another offer."

"I can beat whatever they're paying."

She couldn't find the strength to tell him he really couldn't. She shook her head.

"That's fine. You're a contractor. How long will you be with them? It's going to take me a few months to get things off the ground. Can I snag the next spot in your work queue?"

"This isn't a temporary position." She had to tell him the truth. He deserved to know. "I have a job offer in Italy."

"I see." His expression went flat, and his voice matched it.

I'm sorry stuck in her throat. It didn't seem like the right sentiment.

"If I'd asked you before he did?"

"You did ask me first. A week ago. I wish I could explain it." She barely understood it herself.

"I get it. You do what you have to, for you." He turned and left. No *goodbye*. No glance back.

Light from the hallway spilled in, then vanished

again, cutting her off from him. Something in her heart snapped. She pulled her knees to her chest. If she hugged tight enough, maybe she could keep herself from falling apart.

CHAPTER TWENTY-FIVE

THERE HAD BEEN AN empty pit in Antonio's chest since Justin left his house Monday afternoon. It filled in a bit when Emily said *yes* to his offer.

She stood next to him now, finishing her conversation with Customs.

She intertwined her fingers with his, and he gave her hand a reassuring squeeze. He'd been back to Italy several times since moving to the U.S.— holidays, birthdays, whenever he could find a free week—and it never felt like home until he left Customs.

This time was different. He led her toward baggage claim, and the permanence of the situation sank into his skin, easing the hollowness behind his ribs. He was home. He never expected the words to sound so good. They didn't erase the defeat of leaving Justin behind, but everything else about it felt right.

He glanced at Emily, who was looking everywhere, eyes wide and a tiny smile playing on her lips.

"It's an airport, *passerotta*." He laughed. "Like every other in the world."

She glanced back at him. "I know. But it's what

it represents. Outside these walls, there are things I've never seen before. Never even imagined I'd see in person."

"And a lot that will look too familiar."

She smacked him lightly on the arm. "Don't steal my fun. You seduced me here with promises of seeing the world. Let me see it."

The banter was nice. It blended and melted with the rightness of walking through familiar territory. They grabbed their bags from the carousel and headed outside. Most of their things were being shipped via freight—his now, and hers once she was sure she was comfortable here. He'd sold a lot of it or left it with the house, though.

His sister was waiting by the curb, as she promised. She hopped from the driver's side of the car as they approached, and trotted to meet him. She shared a lot of features with Antonio—almost six feet tall, straight dark hair, and brown eyes—but instead of an olive complexion, she had the same pale skin as their mother. He swept her into a hug, sinking into the comfort of familiarity.

She stepped back and looked Emily over, then extended her hand in greeting. Emily shook it.

"Emily, my older sister Tara," Antonio said. He spoke English, to make sure Emily wasn't excluded. It came naturally. He and his sister were raised in a two-language household, so they'd always spoken both. On top of that, it was required in the office, because the company had a policy of hiring people from around the world. It kept communication straightforward. "She was the bane of my existence until I was about twenty."

Tara smirked. "You loved it, and you know it. You didn't tell me you were bringing a girlfriend. You didn't tell me you *had* a girlfriend."

Pink dotted Emily's cheeks, and she ducked her head. It was such a simple response, but she was gorgeous.

He shook the thought aside. "She's a friend." The words felt wrong, but they were true. Weren't they?

"*Ma che bella.*" Tara dragged her gaze over Emily again, taking her time.

A surge of protectiveness and jealousy surged inside Antonio. "*Giù le mani.*"

"*Se non ci provi, ci provo.*" Tara shrugged and turned away to open the trunk. "Your choice."

"Did I miss something?" Emily asked.

"Did she?" Tara directed a pointed gaze at Antonio. She was in rare form today. He'd have to ask her later what was up.

He shook his head, but couldn't hide his smile, and loaded their luggage into the car. "She says you're pretty, and if I'm not going to make a move, she will." He didn't see a reason to hide the conversation.

Emily's blush darkened. "What did you tell her?"

"Hands off." He opened the back door for Emily and waited until she was in before sliding in next to her. "Her penance is she gets to play driver for the afternoon."

They left the airport and headed toward the city. Tara got him an apartment near the offices, which should be perfect for Emily to dive into the experience and make getting to work easier. Besides, after living in San Jose for so long, he wasn't sure he could handle the shock of removing himself from a crowded city center right away.

Tara met his gaze in the mirror. "I bought you a little time to get settled. I know you've been on the plane all night, but Mom and Dad are expecting you for dinner. Should I tell them you're bringing a guest?"

"It's up to you," he said to Emily. If Tara was a pest about meeting her, his parents would probably fawn and fall over themselves, but it wasn't his decision to make. "My family is friendly, but if you want to sleep off the flight, no one will blame you."

"I'd love to meet them." Emily gave him a huge grin, then turned her attention back to the passing scenery. As they drove, he pointed out different places of note—some historical and others personal. She looked fascinated with each one, snapping pictures whenever the car came to a stop.

The last time he viewed Milan through the eyes of someone new to the city, it was with Justin. The reminder clenched like a fist around Antonio's lungs, but the squeeze wasn't so tight with Emily by his side.

"Tara doesn't sound like an Italian name," Emily said.

Tara glanced in the rear-view mirror. "It's not. Our mother's Irish. Don't worry. I'm sure we'll share all the fun secrets Antonio's kept from you, over dinner."

"I can't wait." Emily sounded excited. Then again, that tone had been in her voice since before they landed.

He wished he could bottle a little of it and use it to smother everything unpleasant that haunted him.

A short while later, Tara dropped them off at the new place, handed over the keys, and wished them both luck. She swept Emily into a huge hug as well, before leaving.

Inside was smaller than Antonio's house in California, maybe only half the size, but it felt perfect. He settled their bags in their separate rooms, and as he turned, he caught Emily yawning.

"We don't have to be anywhere until eight tonight, and the city will still be here tomorrow. You should sleep."

Her persistent grin drooped. "I guess."

"Come on." He wrapped an arm around her waist and dragged her to sit on the edge of the bed. "Shoes off."

She complied, then crawled further onto the mattress and patted the spot next to her. "Keep me company?"

"Sure." As if he could say *no*?

He wasn't aware of falling asleep, until his world shook and startled him awake. Emily flopped down on the mattress next to him. The sun had shifted from one side of the world to the other while he napped, bathing the room in a gorgeous yellow glow.

She settled her head next to his, held up her phone, and said, "Say *cheese*."

"Uh… cheese?" He grimaced.

She snapped the photo of both of them, then bounced away.

He forced the haze of sleep away and sat up. "What was that?"

"Nothing. I need to get ready, don't I? It's five. When do we have to leave?"

He leaped from the bed and lunged for her phone. She squealed and held it above her head, which wasn't much of a threat. He snatched it away, the frowned when he tried to figure out what she wasn't telling him. "It's locked," he said.

"Duh?" She grabbed the device back, swiped the screen, and held it up.

It was a text message from Justin. *Did you get in safe?*

Her reply was the photo she'd taken.

Glad to see it. Tell Antonio I said hi.

Antonio handed the phone back, as a million emotions vied for his attention.

"You okay?" Emily asked, concern in her voice.

He wasn't sure. The snippet of conversation hurt—that Justin reached out to her, that he sent along his greetings after everything that had happened, and simply the reminder Justin wasn't gone, even if he was on the other side of the world. "I thought you two left things on a sour note."

"I couldn't. I told him to keep in touch, and he made me promise to check in when we landed. Is that a problem?"

It hurt that Justin and Emily had that, but while Antonio was still desperate to have Justin here, he wouldn't do it without Emily. Was it selfish to want them both?

"I'll be fine." He forced a smile. "And we have about two hours before we have to leave. Plan accordingly."

How long would it take before something as

basic as hearing Justin's name didn't threaten to devour Antonio from the inside out?

* * * *

JUSTIN HAD DEVELOPED A NEW routine in the two weeks since he'd been unemployed. *Retired? Self-employed?* The last one felt odd, since he'd considered himself his own boss for so long. That had never quite been true, though. There was a lot to adjust to since he gave up APPropriate Designs, but the thing he minded the least was being out from under the board's thumb.

In the mornings, he worked on his business plan. It took a lot of dry research, and his brain could only do so much at a time. Afternoons and nights were for coding. He was in the process of contracting the engine from his former company, and he operated under the assumption it would happen. Lunchtime was his break from it all, and he never skipped lunch these days. He was guaranteed to get Emily on Skype.

She hadn't been able to convince Antonio to join, and that gnawed at Justin, but her company was fantastic. Her being so far away deprived him of the ability to press her to the wall and make her whimper, and—*fuck*—he missed that, but it also meant they talked. He enjoyed the company.

He missed Antonio too. So much, it chewed on his brain and kept him up until he collapsed from exhaustion around two or three every morning. The best way through it, as far as he'd found, was working. Justin expected that to fade with time, but so far, it seemed to intensify as each day passed. Or it was the lack of sleep. It was hard to tell where one stopped and the other started.

His laptop chimed, and a notification popped, telling him Emily had logged on. He gave her a few seconds before he sent the video chat request, and she answered on the first ring.

It didn't matter that the video quality was choppy; seeing her face was calming. "My favorite siren," he said.

"You've got more than one?" Her stuttered image flashed a scowl that was a grin half a second later.

"No. Only you."

"Then, technically, that also makes me your least favorite."

The logic made him chuckle. That felt good. "I'm pretty certain there are holes in your argument."

"Nope." She shook her head fast enough her face became a blur. "Absolutely flawless. Are you going to ask?"

"Ask what?"

"Same thing you ask every time you call. We make jokes, you ask your question—"

"You gloss over it with a generic answer. Should we skip that part today?"

"No. You can't break the cycle."

He sighed. Might as well get it out of the way. He wanted to know, anyway, even though the response was always, *He's well. Same as usual. You know.* "How's Antonio?"

"He misses you. A lot."

Justin swallowed hard, surprised at the gouge the words left in his heart. He should have a clever come back, like, *Of course he does,* but he couldn't find his voice.

"I'm not supposed to tell you. In fact, I've been specifically ordered to not say anything. But you two are being stubborn assholes, him with the not-talking-to-you and you with the refusing-to-admit-how-you-feel, and I'm tired of the drama. Seriously, you're worse than high-school girls with a crush."

"It's not a crush." What Justin meant as a denial took on a whole new meaning as he said it. He was telling the truth; it wasn't. What he felt was so much more.

"Don't go anywhere. I'll be right back." Emily vanished from the screen.

His curiosity grew, but short of shouting for her and hoping she hurried, he didn't have much choice but to wait. Muffled voices carried through the speakers—Emily and Antonio—but Justin couldn't make out the words.

"This is a bad idea." Antonio must be within range of the microphone now.

"Sit," Emily said.

Antonio dropped into the seat in front of the webcam, and Emily crouched next to him.

"Hey." Antonio wore a grimace.

Justin didn't care. This was better than he hoped for when he called. "Ditto. How are things? Work and such?"

"Good." Antonio's tone was flat. "Transition is taking time, but fortunately Dad thought all of this through before he decided to retire."

Justin hid a wince at the implication. "Glad to hear it. You're happy there, then?"

"Never been better. How's Promiscuous Perks or whatever you're calling it?"

"Great. Fantastic. Once I have a final contract in place for the engine, the school Susan teaches at is taking us live. It'll need a new name before then." Justin had to do some serious pleading with Mercy, to convince her helping him make the connection was a good idea. She was skeptical he could pull this off on his own. In fact, she was stunned he didn't leave with Antonio. Told Justin she always figured he'd get it through his thick head one day.

He'd told her she was imagining things. Now, as he watched a low-res Antonio stream through his monitor, Justin wondered if he was the only person who hadn't seen what was there. No. He missed his best friend and hated that things ended the way they did, but that was it.

Fuck. He didn't even believe his own denials anymore. *I miss you. I think I might love you, too.* The confession stuck in his throat, and the realization squeezed like a fist around his heart. "Anyway. Good to see you. I'll let you both get back to your night."

"Yeah. Later." Antonio left.

Emily slid back into the chair, shouting over her shoulder, "You're both stubborn assholes." She looked back at the screen. "That includes you."

"I figured." Justin tried to smile, but he wasn't feeling it. "Will you be around tomorrow?"

"Always."

They finished their conversation, and she logged off. Justin needed to get back to work, but he couldn't unstick his thoughts. Seeing Antonio filled him with a need to say *something*, but anything Justin thought of felt rash. He didn't want his thoughts to come off as impulsive or insincere.

His confusion was amplified by the situation. Was it really love, or did he just hate losing? And if it was real, the sentiment was too private to share with anyone except Antonio, but at the same time, Justin wanted Emily to hear. Not to hurt her. That was the last thing he wanted. He missed her as much, but at least she was still talking to him. He wanted to make sure she was okay with it. She and Antonio were obviously close. Justin couldn't destroy whatever bond they built. And if he said the wrong thing to Antonio, he could lose them both forever.

The momentum Justin relied on was gone. He'd stalled in the middle of a quagmire of uncertainty and couldn't see the path out. He dropped his head into his hands. Was this a flash-in-the-pan impulse?

No. Justin meant this. He felt it in every inch of his body. Antonio wasn't just a friend or business partner. He was more. He'd always been more. That *I love you* he refused to say was real. He couldn't keep pretending otherwise.

But Emily… Justin needed her as well. The three of them made it work for fun. Could it be more? Did it even matter, if it was too late to make things right?

CHAPTER TWENTY-SIX

ANTONIO LEANED AGAINST THE doorframe to Emily's bedroom and watched her as she pinned another photo to the plaster. She was building a collage of her favorite images from around the city, and her goal was to cover an entire wall. If she didn't slow down, that wouldn't take long. He loved seeing her enthusiasm. Her excitement. And her.

She whirled and squeaked. Her hand flew to her chest, and she gave a nervous laugh. "Standing there, watching, without saying anything? That's kind of creepy."

"I'd apologize, but..." He pushed away from the wall and strode toward her.

"But you're not sorry."

He stopped a few scant inches from her and brushed a loose curl of red from her cheek. "I'm really not. The scenery is too breathtaking to regret looking." They'd been here a month, and while certain pains never lessened, every day with her was easier than the one before. He wasn't sure when it happened—or maybe there was no single point in time—but somewhere along the way, he fell in love with her. He prayed telling her wouldn't backfire, like last time he spilled his guts to someone about love. He didn't have the same doubts, though, and even if the confession didn't go well, for some reason he couldn't fathom, he refused to hold back this time.

She watched him, green eyes wide and sparkling with amusement. "You're still staring."

"I'm still enjoying the view." They shared a bed half the time, but it was only for sleep. They hadn't had sex since they moved here. He always had an underlying fear he might use her to replace Justin, and end up hurting her. That concern was gone now. "Would you rather I was doing something else?"

"Depends on what you have in mind."

"This." He cupped her cheek with his palm and brushed his mouth over hers, then pulled back to gauge her response.

She caught her bottom lip between her teeth. "That's pretty good."

"Then you'd be amenable to more of the same?"

She hesitated.

He probably missed a few steps along the way. He glided his hands down her arms and tangled his fingers with hers. "I need you to know I love you. I've been thinking about this a lot, and I wouldn't say it if I didn't mean it completely. I can't imagine my life without you in it, and I won't let you slip away if I can help it."

"I'm not going anywhere."

It wasn't exactly the response he hoped for, but it was better than some of the other possibilities. He gave her hand a gentle squeeze. "I'm not using you to fill a void. The place where you sit in my heart is for you."

She let out a laugh and kissed him. It was a feather-light hint of skin on skin, and she pulled away before he could respond, enough to look him in the eye. "I love you too."

His pulse soared, and he felt lighter than he had in weeks. It had never occurred to him how powerful hearing those words aloud would be. He crushed his mouth to hers, starving and frantic. Needing to be a part of her.

She raked her nails up his chest, pushing his shirt out of the way, and he broke away long enough to tear the clothing over his head. She trailed her mouth along his tattoo, following the path of the dragon's tail as it looped down his side. Each touch permeated his thoughts.

"I don't have the patience for that tonight." He nudged her back and pulled her shirt off. Knotting one hand in her hair, he kissed her again. Holding her close as if she was his air. Diving into the moment. With his other hand, he unclasped her bra.

She giggled and murmured against his lips, "You've got nimble fingers."

"I can do a lot more than that with them." He slid her bra straps down her arms, and tossed the garment into the growing pile a few feet away.

She stepped away, playful smirk dancing on her swollen lips. "Like what?"

He let his gaze linger on her breasts, round and full, tipped with eager pink nipples. Christ, she was gorgeous. He grabbed her hips and pushed her toward the bed. He kissed her again as they sat on the edge of the mattress. He could do this all night, even if they never went beyond this intense making out. Her mouth against his, their tongues wrestling, it decompiled his thoughts, leaving raw, exposed data in its wake.

She gripped his erection through his jeans. He bucked against her hand with a sharp gasp, and she stroked.

He grasped her wrist and jerked away from her touch with a growl.

She pouted. It was childish but alluring, and he kissed her bottom lip. "If you do that, I'll finish before I'm ready," he said.

"I have a hard time believing you have that little self-control."

"Only with you."

*

EVERY CARESS WAS A NEW SENSATION to Emily. It didn't matter if she'd been touched somewhere before, it was different this time. He lowered her onto the bed, then licked a line along her collarbone, down her chest, and over her breasts, to drag a nipple into his mouth. She squirmed under the attention, need throbbing between her legs, slippery and anxious.

When he said *I love you*, she thought her heart might explode. Which was cliché, but she didn't care. She'd been on the cusp of falling for him for what seemed like an eternity, not daring to think the words, because of Antonio's baggage. When he made the confession, truth rang through his voice.

He sucked and scraped his teeth along the

swollen nub on her chest, undoing her jeans at the same time. There was a tenderness to each movement, despite the frenzied desire to remove everything keeping them from feeling each other. It terrified the hell out of her, and she loved every minute of it.

He dragged her jeans and panties off, then kissed along the inside of her thigh on his way back up. When he glided his tongue up her slit, she arched her back in pleasure, pressing into his face.

"I was promised magic fingers," she managed between gasps for air.

"Are you complaining?" His mouth vibrated against her labia when he spoke, teasing her.

"Definitely not."

He finally reached her clit and sucked on it, then flicked his tongue over the tender bud. He kept up the attention for several minutes, driving her to the edge of orgasm and leaving her head in the clouds, as all the blood and oxygen rushed to other parts of her body. She gripped his short strands of hair, needing something to hold onto, and he increased his speed.

"Please, let me come?" she whimpered.

He glided two fingers inside her, hooked them up, and hit her G-spot. Climax spilled through her, and she cried out, grinding into his face and falling into his touch until it was too much.

He eased back, and she shuddered with pleasure. Tingles raced through her limbs, and her legs refused to respond. He moved his mouth back up her stomach, over her chest, and to her lips. She dove into the taste of her plus him. It was official—his kisses were one of the most delicious things she'd ever had.

"You're beautiful." He leaned over her, looking down.

Regardless of the fact she lay naked in front of him and the two of them had done things with Justin that would make a Play Girl editor blush, the simple compliment made her feel exposed and vulnerable. "Thank you."

She reached for him again, found his erection, and traced its outline through denim. He pulled away with a throaty laugh. "You're not satisfied?"

"You were—are—amazing. I'm thinking about you."

He stood and stripped off his jeans. His cock sprung to attention, and he wrapped one hand around the shaft, gaze lingering on her body. "Not that I mind you thinking about me, but I'd rather you enjoy this too."

"I will. I don't doubt it for a second."

He knelt next to her, then flopped back on the mattress with a groan. "Fuck."

"That's the point." She propped herself up to look at him.

He shook his head. "I don't have any condoms."

She raised her brows in disbelief. "That's not like you—not planning well."

"I wasn't really planning. I got as far as confessing my love and didn't dare think beyond that point."

She fell onto her back and pointed toward her bathroom. "Box. Top drawer. You might not have had expectations, but I've been hoping pretty much since we got here."

"You are brilliant and sexy and scary." He gave her a quick kiss, then stood and disappeared into the bathroom. He emerged seconds later, rolling the protection on, and nudged her thighs apart with his knee.

One hand next to her head, to support his weight, he teased her opening with his cock. She swore he slid inside a millimeter at a time. The slow penetration built a dam of tension. He locked his gaze on hers, as he increased the pace, building from a gentle rock to a steady rhythm.

The tease was nice, but she wanted fast and furious. She wrapped her legs around his waist and prompted a change in speed.

He gave her an evil grin, straightened up, and pinned her knees to her chest. With the new angle, he hit deep inside her, pressing an already tender button. Orgasm built again, this time a slow burn that felt like it would never reach the finish line. Her muscles clenched around him involuntarily, drawing him in, then forcing him out.

"Jesus, *passerotta*. I can't..." He let go of her legs and rested his palms on either side of her head again. His pounding reached a frantic pace, punctuated by grunts of pleasure. She felt like she was drowning in his dark eyes.

The rapid-fire thrusts yanked out her orgasm, and she gripped his arms, digging her nails into his biceps as ecstasy rolled over her. She recognized the familiar sound of his climax, and he seemed to slide into a different pace when he came, driving hard, then giving a few short thrusts, before slowing to a stop.

He knelt for a moment, staring in to her eyes, his panting matching hers. She wasn't sure what broke the spell, but he leaned in and gave her a quick kiss, before falling next to her on the mattress. They lay side by side, her gaze frozen on the ceiling. He sought out her hand, and she squeezed back, gripping for everything the gesture represented.

"You really are amazing, *passerotta*." His voice was gravel.

She had to swallow several times, to unstick her throat. "What does that mean? It sounds pretty when you say it, but you could probably read me a shopping list in Italian, and I'd think it was pretty." Now that she mentioned it, she should have him do that.

"It means *sparrow*. It's a term of endearment."

She liked the sound of that. "I'm a little bird?"

"Yes." He shifted from the mattress, helped her sit, moved up to the pillows, and pulled her down to rest her head on his chest.

"Why?" she asked.

"Why do I call you that? It seems fitting." He trailed his fingers along her arm. "This is how I see it. The dragon is power, strength, and good luck. The phoenix burns bright, burns out, and rises from the ashes. But a sparrow is spry and intelligent. Fast and quick. Rising above it all and soaring to heights the dragon and phoenix can't imagine."

"Why did you phrase it that way?" It felt odd to be placed in the middle of something he and Justin had shared, like matching yin yang symbols. She didn't mind.

Antonio had to know he was doing it, didn't he?

"It seemed appropriate." Apparently he did.

Silence settled between them. It felt right, as it always did. She'd never been more comfortable not saying anything when there was someone else in the room. The comment about the dragon and phoenix sparked a thought she didn't want to have, though. It brought Justin back into the bedroom. She had to know something, and it might spoil the mood, but she suspected it would be okay. "It still hurts you to think about him."

Antonio's hand froze, and then he resumed tracing light circles along her skin. "It does. But that doesn't diminish how I feel about you. I meant it earlier. I love you."

"I don't doubt it." She didn't think she'd get tired of hearing it, either.

"You miss him too. Even though you talk to him almost every day."

Which reminded her—this meant she'd missed Justin's call. He would wait. "If he showed up tomorrow, out of the blue, and said he was wrong—he does love you—what would you do? Who would you choose?" She wanted to slap herself as soon as the question was out. Way to spoil the best, cuddliest-ever post-coital conversation.

"Why do I have to choose?" he asked.

She sat up and stared at him, as the question jolted through her. The words didn't make sense, but they did. "What?"

"Why do I have to choose? If you could have us both, would you pick?"

"I don't think I could. You each speak to a different part of me."

"Exactly." He tugged her back down. "It doesn't matter, though. You're here, he's not, and it's all hypothetical. The most important thing is I'm not giving you up, and you said you'd always be here."

"I will." She nestled closer, meaning the words more than anything.

CHAPTER TWENTY-SEVEN

JUSTIN COULDN'T BELIEVE HE was doing this. *Please don't let it blow up in my face.* He sat in the lobby to an office he hadn't visited in five years, trying not to fidget. He was more nervous than the first time he interviewed here. Back then, Antonio had his back. Justin only had to make a good impression, and the job was his.

This time, Antonio didn't know Justin was here. Justin used his new project name to get himself on Antonio's appointment calendar. This kind of uncertainty was new for him. It was deceptive to not give his name, but if Antonio said *no* before Justin got in the door, this thing would fall apart. He hoped the face-to-face visit would carry his sincerity with it.

"Mr. Bianchi will see you now." Antonio's assistant nodded to the closed door.

Justin steeled himself, pushed into the room, and shut Antonio and himself off from the rest of the world.

Antonio looked up, and his shock blinked into an impassive mask. Even trying to appear emotionless, he looked incredible.

How had Justin missed this part of himself for so long?

"Hear me out," Justin said, before Antonio could speak. "Please?"

Antonio clenched his jaw. "Is this about business?"

"Some of it." *A teeny, tiny bit.* The visit did include a proposal, but Justin didn't expect to get too far into it. Antonio knew most of the information Justin had to pitch.

"And the rest of it?"

I love you, and I was an idiot not to recognize it. Tell me what it will take to earn your trust and friendship back, and then we can work from there. "How are you doing? Both of you."

"You didn't fly to Italy to ask how I was, and you already know how Emily is."

But Justin didn't. Over the last few days, she'd faded off. Cut their conversations short and missed more of them than she made. That hurt too, as much as losing Antonio but in a different way. Justin was surprised at the emptiness her absence left inside. "I'm asking anyway. I want to know."

"I'm good. *We're* good." Antonio's expression relaxed enough that the corners of his mouth teased up. "We're together now. An actual, honest-to-Christ couple."

"That's amazing. Fantastic. I'm glad to hear it." Justin forced the lie to sound sincere. He swallowed the rest of his prepared speech and tried to ignore how much of him shriveled up at the news Antonio and Emily had both moved on. At least it was with each other. Something about that felt right, even in center of disappointment.

"Thank you. We're really happy together." Antonio smiled.

Justin swore there was a hint of sadness in his friend's eyes, but that was probably wishful thinking. He wouldn't fuck up their lives anymore by being the asshole who said, *I changed my mind. I was wrong; I love you,* after Antonio had moved on. "Well, then, I suspect your day is as busy as always. Do you have time to hear the business part of my pitch?"

"You're on my calendar. I've got at least another forty-five minutes." Antonio gestured to the chair across from his desk. It was odd, seeing him behind the desk his father occupied for so many years, but it was appropriate. Justin never should have tried to take him from here. "I have a question before you start, though," Antonio said.

"Fire away." Justin shoved his glimmer of hope to the bottom of his shoes and stomped on it. There was no reason to make assumptions about what kind of question it would be.

Antonio leaned in, fingers clasped. "Does this proposal of yours sound anything like, *Let me introduce you to Promiscuous Perks—a predictive education algorithm, driven by years of data gathering in the consumer market.*"

"It's not *exactly* like that." Justin laughed.

"Because you had to change the name, to sell it to schools."

Justin could do this. It would take time and adjusting, but they could go back to what they had before. Antonio did it for years. Justin could learn. "Pretty much. I'm rolling out with Ballet West's Park

City academy, and I have three other schools along the West Coast and mountain states that are ready to sign on."

"In other words, you've already done the legwork and have the code in place. As long as you work on a lean budget, you've got the capital, and you'll be profitable soon. I've seen the betas. I know. What do you need us for?"

Because I was an idiot and thought you'd wait for me for more than four weeks. But Antonio put up with Justin for a decade, holding out hope. "You've got the infrastructure, your company thrives on partnerships like this, and"—Justin forced calm confidence through his veins—"I don't want to do this without you. I've never wanted to do this without you." He clamped his mouth shut before he could say too much.

Antonio stared back, lips pursed and hands clasped.

Why wasn't he saying anything?

*

ANTONIO WAS SURPRISED JUSTIN wasn't standing up and pacing. Antonio was making him squirm, and it was probably a little cruel on his part, but Justin deserved to sweat a little, since Antonio wasn't interested in actually turning him away.

When Justin walked into his office, Antonio expected the pain to be overwhelming. That had faded, much to his relief. The love was still there. He was grateful he'd been honest with Emily about that. It wasn't the intense, gnawing desperation he felt in the past. Mostly, he was relieved to see Justin again.

"I can't give you an answer right now. I have to take your proposal in front of the board," Antonio said.

Justin raised his brows. "It's a privately held company. Old-family money. Never been owned by anyone else. *You're* the board."

"I am. And you're the asshole who almost cost us everything because you didn't like working within the confines of someone else's timeline." It was far less emotional than what Antonio wanted to say. *You're the asshole who broke my heart and didn't flinch.*

"Technically, the only thing we lost was—"

"*Stop.*" Antonio barked the word. "They took APPropriate Designs from us and left us with a little money as a weak apology. Five years of work, and now we have to pay them if we want to use what we built."

"You know why I did it. We hashed this out already. I thought you understood."

"I do." Antonio hated admitting that, because it felt like a concession and he was still mad at Justin. Besides, this felt like giving Justin an out, when he hadn't earned the right to shrug off any responsibility for what happened.

Justin frowned. "I fucked up. Everywhere. I should have handled my resignation differently. I shouldn't have brushed you aside the way I did." He hissed through his teeth. "I can't say I'm sorry about the results, except that I never wanted to send you back home, but I did a lot of things wrong. You deserved better. And it sounds like you have it now."

Antonio wanted to cling to his anger, but the longer Justin sat here, the more difficult it was. Antonio'd had time to deal with the awkward heartbreak, and while it still hurt, he couldn't blame that on Justin, as much as he wanted to. Justin knew what he'd done and was trying to make things better, in his own way.

If Antonio dragged this out much longer, he might push away his friend again. Which would serve Justin right but wouldn't make Antonio happy. "I want to see your numbers before I sign anything, but I'm willing to shake on it and give you a *probably yes.*" He extended his hand.

"Thank God." Justin's grip was warm and comfortable. A ghost of a temptation and a reminder of the weekends they shared with Emily. Antonio allowed the memories to linger, rather than banish them the way he normally did.

"What about us?" Justin asked.

Not words Antonio wanted to process. Not a question he could afford to make assumptions about. "What do you mean?"

"Are you and I good? Or can we be?"

That would be nice. "We'll get there. Yes, we can be."

Justin's smile—the actual, genuine version of it—was a nice sight. Something Antonio hadn't wanted to admit how much he missed it.

They chatted a while longer, eating into the rest of the time on the calendar and pushing back to more neutral ground. Antonio had to kick him out for his next appointment.

"I have one more favor." Justin stood. "Tell me

where Emily's sitting, so I can say *hi*?"

"Did she know you were coming?" Antonio would be impressed if she kept a secret like that to herself.

"No. She pretty much stopped talking to me. How long have you been together?"

"A week."

"That explains it." Justin sighed.

Inspiration struck Antonio. "How long are you in town?"

"Indefinitely. Long enough to convince you to partner with me. Longer, if I decide I missed the place too much to leave."

Antonio liked the sound of *indefinitely* but refused to let himself get sucked into the possibilities. Especially without Emily. "That means you're free for dinner tonight. Come over to the apartment. Surprise her. We'll catch up."

"I'd love that."

Antonio scribbled out their address along with instructions and came around the desk to hand it over. Justin stood and pulled him into a tight hug. The intensity and intimacy caught Antonio off guard.

"I missed you," Justin said. A current of emotion ran through his voice.

It filled Antonio with an ache he couldn't ignore but made him smile at the same time. "Me too."

*

AN UNEASINESS CRAWLED THROUGH Emily, and she couldn't find a source for it as she stood in the kitchen entrance, watching Antonio cook dinner.

He was making something with a red wine sauce that smelled amazing, and that she struggled to pronounce the name of. His mother was an amazing cook and refused to let her boy grow up inept in the kitchen, so she'd passed the skills on to him.

He'd been quiet since they got home, where they usually chatted and caught up while they made food.

"Are you all right?" she asked.

He added a dash of something else to the steak. "Fine. Why?" His tone was light, but a tension that matched hers ran through it.

"You seem—I don't know—someplace else, I guess."

He turned long enough to squeeze her hand, before giving his attention to the meal again. "It's all good. I promise. Will you grab an extra plate and such for the table?"

She eyed his back with curiosity. "Are we hosting an imaginary friend?"

"A real one. I invited an old buddy over for dinner tonight. I thought I said something. I hope it's okay."

She was certain he hadn't told her. "No worries." It made sense the longer they were here, the more people from his past he'd run into.

Antonio was finishing up, when someone rang the bell. He had his hands full, so Emily said, "I'll get it."

"Wait," Antonio called.

Emily was already answering the door.

Justin stood in the hallway, looking better than she remembered and wearing a sheepish grin.

"Surprise."

Her heart dropped into her shoes, and her mind stalled. "I don't think now's a good time. We're expecting company." *Stupid thing to say.* She didn't have the mental capacity to figure out why.

"You're early." Antonio's voice carried from behind her.

Justin shrugged. "I think I'm the company."

"Oh." She moved aside to let him in. She was hung up on the surreal contrast of the moment. It felt right to see Justin here. As if it was always meant to be. At the same time, it was wrong. Antonio refused to say more than a few sentences to him over the last month, and that was with Justin halfway around the world.

Now he stood in their living room, Antonio greeting him as if nothing happened.

Justin held out a bunch of wildflowers and a bottle of wine. "For my charming hosts."

Antonio moved to Emily's side and took the drink. She grabbed the bouquet, to have something to do, and turned away. "I'll see if we have a vase."

Her mind kicked into overdrive when she broke eye contact with Justin, several thoughts spilling into her head at once. Both men knew this was coming. Why did Antonio keep it a secret? Did he know last week, when he told her how he felt? That didn't make sense, but neither did any of this.

Irrational panic gripped her stomach, and suddenly dinner didn't smell so good. Would this cost her Antonio? They'd talked about not having to choose, if Justin came back into their lives, and she believed Antonio meant what he said, but with every emotion filling her, it was difficult to remember those simple promises.

Antonio wrapped his arms around her waist from behind and pulled her close. "Are you all right?"

"I don't think we have any vases." It wasn't the right answer, but she was fortunate to form words at all.

He took the flowers from her and set them on the counter. "They'll be okay here for now. Come keep our guest company, while I bring out dinner."

"Sure. Okay." She let herself be led to the table and took a seat across from Justin.

"I'm not used to seeing you at a loss for words," he said, teasing in his voice.

She gave him a weak smile.

Through the meal, both men tried to draw her into the conversation. They chatted about the fact that Justin was partnering with the company, and asked for her thoughts. They talked about what had changed since Justin was last here and asked about her favorite parts of the city so far. It only lasted an hour or so, but the meal seemed to Emily to stretch on for an eternity.

It was as if they were never angry at each other. As much as she tried to tell herself she was overreacting, she couldn't silence the part of her asking if she was about to lose something wonderful.

CHAPTER TWENTY-EIGHT

JUSTIN HAD EXPECTED ANTONIO to be antagonistic this afternoon in the office. When the meeting went better than Justin dared hope for, he dropped his defenses. Which meant he was doubly unprepared for the lukewarm reception from Emily. Her cool, single-word responses and refusal to make eye contact during dinner dug deep, jarring him more than he expected.

He followed Antonio's lead through the meal, keeping up his half of the conversation. Dessert was served, and Justin sectioned off a forkful of tiramisu. "I missed your cooking."

"There are leftovers. I'll wrap some up for you," Antonio said.

Emily pushed back from the table without touching her food. "If you'll excuse me, I need to do a thing."

"Em, wait." Antonio hurried after her and stopped her halfway between the dining room table and what Justin assumed were the bedrooms. Antonio grabbed her arm. "What's wrong?" He kept his voice quiet.

Justin couldn't help but hear, anyway, in the

small space. He tried to busy himself with his food, rather than eavesdrop.

"This is a bit out of the blue is all." Emily's grumble carried through the room.

Unless Justin plugged his ears, he was going to hear the conversation. "I'm not here to cause a rift. I can leave, if you'd prefer."

"No." Antonio glanced at him, then turned back to Emily. "We talked about—"

"I know what we talked about. I was there." Emily's tone was curt.

"It doesn't matter. That's not why he's here," Antonio said.

Justin should stay out of this, but his curiosity got the better of him. "Why am I here?"

"To visit. As a friend." Antonio kept his gaze fixed on Emily. "I didn't know he was coming until he showed up in my office today. I thought inviting him over would be a pleasant surprise. I promise I didn't invite him as a way to trap you into making good on a hypothetical conversation."

Intriguing.

Emily looked past Antonio to Justin, making eye contact for the first time that evening. "Pretend I'm a tad insecure about reaching a new level in this relationship, and assure me you're not here to screw things up. That you didn't fly halfway around the world, without warning either of us, because you hoped—I don't know—that being face to face would make Antonio more likely to listen when you told him you were wrong. That you love him too."

How the fuck did she know that?

"That's not what this is about." A waver ran

through Antonio's words.

"I'm asking Justin," Emily said pointedly.

Justin reached for denial, to make her feel better, but he didn't grasp it quickly enough.

"Fuck." Emily stepped back, face twisting in pain.

"But you two look so good together, I couldn't say anything." Justin struggled for the right words to fix the situation.

"I can't do this." Emily spun and strode into one of the rooms, shutting the door behind her.

At least she didn't slam it.

Antonio sank onto the couch. "Wow. You have shitty timing. Ten years, and you pick *now* to figure things out."

Justin cringed at the words. Antonio wasn't kicking him out or telling him to go fuck himself. The realization offered little consolation. "This isn't what I wanted. And don't tell me I should have thought it through first. I've spent the last month missing you and trying to figure out why and admitting to myself how I feel. I wouldn't be here, though, if I thought… I should have known the two of you would wind up together. You wouldn't have made the move if you weren't falling, and you always got along better with Emily than I did."

"Jealous?"

"Immensely." The answer slipped out without thought. Justin realized how true it was. He flew here to confess his love to Antonio, and now he was envious he didn't have Emily. Fuck, he was a selfish prick.

"You couldn't have known." Antonio sounded

sympathetic. "You took her at her word that we were friends. What else could you do?"

"You're taking this well."

Antonio gave a barking laugh. "I'm screaming on the inside. I don't know whether to deck you or kiss you, and neither one matters, because Emily needs me. I need to talk to her."

Justin stood and crossed the room in time to grab Antonio's arm before he could knock on the bedroom door. "Let me?" Justin didn't know what he was going to say, but he broke this; he needed to fix it.

Antonio held up his hands in surrender and backed away.

Justin knocked. "Can I come in?"

There was no response.

"Emily?" he said.

Seconds later, the latch snicked, and the door creaked open an inch. Justin nudged it wider and saw her standing at the other side of the room, facing a wall covered with photographs of Milan. He walked toward her but stopped about a foot back. He was intensely aware of Antonio watching from the doorway.

She pointed at one of the photos. "I took that the day we got here. I was completely jetlagged, and riding the high of being someplace new." She gestured toward another one. "We took a weekend trip to Rome. I saw the freaking Sistine Chapel and the Colosseum."

He looked at the collage of images. Some were of Antonio, others of her or the both of them or buildings and landscapes. All of them radiated her passion.

She slumped her shoulders. "This is a lifetime of memories from less than a month. I'm not saying I live in some sort of magical utopia, but I'm really fucking happy with our life here."

"Tell me what I have to say to make this right."

Emily shook her head. "I don't know."

That was better than *you can't*. Justin hated confronting this frigid side of her. It was worse than in those early days, when the two of them clashed. Back then, the last thing he wanted was to like her, even professionally.

Now, if she refused to forgive him, it would hurt as much as Antonio leaving. The revelation hit him like a fist to the gut. "Help me figure it out."

"You scare me, Justin. No, that's not quite right. You terrify the hell out of me." She whirled to face him, and he was stunned to see the red rimming her eyes.

"Why?" Justin would do whatever it took to make this right.

"Because you have the ability to take away the best thing that's ever happened to me, and you act like it's nothing. Like that's not the most important power in the universe. And at the same time, you have the ability to be the other half of that same best thing ever, and that's chills me to my core."

"I'm not going anywhere." Antonio's voice carried from the back of the room.

Emily looked past Justin. "Living it is different than saying it."

"And I'm not trying to break the two of you up." Justin poured sincerity into his words. "Though if you're looking for a third…" No. Stupid. Bad. This was the worst way to go about making this better.

The twist of her lips said she agreed. "I can't do what we did before. I won't be an excuse for the two of you to be together without admitting that's what you're doing."

"Never." Antonio moved next to Justin. "I promised you that, and I *do* mean it. I won't break your heart. I don't want to. I need you."

The passion in his words threatened to snap Justin's heart in two. How could he hope to come between them? *Wait.* He was still looking at it wrong. He didn't want to drive Antonio and Emily apart, obviously. But he wanted to be a part of this thing they shared. To have them both.

Emily crossed her arms. "I don't know that letting Justin into our lives works on anything beyond a hypothetical level."

They discussed him that way? Justin couldn't ignore the overjoyed feeling inside, but he did manage to keep it from his face. "It can work, if you're interested." He was in his element. Shooting from the hip. Letting momentum drive his reply. "The two of you have this deep, passionate bond, and that doesn't have to change.

"You and me?" He made sure he had Emily's eye. "That doesn't have to change either. I miss that heat. I miss you as much as I do Antonio. And all three of us, when we put our pretenses and insecurities aside—we're brilliant together. If you're willing to hang onto all of that and let him and me explore what I've been slow to recognize, then we can find that intimacy that comes from watching and being part of it at the same time." He summoned her words from the first night they met.

She smiled. "You remember."

"It's only been a few months. God, has it really only been three months? Yeah, I remember."

Antonio glided his palm down her arm, pulling her out of the defensive pose. "We all have to agree to this, *passerotta.* Your opinion matters as much as Justin's."

"I do want it." Her confession made Justin's heart soar. "But it still terrifies me."

"Like moving to Italy on a whim?" Justin asked. "Or falling in love, in the first place? Do you think it doesn't scare the fuck out of me?"

"I'm starting to wonder if anything frightens you." Emily gave a nervous laugh.

"Loving you does, and I do love you." It felt incredible to say the words. Justin looked at Antonio. "Loving him at least as much—frightening as hell. And I know what I said before you left, and I lied. I was wrong. I love you, and I think I always have, and I'm sorry I was too dense to see it sooner."

The corners of Antonio's mouth twitched up. "It's hard to plan ahead when you spend so much time being impulsive, rash, and irresistible."

"Not quite what I was going for." Justin grinned. "But I'll take it. Can we give this a chance?" He turned back to Emily. "All of us?"

She screwed up her face, and the seconds ticked away without an answer. Finally, her expression softened. "Do I get to watch the two of you make out? Because I've never seen that, and I bet it's pretty hot."

"It is." Justin faced Antonio, tangled his fingers in his friend's hair, and crushed their mouths together. Relief and need crashed around him, dragging a groan from his chest.

Antonio glided his palms down Justin's back, gripped his ass, and pulled him close until their bodies molded together as one. Antonio's erection dug into Justin's pelvis, hard and insistent.

When Emily said this was scary, she had no idea. Justin couldn't fathom what he was about to walk into. But with his cock pressed between him and Antonio, he couldn't wait to explore and figure it out.

"Oh, hell. I was right. *You* were right." Emily's breathy exclamation penetrated Justin's haze of enjoyment.

Antonio broke the kiss to look at her. "About what?"

She smirked, mischief dancing in her eyes. "First night we met? Justin told me he had a sexy Italian friend he'd go gay for. And we screwed to a fantasy of you sucking him off."

Justin couldn't believe she'd shared that. Then again, maybe he should be surprised she kept it to herself for so long. "It was a heat-of–the-moment kind of thing." He didn't want to deny it. He was grateful to have it out in the open. "I should have paid closer attention to myself."

"No. Being right once doesn't mean it's smart to listen to you inebriated the rest of the time." There was no malice in Antonio's voice.

"As I was saying"—Emily interrupted—"watching you two together is making me kind of wet and squirmy. So if you want to keep it up, maybe shed a few—or most—of your clothes, I won't complain." She pulled out a chair from her desk. "I'll be here, playing with myself, while you figure out which tab goes into which slot."

Justin's skin heated to volcanic, and his cock threatened to burst his zipper. He pulled Antonio into another kiss, memorizing the taste, the smell, the sounds… All of it.

CHAPTER TWENTY-NINE

ANTONIO ALMOST BELIEVED THIS was a dream—the most exquisite he could have landed in. Kissing Justin. Exploring every inch of his body, as clothes came off. Not having to question what it meant or if it would last past tonight.

His lips burned from the scrape of five o'clock shadow and a string of hungry kisses that seemed to go on forever but at the same time not long enough. Justin studied him as if he were dessert and the only dilemma was where to start.

Thanks to Emily's not-so-subtle nudging when the three started working together, Antonio already had the memory of Justin's naked form etched in his mind. It was low-res and disappointing, in comparison to standing in front of the real thing.

Antonio traced his fingers along the lines of Justin's tattoos, following the same path with his gaze. Antonio glided down a chiseled chest and over a flat stomach, to tease Justin's cock with a feather-light touch.

Justin mimicked the contact without hesitation and groaned at each new caress. Antonio was torn between the desire to spend hours exploring, and finding release for the diamond-hard insistence throbbing between his legs. Fortunately, this wasn't a one-off experience.

Antonio thought he might pass out when Justin said, *I love you*—words he'd waited forever to hear in that voice and never expected to.

Justin's dick was longer, but not as wide as Antonio's, and the girth was an intoxicating warmth against Antonio's palm.

"In case you're missing something…" Emily's voice blended into the moment, instead of shattering it.

Antonio turned his head to see her standing next to them, clothes gone and stunning body on display. He was so busy staring, it took him a moment to realize she held something.

"One of many reasons we can't do this without you. You're the details lady." Justin kissed her on the forehead, the tip of the nose, and then the lips, before taking the lube and condom from her.

She gave Antonio a playful smile and walked away. He watched the wiggle of her ass. She dropped into her chair and cupped her breast, gently kneading as she watched the show. Justin pulled from Antonio's grip, settled a palm on Antonio's cheek, and turned his head.

"I'm over here," Justin said. He captured Antonio's mouth with his again, then broke away. "Turn around."

Antonio's anticipation spiked through his chest, and he obeyed.

Emily looked enraptured with the show. She parted her legs and slid her hands along the inside of her thighs, giving him a teasing glimpse of her gorgeous pussy.

"I'm not sure I'm doing this right." Justin's breath caressed Antonio's ear. "So tell me if it hurts." He bit into Antonio's shoulder, and a sharp, delicious pain spread from the fresh mark.

Antonio tilted his head back with a groan. "It hurts."

"Do you want me to stop?" Justin asked.

"Christ, no."

Justin's chuckle rolled over Antonio, raising goosebumps in its wake. A second later, cold lube delivered with fingers met Antonio's ass, and he hissed through gritted teeth. A groan tore from his throat when Justin nudged his opening, pushing inside enough to tempt.

Emily watched, lips parted in a silent gasp, and spread her legs wider, giving Antonio a perfect view of her glistening sex. When Justin pressed against Antonio's hole with the head of his cock, Antonio forced himself to relax. He'd been with enough men that the experience wasn't new, but with Justin it might as well be.

Justin hesitated, and Antonio pressed back into him, setting the pace and letting Justin in one excruciatingly slow inch at a time.

Emily's chest heaved, and she fingered her clit. Antonio knew that tempting, flushed look. She was near climax. That the moment turned her on as much as it did him made him so hard it ached.

Justin buried himself to the hilt and grabbed Antonio's hips. Antonio moaned, eyes closed, letting the sensation glide from his fingertips to his toes and focus on his dick.

Justin rocked against Antonio slowly, stretching him out and stealing his reason. Something warm and wet slipped along his shaft, and he opened his eyes to see Emily kneeling at his feet, watching him with hungry green eyes as she stroked him.

"I don't want to come without you." She gave him an exaggerated pout, before pulling her bottom lip up his length, and then taking him in her mouth.

"Fuck." Justin let out a guttural groan. "Watching you two is better than good whiskey."

Antonio didn't know if he wanted to pound into Emily's sucking, or grind back against Justin's cock. He twisted his fingers in Emily's hair and found a rhythm that let him do both.

Antonio held her gaze, captivated, as she continued to stroke and lick. She dropped her free hand between her legs again, and the moan that rumbled through his shaft confirmed what he could only glimpse—she was fingering herself.

He didn't know which sensations to give his attention to. Her soft lips and hungry licks. Justin pounding into his ass. The sound of grunts mingling with the scent of arousal from the two people he loved.

Emily gave a muffled whimper when she came, shuddering against his grip, and increasing her attentions on his dick.

Justin clenched his fingers into Antonio's hips hard enough to dig into his pelvis. That explained the tiny purple bruises Emily had sported the three weeks they worked together on PP together. The realization dialed up Antonio's arousal another notch.

He pulled Emily to her feet, grasped her wrist, and drew her fingers into his mouth one at a time. She tasted incredible. He wrapped an arm around her waist and pulled her close. His cock dug into her stomach, and she wrapped a fist around it, pumping and driving the head into her belly.

Justin's thrusting was frantic now, and combined with Emily's ministrations, made it impossible for Antonio to back. Orgasm spilled through and out of him, coating Emily's hand and leaving a sticky mess between them.

Justin slammed into Antonio hard and fast, his groans shifting to punctuated grunts. He let out a long, low yell, before slowing to a stop. He rested his head against Antonio's shoulder, his gasps for breath hot and heavy on Antonio's back.

"God, I'm an idiot." Justin's lips moved against Antonio's shoulder. "Taking so long to figure out what you already knew—that I love you."

Antonio was never going to get tired of hearing that.

"Yeah, you are." Emily smirked. She looked at Antonio. "But I suppose we've all been a bit dense."

Antonio expected a flash of jealousy at the playful teasing Emily and Justin slid into without effort. What he felt instead was a light heart and a release he never expected.

Justin kissed up his neck, then nipped at his earlobe. "I'd be lost without you. I literally was."

"Figuratively," Emily corrected him.

"Me too," Antonio said, knowing it didn't quite make sense in the flow of conversation. They'd understand him anyway. He didn't doubt it. This was perfect and then some.

*

EMILY LOVED WAKING UP next to Antonio, but she hadn't realized how much she missed opening her eyes to him wrapped around her and seeing Justin next to her as well. Her heart stuttered with joy at the sight of the morning sunlight falling across his face and making his blue eyes as pale as ice.

It was difficult to focus on that this morning. She'd awoken to Antonio's arm draped over her hip, fingers teasing her mound. She squeezed her legs together. She was already wet from the attention.

Justin brushed a curl off her forehead. "I've never forgotten how gorgeous you are first thing in the morning."

"Me or him?" Heat flooded her cheeks.

"Both of you." Justin kissed her.

Antonio pulled away abruptly, stopping the attention on her tingling clit and letting the cool air rush in when the blankets fell away. He slapped her ass lightly. "We're going to be late for work."

She rolled onto her back and gave him an exaggerated pout. "But I'm sleeping with the boss. Doesn't that buy me an extra hour or two?"

"Not when I have morning meetings." Antonio offered her a hand and pulled her into a sitting position. He stood next to the bed, looking glorious and unashamed of the fact he wore nothing.

"I can't believe you two are talking business in bed," Justin said.

Emily looked back at him, brows raised. "Since

when?"

His scowl melted to laughter. "Sorry. I was trying to keep a straight face, but nope. Not happening."

"I really do have to get ready." Antonio sounded disappointed. "I'd invite one or both of you to join me in the shower, but we tried that, and there's not enough room."

"In that case, we're going to need a bigger apartment, with a huge master bath," Justin said.

Emily eyed him. "We?"

Justin stared back unflinching. "And a bigger bed. King sized, for sure."

"You've put a lot of thought into this." Emily loved the certainty in his statements.

"Nope. I'm making it up as I go along, and leaving the details up to the two of you."

"Sweet of you." Antonio tugged Emily to her feet. "Some of us decided to get jobs, rather than live off fat buyout checks, so we really do need to get going." His stern expression melted into a smile. "Have your lawyer call mine, so I can get you on a similar schedule sooner rather than later?"

"I will." Justin said. "Set a spare desk aside for me."

Contentment and satisfaction rolled through Emily. The arrangement might be atypical, and getting here had been a bit rough, but she was exactly where she belonged and had no doubt Antonio and Justin felt the same way.

EPILOGUE

EMILY RESTED IN THE tattoo chair, trying to focus on the hum of the needle, rather than the piercing sensation as Tara dragged it along her breastbone. This was the last sitting Emily needed, before the artwork was in place.

Tara had drawn the design at Antonio's request. A birthday present to Emily. A dragon wrapped around the left side of her neck, body and head slithering down her collarbone. She'd had that one done first, despite Justin's very vocal and less-than-serious protests about her picking the phoenix second.

The bird's tail intertwined with the beasts on the back of her neck, and the feathered flames ran along the right side. Their heads came together between her breasts, leaving room for the sparrow that soared up her sternum.

Emily was in awe of Tara's talent, not only with the design, but also with the tattoo gun. Tara was a graphic artist, and had been with the company for years. When her marriage fell apart a few months ago, she needed an escape. She surrendered it all and started the tattoo parlor.

Emily got the impression there was a lot more to the marriage story than she'd heard, but Tara was tightlipped about the details, and that was her right. Emily was happy to see her pull out of the mire. She liked Antonio's family, and especially his sister.

The needle hit bone again. Emily clenched her jaw and squeezed Antonio's hand. Justin had tried to warn her that anything so close to bone was going to hurt more than a fleshy region. He suggested she start smaller, like with a simple image on her calf.

She told him a little pain never hurt anyone, and he stopped arguing.

Right now, he straddled the chair across from her, chin and arms resting on the back and gaze holding hers, to help her focus.

He looked away and reached for his phone. She rolled her eyes but didn't mind that he was as addicted to the job as he'd ever been. Having Antonio's infrastructure and international contacts gave Justin a freedom he never had before, and she saw how happy it made him. Besides, all three of them were a part of the same machine, as intertwined with the job as they were with each other.

She fell back into the pain, gripping Antonio's hand until she was concerned she'd cut off his circulation.

"All done," Tara said, at the same time Justin said, "Fuck me."

"At least let me finish, before you share whatever that news is," Tara told him. She cleaned up Emily's chest, then helped her sit and face a mirror.

"It's amazing," Emily said, awe filling her.

"Thank you." Tara covered it up. "You know the rules for care. I'm sure you can find someone to help you keep lotion on it if you're having trouble." She didn't bat an eye when Antonio told her about the relationship, but Emily swore she occasionally caught Tara watching them with a trace of envy.

Antonio helped her to her feet and hovered his hand over the plastic. "I wish these didn't take so long to heal."

"Take that sappy shit home. Or anywhere but here." Tara's retort was gruff, but affection lay underneath.

Justin joined them, pressing his fingers into Emily's skin along the edges of the fresh scars. She gasped at the rush of pain and endorphins. It only took her first visit to the parlor, to realize he knew where to touch, to draw a groan without doing damage.

"That goes for both of you," Tara snapped. "Not in my shop."

"We're behaving. Thank you again. For everything." Emily gave her a hug. Goodbyes were exchanged, and Emily left with Justin and Antonio.

They were within walking distance of their apartment. Though it was winter, and colder here than Emily was used to, it wasn't too chilly for a stroll. She still enjoyed seeing the city covered in glistening crystals of ice and sunshine.

She strolled a few feet ahead, her attention flitting wherever it was drawn. It was lovely to be hand in hand with Antonio, Justin, or both of them, but it was just as much fun to watch them hold hands.

Today she took in the scenery, while the men enjoyed each other's company.

"Is someone going to ask?" Justin's question carried from behind.

She glanced over her shoulder, but before she could reply, Antonio said, "Maybe. After you've squirmed with the news a little longer."

"You're such a dick." There was no malice in Justin's voice.

"I want to know." Emily paused, to snap a picture of the sunlight streaming between buildings and striking the stone at her feet.

"Thank you." Justin sounded smug. "How would you, my favorite siren, like to take an implementation team and go to London for a month?"

She whirled to face him, grin stuck on her face. "You landed Oxford?"

"*We* did," he said.

"Why didn't you say so?" Antonio asked.

Justin laughed. "I take it back. You're not a dick. You're a massive dick."

"You'd know," Antonio said, teasing in his voice.

The comment was enough to make Justin pause. These were the only times Emily saw Justin hesitate—the jokes about liking men still tripped him up. He didn't care who knew about him and Antonio, but he wasn't used to being on that side of the teasing.

She thought it was adorable, which he didn't appreciate. "London sounds amazing." She pulled the topic back to his news. They'd discussed how this would work. Justin would travel with her and a small team, to bring the school online with their new product. Antonio couldn't leave the office in stretches like that, but he'd visit on weekends and whenever his schedule allowed.

The entire setup—not just the foreign accounts, but also, and most importantly, the two wonderful men next to her—was something she never would have dared imagine for herself. But now that she'd tasted it—lived it—she wouldn't give it up for anything. This was exactly where and what she wanted to be.

THE END

~*~

If you'd like to see Cynthia figure out love is more than just an equation, check out *Their Matchmaker*. Keep reading for a free sneak peek

their
MATCHMAKER

ALLYSON LINDT
USA TODAY BESTSELLING AUTHOR

CHAPTER ONE

REGARDLESS OF HOW MUCH MONEY the participants had, the game never changed; the stakes just got higher. Curiosity made Aaron want to watch the scam play out, but propriety and the lack of desire to see someone hustled won. He joined the group of gentlemen clustered around a woman in a blue dress with a plunging neckline.

The pack stood near the back of the art gallery. They all wore tailored suits, and the woman in the middle—Aaron was calling her *Ms. Blue* while he observed—held their attention. Except for one man, who spent more time searching the faces of those around him, than trying to catch a glimpse down the front of Ms. Blue's dress. That must be her partner.

"It's a tragic story." Aaron pulled his wallet from his back pocket and plucked out a bill. "I'll give you twenty dollars and two cough drops for the painting. I hate to see a lady in distress."

Her partner snorted. "You're insulting a mourning woman."

Murmurs of agreement rippled among her pack.

"I'm truly sorry for your loss, miss." Aaron kept the sympathy in his tone. "I feel for your situation, but if the painting isn't worth anything…" If he walked into the middle of the group and proclaimed her a gold-digger, out to steal someone's money, no one would listen. She had them captivated. But if he looked like he was on her side, trying to stop these men from taking advantage of a grieving woman, the hustle would break up, and he and his business partners wouldn't have to deal with it happening on their property.

"This isn't about the worth of the painting." Her partner pushed. To the woman, he said, "You don't need any more grief in your life. I'll give you two thousand, for this unremarkable piece of art."

She choked on her champagne. "How much? For a worthless piece of canvas? But why?"

The mark cut in. "Because he's a cheapskate. I'll give you five thousand."

Aaron feigned shock. "So many generous strangers." He leaned closer to Ms. Blue, and spoke in a stage whisper. "I'd be careful, miss. I believe in charity, but if he's willing to pay you more than a couple of bucks for a worthless painting… perhaps it's worth more than he's saying."

The mark flushed bright red. "Are you implying I'd take advantage of this poor woman?"

"I would never." Aaron kept just as much indignation in his voice. Then he winked at Ms. Blue. "I totally am. I'd get out now, if I were you, before this man tries to steal more than your *priceless* Picasso."

Ms. Blue nodded at Aaron, no longer looking at anyone else. "Thank you." The sweetness vanished from her voice. "Apparently I almost made a terrible mistake."

"Don't mention it." He turned his attention back to the photography exhibition, as the group dispersed. He'd enjoyed watching the hustle as a throwback to his teenage years. However, he was here for the art. It held a kind of joy and innocence the world didn't display in long stretches. A charm that was pleasant to drift into for moments at a time.

A hand on his arm drew his attention. "Aaron Birch." It was Ms. Blue. "I'm Katy. I'd have ditched the loser and low-end hustle, and come learn from you, if I'd known the Four-Billion-Dollar Master would be here tonight."

He hated that nickname. "I don't normally give lessons."

"I can make it worth your time." She traced a finger along the plunging *V* of her dress.

If her version of playful banter was as good as or better than her hustle, he'd see this through, to find out whose bedroom they ended up in. "What kind of conversion rate do I get on that?"

"Excuse me?"

"Is this a penny-per-minute thing? Three-ninety-nine an hour?"

She frowned. "I'm not a whore."

"I never said you were. It's about the back and forth, see? *Worth my time* leads to *conversion rate*, which segues to *value*..." He shook his head. It was no fun if it had to be explained. "I'm sorry, Ms. Blue. I don't think we're on the same page."

"It's Katy. I'm just a little tired. Not paying attention. I get it."

Aaron trailed his gaze around the room,

stopping on each face before moving to the next. "We both know you're as much a Ms. Blue as a Katy. Thank you for adding a little spice to my evening, but my date is waiting, and—fair warning—she's the jealous type." And there she was. Or rather, he hoped she'd act like his companion long enough to kill Ms. Blue's interest.

The woman he spotted was spending more time looking at the art than the people. Her glass was still full. She was the least likely to push him away before she had a chance to analyze the situation. It didn't hurt that she was gorgeous—golden hair piled high, with a few ringlets loose around her face; a long, slender neck; and a dress that hugged every inch of curve, without showing a whole lot of skin. Elegant and classy.

He strolled up to her, the clack of heels behind him telling him *Katy* followed. The stranger met his gaze, and he said, "I'm glad you made it, love. I was worried I wouldn't see you tonight."

The stranger wore a half-scowl as she looked between him and Ms. Blue. "Love, this is Katy," he said.

"Cynthia." The blonde extended her hand. She was playing along. Perfect.

Ms. Blue's smile slipped, and she returned the handshake. "Pleasure."

Aaron rested a hand on the small of Cynthia's back, hoping to strike the balance between looking involved and not pissing the woman off before the gig was up. "My tempting Cyn and I are going to enjoy the rest of the show. Good luck selling your priceless Picasso, Ms. Blue."

*

IT WASN'T THAT CYNTHIA disliked people. They were fine, one at a time. But she preferred numbers. If she added one to one, she got two. Not three, or seven, or a brokenhearted point five. *Two.* She turned to the man who'd adopted her as an accessory. "She owns a Picasso?" Not the most brilliant thing she could have said, but she was piecing together what happened.

"No. But she wants people to think she does. Thank you for saving me, by the way. Aaron."

He was attractive. Dark hair brushed his ears, and he had pale-green eyes she had to tilt her head up to see. It was rare for her to meet a guy taller than her, especially when she wore heels. His suit was made to accentuate and hang from every place a good suit should, showing off broad shoulders and a narrow waist.

"Cynthia. But you already know that." Why was she flustered? She was familiar with his type. They thought they were smooth as shit until someone called them on it, and then they fell apart. Their reaction to someone seeing through their façade was an unknown variable in a world she preferred to keep ordered.

He looked her over, gaze lingering on her hips and breasts before returning to her face. "And you *are* a sinful temptation."

The cheesy play on her name was enough to snap her reason back on. The attention was flattering, but she knew better than to be sucked in. When she'd started her matchmaking firm, she let guys like this Aaron in the door, along with every other client. Everyone deserved a chance, and she didn't make sweeping assumptions about people.

She'd never been able to match one, though. Guys like him didn't work with her algorithm, because they were so focused on impressing the world, they had no substance of their own. These days she sent them on their way with a smile, an apology, and the assurance they'd have better luck without her computer's interference. "Is that considered an opening line in a place like this?" she asked Aaron.

He raised his brows in question.

"*Hi. I'm Katy, and I own a priceless Picasso.* Is that how the pick-up works here?"

He chuckled—a casual, throaty sound that sent pleasant tingles across her skin in a way she tried to ignore. "Not in the way you're thinking," he said. "It's a hustle."

"Like… *guess which cup the ball is under?*" She couldn't keep the disbelief from her voice. He was comparing high-end art to street tricks.

"Exactly like that that, but with a more impressive payout. She finds her way into a gathering like this, usually with a friend to help nudge the crowd, and convinces people she owns said priceless Picasso but has no idea how much it's worth. They believe they underbid her. To them, it's worth twenty million dollars, and they offer her five or ten grand. When they go to pick up the art, she either hands them one of fifty convincing replicas, or more likely, she takes their money and runs."

"That's horrible." She couldn't believe the casual way he said it. "And you let her walk away?"

"She didn't do it yet. And any of those men she was talking to thought they were scamming her, too."

The concept left a bad taste in her mouth. "But still…"

"You think I should call the police? She hasn't done anything wrong this evening." He looked at Cynthia like she was the one not making sense.

She definitely preferred numbers. It was time to wrap this up. "Enjoy the rest of your evening."

"Wait. You're right. It is disturbing. On both their parts."

She should keep walking. So why was she facing him? "You're only saying that because you think it's what I want to hear."

"I'm saying it because I stopped her from doing it. Doesn't matter if everyone in that group was trying to screw everyone else over, it still wasn't right." He quirked his mouth in a smile he probably thought was seductive. It was kind of cute. "If I was saying what I thought you wanted to hear, I'd feed you a line about being one of the owners of this building, ask if you wanted the grand tour, and watch you get flustered again."

"Is giving me a *tour of the building* a euphemism for trying to talk me out of my dress?" She was making a bit of a leap in logic, that his hitting on her was meant to lead to more. She was bothered that part of her liked his line, though. The notion of being talked out of her dress by this gentleman who knew exactly how to flatter her was more tempting than she wanted.

"You're assuming a lot. What makes you think I don't have a date?" he asked.

She raised her brows in disbelief. "You're here with me. I'm your girlfriend. Isn't that what you told Katy?" Earning her living hooking people up had taught her a lot of important lessons, number one being that a successful Evening One didn't have to lead to an Evening Two, as long as everyone was on the same page.

"In that case, I don't have to use euphemisms to get you to join me upstairs. You already know how incredible I am, and you're curious to see what we get up to next. You're wondering if we can top how much fun we had at that last place." His smile shifted to something almost challenging.

"Is that what I'm wondering? Considering I struggle to remember the last place… Oh wait—the back room of that place in Chinatown?"

"I love that place. Best dumplings. Do they have a back room?"

This was more fun than she expected. He didn't flinch, and he had a counter at each roadblock. "If neither one of us remembers the back room, it won't be a hard night to top." Despite the derision in her words, she hoped he kept playing along, rather than getting offended.

"We can't have *completely forgettable*. Let me make it up to you. *That* was the pickup line, if you're keeping track."

"I need to start, if you're going to show me a night I'll remember forever."

His frown caught her off guard. "I don't know. I don't think I'm your type."

He was right, but now seemed like an odd time to point it out. She couldn't hide her curiosity. "What is my type?" According to the program she used to match clients, no one she'd met came close. Not that she would date a client—talk about unethical—but she kept her name in the database for strictly educational purposes.

"Intelligent," he said.

"And that's not you?"

He shook his head. "You don't just want someone who keeps you on your toes with his wit. You want someone who knows the difference between"—he studied her again, this time keeping his attention on her face—"tabs and spaces."

Tabs. Always tabs. "They're two different keys on a keyboard. Mystery solved. I didn't realize you were offering anything long term enough for that to matter." Every time she opened her mouth, she got sucked further into this ridiculous but tantalizing conversation. All she had to do was stop talking and walk away, but no. Something propelled her to say new things.

"I'm not. Does that mean your criteria for letting a random stranger make you moan are different?"

"After that night in Chinatown, my criteria are higher than they used to be." She smiled, to let him know she was still teasing.

"I like it." He dipped his head, and she caught the faint scent of musk. He smelled good too. It wasn't fair. "If you're considering saying *yes*"—his warm breath caressed his skin, and his voice was low—"let's pretend I already talked you into it.

There's an office on the fourth floor that's staged for rental, and I'm curious about whether the couch is good for anything besides sitting on."

And there was the arrogance she was looking for. The assumption the conversation would lead to sex. It should bother her more than it did. "Why would I say *yes*?"

"Because you think there's nothing to me but what's on the surface, and the curious bits of you are begging for proof that I'm all talk."

He was perceptive. That probably made a lot of things easier for him. She wouldn't be one of them, despite enjoying the conversation. "In other words, you think I'll go upstairs with you in hopes of being disappointed?"

"I do. And you've set your expectations pretty high."

"You make me sound cynical." Which she was, but it was jarring for someone else to point it out.

"Not at all. Just realistic."

It was time to wrap this up. "Disappoint me before we make it upstairs, and it'll save us both time."

"And how do you propose I do that?"

"If I have to tell you, it's not your idea, is it?" She had no clue what the challenge would get her. Being unable to second-guess him was exhilarating.

He rested one hand on her hip, thumb tracing tiny circles, and cupped her cheek with the other. When he locked his gaze on hers, her breath jammed in her chest. *Captivating.* He dipped his head, then brushed his lips over hers. The barely-there touch raced through every inch of her, drawing her senses to life.

He stepped back, challenging smirk returning, and cool air mingled with disappointment to take his place. "I'm not interested in talking anyone into an evening they don't want." He grasped her fingers and kissed the tips before releasing her. "Enjoy the rest of the exhibit, my temptation."

She leaned against a nearby wall with a soft *oof* as soon as he was out of sight. What the hell was that?

The story continues in Chapter Two

ABOUT ALLYSON LINDT

ALLYSON LINDT IS A FULL-TIME GEEK and a fuller-time contemporary romance author. She likes her stories with sweet geekiness and heavy spice, because cubicle dwellers need love too. She loves a sexy happily-ever-after and helping deserving cubicle dwellers find their futures together.

www.ingramcontent.com/pod-product-compliance
Lightning Source LLC
Chambersburg PA
CBHW032104180726
48284CB00002B/434